The Sentence of the Court by Fred M White

Fred Merrick White was born in 1859 in West Bromwich in the Midlands of England to Joseph White and Helen Merrick who had married the previous year.

Joseph was a solicitor's managing clerk, who by the time the family moved to Hereford a few years later, had become a solicitor's article clerk.

Little is known of White's early years but what is known is that he followed in his father's footsteps and worked as a solicitor's clerk in Hereford. His father by now had also become a solicitor and times seemed quite prosperous for the family.

However in the late 1880's something went badly wrong for his father and he was imprisoned.

White had by now decided that writing was a more preferable career for him than the law. By 1891 Fred M. White, now 31 years old, was working full-time as a journalist and author, earning enough to support himself and his mother, Helen. By this time Fred's younger brother, Joseph A. White, had left home and working as a glass-blower.

In 1892, White married Clara Jane Smith. The wedding took place at King's Norton, Worcestershire, and the couple went on to have two children; Sydney Eric White (1893) and Ormond John White (1895).

As the century closed Fred's father had been released from prison and was living as a "retired solicitor", together with Helen, in Worthington in West Sussex.

By the time of the 1911 census, Fred M. White, now 52 years old, and his wife Clara were living at Uckfield, a town in the Wealden district of East Sussex. As the ominous shadows of the First World War gathered White had established himself as a popular and extremely prolific author. Indeed whether it was novels or short stories they flowed from his pen with a startling speed and many of them were initially serialized in the popular weekly and monthly magazines. His clever use of science to create imaginative and highly adventurous story lines was a particular talent of his.

During the First World War, both of his sons served as junior officers in The Royal Inniskilling Fusiliers.

The titanic struggle of the First World War and his sons' war-time experiences in it greatly influenced this phase of his writing. His novel The Seed of Empire (1916), describes early trench warfare in great and gritty detail. He went on to describe how the social changes after the war created many problems for returning soldiers as they attempted to fit back into a now peaceful society.

Fred and Clara spent their twilight years in Barnstaple in Devon, an area which also provided the backdrop for his novels The Mystery Of Crocksands, The Riddle Of The Rail, and The Shadow Of The Dead Hand.

Fred Merrick White died in Barnstaple in 1935.

Index of Contents

CHAPTER I

Everard Gilray struggled to be free. What did this outrage mean? Who was this ragged, seedy fellow, who had thus dared to attack him on his own doorstep on the stroke of twelve? And this was not some slum in the East End—it was the respectable, dull, decorous Harley-street. Gilray had had slipped his Yale key in the front door, the polished mahogany portal stood open, showing the luxury and comfort and elegance of the hall in the dim, shaded electric light when this ragged nomad had emerged from the shadows and gripped him by the shoulder.

A beggar no doubt, some impudent fellow relying on the lateness of the hour and the stillness of the street to enforce a demand for alms.

Gilray turned fiercely upon him, his left shot out, and the ruffian staggered under the force of the blow. The street outside was absolutely deserted, there was no sign of a policeman anywhere. And Gilray's house contained things of price. The servants had long gone to bed, it was impossible to alarm them.

The man was evidently desperate, his courage was growing in proportion to the lack of danger. All this Gilray could read in his hungry, glittering eyes. This was the kind of thing that led to murder. Here, in Harley-street. Gilray wondered what people would say...his patients...constituents, his many friends in society. Possibly—

He staggered back under a furious onslaught, and fell against a table in the hall. The shabby man followed quickly in, and shut the front door. He looked a little less dangerous and desperate now, but there was a grim smile on his face.

"Seems to have been a bit of a misunderstanding, sir," he gasped.

"You infernal scoundrel," Gilray cried. "What do you mean by it? If you had asked me civilly for assistance I would have helped you. But to attack me like this—"

"Who attacked you?" the man demanded sulkily. "I put my hand on your shoulder. I always put my hands on their shoulders, same as detectives do. 'Tis allowed by the law. 'Tis a symbol, that's what it is. Tells as 'ow you're my prisoner without using the word."

Gilray gasped. A curious feeling of nausea oppressed him. He felt sick and giddy and curiously unreal, as if he were some unworthy person masquerading as himself. The man was quite calm and collected now, and, in his way, not disrespectful.

"I am your prisoner, then," he said, hoarsely.

"If you please, sir, Sheriff of London. What's called a Writ of Attachment. You see, as there is a Bill of Sale on your goods 'ere, there was no other way. Two hundred and thirty-eight pounds four shillings. You've got to come with me to Brixton Prison. Get the money from your friends to-morrow. Sorry to be so late, sir, but I missed you as you was going out to dinner. You got away in your taxi, only a few seconds in front of me."

Gilray shuddered. He wondered if that pallid face in the Venetian mirror opposite was his own. That immaculately cut dress suit was a mockery. The pink-shaded hall, the thick Persian carpet, the pictures and the flowers were all a mockery. He was no longer Everard Gilray, the petted and fashionable eye specialist, a popular Member of Parliament, one of the idols of the hour. He was a hunted wretch with disgrace and worse before him. To-morrow he would be a byword, a failure, his specific services would be required no longer.

He pointed a shaking finger in the direction of the dining-room, that wonderful room in crimson and old oak that was the admiration of all his lady patients. Gilray was a born collector, he never could resist the artistic and the beautiful—he never could resist anything that cost money. He made 10,000 pounds a year, and he was doubly that in debt.

The more money he made the more hopeless grew his position. Betting, gambling, the Stock Exchange— every desperate remedy had been tried. And every venture found him nearer the brink. He was a humbug, a fraud—if nothing worse.

"Sit down," he said hoarsely, "sit down and help yourself. Brandy, whisky, a cigar—anything. I suppose you could not accept a cheque?"

"I could not, sir," the man said. "They never take cheques in these cases. Cash down and paid to the Sheriff. To-morrow—"

"Oh, curse it, man, there can be no to-morrow in my case," Gilray burst out passionately, "Can't you see that this means absolute ruin to me? Why, to-morrow I go to a palace to operate on Royalty. I shall not be there. Enquiries will be made the story will get abroad, and my practice will be dead. I represent a constituency in the north—a stern and rigid set who would turn and rend me if they knew to truth. Can't you see that I must have time, man? Go away and come back to-morrow night. I'll have the matter settled by then."

The man with the glass in his hand shook his head resolutely. "Can't be done, governor," he said. "More'n my place is worth; I've got a missis and three kids, and one of 'em's a cripple. Not for all the money—"

Just for an instant something like murder gleamed in Gilray's eyes. He seemed to be moving in a blood-red mist out of which loomed that man's lean and narrow throat. Why not kill him and pretend that he had found him here stealing the plate? No, that would not do. Inquiries would be made, and the whole story come out. The man must be bribed; there was money yonder in the oak secretaire. Gilray pulled open the desk and tossed aside a heap of papers. Bills, bills, bills! Threatening letters, money-lending circulars, pressing hints from solicitors. Curse the bills! Curse the money-lenders who were sucking the life's blood out of him!

But they could keep; nothing mattered now as long as this fellow could be got rid of. He was there at the instance of the one creditor whom Gilray had least feared. That was always the way. Yes, here was the money almost thrown at him earlier in the day by a grateful American patient. Twenty pounds in gold and some notes. Gilray took the sovereigns, and laid them in a neat pattern on the polished oak table. They glittered and gleamed temptingly in the light.

"Look at them!" Gilray said hoarsely. "Just think what they mean to a man like you. They are a small fortune. And they are yours for the asking. Take them and put them in your pocket!"

The man's fingers went mechanically in the direction of the good red gold. The dirty hands hovered over the shining coins; Gilray could hear the fellow's quick and strenuous breathing.

"Take 'em away!" he said. "Take 'em away, or I'll do you a mischief! What do you mean by temptin' a poor man in this way. It's cruel of you, sir."

"But where is the harm?" Gilray pleaded hoarsely. "And how are you going to suffer? Nobody saw you come here, and nobody will see you go away. You have not been able to execute your warrant. Circumstances have been against you. To-morrow I am at the palace. I'm not going to run away, you know. If the money owing is not paid by mid-day, come back here and take me. Don't be a fool, man— don't stand in your own light."

The sheriff's minion was hesitating now, his eyes twinkled and watered as if the gold dazzled them. Gilray snatched up the heavy, clinking coins, and thrust them in the other's hand.

"There!" he said. "I knew that you would think better of it. Did you ever have so much money before? Did you ever make it so easily? And all for waiting a few hours. There is no danger to yourself, and you help me. Do you suppose that I don't mean to meet this liability? I've got to do it. If not, I might just as well jump into the Thames. Put the gold in your pocket."

Gilray turned his back, knowing that he had won. He heard the muffled clink of the sovereigns as they dropped in the tipstaff's pocket. For the moment, at any rate, the situation was saved!

Gilray was alone—the man had gone. He breathed more freely as he came back to the dining-room and helped himself liberally to brandy. This was not one of his usual habits, he was very rigid about that kind of thing. His was a popular figure at West End dining-tables, but he had never been known to exceed one glass of claret or hock. He was practically a non-smoker—one could not indulge in that kind of thing and retain the steady, steel-like hand necessary for the delicate eye operations. And tomorrow, for the first time, he was called upon to attend a Royal patient.

And to-morrow he had to find that money. It was a mere trifle, and yet it was as big as a mountain. He had absolutely reached the end of his resources. There was not a money lender in London who would look at his paper, not a friend from whom he could borrow.

He knew what a dainty, delicate plant was an operating surgeon's reputation. Here he was surrounded with every luxury in a house full of costly trifles, pictures, work of art, rare silver, and he could not touch a single object there. They were only nominally his—they belonged to a creditor under an assignment. To take one of those precious treasures and raise money on it would be fraud.

Where was the money to come from? About two hundred and fifty pounds. A mere bagatelle. Gilray had spent that a score of times on a ring or cameo. And now—

He came back with a start to the reality of things. The house became a human habitation again, and somebody was moving in the basement. There was now no light in the hall, and the thick curtains in the dining-room effectively screened the gleam of the electrics from the road outside. Doubtless some burglar was at work below there under the impression that everybody was asleep. Well, Gilray would know how to deal with him. He wanted something to vent his rage and passion upon. He had run up against a night of adventure, and he would see the trouble through.

He crept to the door of the dining-room and waited. In the black, velvety darkness of the house he seemed to hear all the more clearly. Beyond question somebody was fumbling his way upstairs. It was possible to make out a soft footfall, the crack of a board, a sound of somebody breathing hard.

There was a smell of humanity there too, humanity that sleeps out of doors and wears its clothes far too long. Gilray touched the switch.

Just for a moment the blinding flood of light dazzled him. He made out a tall, spare figure in a shabby tightly-buttoned frock coat, once of fashionable cut, and with the evidence of the hand of Bond-street upon it.

He saw a dark, clean-shaven face, a pair of keen, glittering eyes, glistening in a face that bore evidence of recent illness or privation. And in one of the long, lean, capable-looking hands was a Browning automatic pistol.

"What is the meaning of this?" Gilray demanded.

"We'll come to that presently," the stranger said.

An educated man with the public school label on him, Gilray thought.

"No occasion for violence, Doctor Gilray. I rather fancy I can find you the money you are just now so sorely in need of."

CHAPTER II

THE WHITE HAND

Gilray stared wonderingly at the speaker. He could only wait for the other man to speak. It looked that night as if all the world had gone mad, as if law and order, and the sacred rights of property were no more. For this man was not shirking or abashed; there was no suggestion of an apology about him. On the contrary, his manner was coolly contemptuous, even superior; it was as if a magistrate were addressing a first offender.

He was a waster, of course, and a failure—even his cool and easy audacity could not conceal that. But he was undoubtedly a strong man, and Gilray did not fail to recognise the fact.

"How did you get here?" he stammered.

"Does it matter?" the other asked. "Let it suffice that I am here. Before long you will be glad I came. Permit me to introduce myself. Mr. Horace Vorley, whilom Doctor Vorley, very much at your service.

"You mean that you are not on the Medical Register now?"

"Precisely. You catch my meaning exactly. The old story of two men and one woman, and that woman happened to be my wife. I took matters in my own hands...Since then I have had a series of adventures in many lands, mostly taking the form of strife between myself on the one side and the authorities on the other. If you would give me a biscuit—"

"There are light refreshments in the dining-room," Gilray said, "and—and whisky."

"Thank you very much. I have eaten practically nothing to-day. I was searching for food in your kitchen. You see, I thought that Warner—the bailiff who was here just now—would have remained a little longer. When you left the front door open I followed you into the house. I also took the liberty of listening to your conversation with Warner. It looked like being a big struggle between you, so I stopped down in the kitchen. What did you give him to buy him off?"

Gilray exploded with impatient passion. How dared Vorley come here like this. What did he mean by treating the house as if it were some hotel? What business was it of his? Did he want the police to be telephoned for?

"Not a bit of good," Vorley coolly said, as he finished the sandwiches. "Upon my word, you have a pretty taste in whisky, sir. And these are really Villar Corona cigars. Let me ask you a question. Where are you going to get the money to pay that debt to-morrow? If it is not discharged by four o'clock the bailiff will be back again. At the present moment you have not one penny in the world. If the truth leaks out you are professionally ruined. Now, don't bluster, and don't lie about it. I was looking in here when you were discussing matters with Warner. Oh, if you could only have seen the white, anxious misery of your face; if you could only have heard the hoarse despair in your voice! You were pleading desperately for your social life. Man, do you want me to get you that money?"

Gilray laughed somewhat mirthlessly. He was beginning to like this blunt, outspoken man.

"That money! I'd give anything for it," he said. "Still, it is absurd to hear you talk of finding it! You are palpably penniless, seedy, desperate; and until a few moments ago, hungry. And you talk of finding me money! You find two hundred and fifty pounds! Ridiculous."

"Nevertheless, I can," Vorley said emphatically. "Before daybreak. That is, if you are prepared to perform a secret operation and to forget all about it afterwards."

"You came here to ask me to do this?"

"In a measure—yes. There is a man in whom I am deeply interested who has met with an accident to his eyes. He cannot for certain reasons show up in public, in fact he is hiding in a shady quarter near the river. No occasion to go into details. It's a queer business altogether. But this man needs the very highest skill, and I came West to-night to get it for him. My idea was to call on Evershed—he's a good chap, and we were pals at one time. I was hanging about on his doorstep making up my mind. Then I saw Warner stop you, and my way was clear."

"Warner is an old acquaintance of yours, I presume," Gilray sneered.

"Once more you show your quickness and intelligence," Vorley said urbanely. "When I was going headlong to perdition, Warner was a frequent guest in my house. We were good friends. So when I saw him to-night fighting with you on your doorstep I saw my way. Here was the fashionable and popular Dr. Gilray being arrested on a writ of attachment! You see, I know all the jargon. What a revelation! People don't let things go so far as writs of attachment unless they are in desperate need of money. My chance lay plain before me, and I took it in both hands. Now, do you need that money?"

"I would give my soul for it," Gilray said hoarsely. "If you can prove to me that you—"

"Man, you must take my word for it. And you must ask no questions. I cannot get a shilling for myself, but I can get you three hundred guineas for the secret operation. The man who handles the cash is a miser of the worst possible type. But the operation means much to him. I told him what I proposed to do, and he scoffed at the suggestion. No surgeon of good repute, he held, would come at dead of night to one of London's deadliest slums and perform such an operation as that required."

"But the patient might come here?"

"The patient is ill, he has had a bad accident. And there are other reasons why the thing should be carried out with every precaution. The danger of it—"

"Oh, there is danger, then? I see I am going to earn my money."

"Glad to hear that you have made up your mind," Vorley said, smiling for the first time. "'My poverty, and not my will consents,' as Shakespeare's Apothecary said. As a matter of fact, everything that I could see to is ready for you. You will need an anaesthetist, and you could not have a better one than myself. All the needful appliances are on the spot. So come along."

Gilray hesitated no longer. The hand of Fate was clearly directing the thing, fortune for once in a way was fighting on his side. The difficulty that had been before him threatening his ruin was solved—he would be able to keep faith with Warner.

"Very well," he said. "I will trust to your word. The money will be paid to me—"

"In gold, if you like, as soon as the operation is over. But we are wasting time here. Come on."

Gilray, after that, waited only to get his necessary instruments together, and presently he and Vorley were walking eastward together. A passing taxi was hailed by Vorley, and an address given that was somewhere at the back of the Tower of London. They were in a maze of mean streets presently, dark and narrow thoroughfares, dirty and ill-smelling, with dim lights gleaming here and there behind faded curtains. A few gas lamps struggled fitfully against the pervading gloom. Even these ineffectual gleams were lost presently, for, dismissing the taxi, Vorley turned through a broken-down gateway that seemed to give on to some open space, evidently a disused wharf or shipbreaker's yard, littered with refuse, amongst which Gilray stumbled along painfully, sweating, and uncertain on his feet. He could faintly catch the glimmer and hear the drip of water somewhere as he groped his way blindly in the dark.

"Where are you leading me?" he asked hoarsely.

"Take my hand," Vorley whispered. "I know every inch of the way. This is a treacherous place at night. A false step to the right or left and you are over the edge, and into one or the disused old locks. At one time a prosperous trade in the building of ships was carried on here, now the place is deserted and derelict. We are just about to cross the sluice-plank over one of the waterways. Be careful, man, be careful! Put your hand on my shoulder and shuffle your feet along."

Gilray with a shudder complied. He was suffering all the tortures of a vivid imagination. He would have given five years of his life to be back in his own house again. But there was no turning back now, and the vision of the rich reward to come spurred him on.

They were on firmer ground presently with something that looked like the outline of a house ahead. It seemed to be a fair-sized building, but there were no lights anywhere and the place was all in darkness. At this point Vorley paused and struck a match which he concealed as far as possible in the hollow of his hand. The fitful light disclosed what appeared to be a kind of basement to the house, with a door to which a flight of steps gave access. A sudden puff of wind and out went the match. Vorley swore under his breath.

But Gilray was no longer attending to the movements of his guide. He stood almost transfixed to the spot, all his fear gone, listening and wondering. For in the house away back in the darkness a girl was staging the 'Jewel Song,' from 'Faust.' The voice was glorious, divine. Its free abandon, its exquisite quality and purity of tone amazed Gilray. Here, wasting the silver of her notes, was assuredly some great star of Opera.

"Come on," Vorley whispered, noting his companion's amazement. "I'll show you queerer things than that yet. Now, get inside and wait till I come for you. The basement is dark and damp, but you can sit there for a moment. As to myself, I shall have to enter the house another way."

Gilray followed with blind obedience. He was thrust without ceremony into a dark room, and the door was locked behind him. Then, as Vorley's footsteps died away it seemed to him that he was neglected and deserted in a world of darkness and desolation. He heard something squeak and scurry, he felt something warm move over his foot. Gilray shuddered and his hair stiffened as he recognised the fact that the place was full of rats. He could hear them scrambling up the damp walls, and high above all he could hear the owner of that divine voice singing the passionate music as if her soul were in it.

Well, here was a link with the better side of humanity at any rate. So long as that glorious music continued Gilray could take heart of grace. He strained his ears, he heard the liquid notes break off suddenly and a woman's voice screaming in deadly fear. The screams went on for a moment or two, then ceased with a gurgling cry. It was as if a hand had been placed on the throat of a nightingale to stop its melody.

Every individual hair seemed to stand up straight on Gilray's head. He could hear the heavy tread of feet above him as if several persons were engaged in a deadly struggle, he could hear muffled curses and something that might have been the crack of a revolver.

Evidently he had been forgotten, murder was being done upstairs, and whatever the danger, he must not be found there. He fumbled for the door, only to find it fast locked, so he groped for some other outlet. As he did so there was a heavy fall in the room above, and after that silence like that of the grave. It was so silent that Gilray fancied he could hear the blood pulsing through his brain.

Something snapped, and a gleam of light darted like a lance across the floor and flooded the dark brick floor of the cellar-like room. A huddle of rats scampered away into the shadows. A trapdoor opened and a hand and arm appeared through the opening—a slim, white, velvet-skinned arm and hand traced with delicate blue veins a hand that had known no labour, daintily manicured, pink as to the polished nails, a hand moreover blazing with a glittering of antique diamond rings.

"Lord," Gilray gasped "Lord, I'd give my reputation and my good name to be well out of this!"

CHAPTER III

THE SARD INTAGLIO

Gilray moved back as if that long, slim hand was some fearful thing fraught with peril. Yet he was strangely fascinated by it, it aroused all his artistic sense and love of the beautiful. Nor was he blind to the value of those beautiful old rings that decked it with their glittering brilliants. It seemed to him that he had seen one of them before in a famous collection of jewels. Surely the one with the panel of stones had been part of the D'Alencus treasures.

Gilray could have sworn that he had once had it in his hand for inspection; that it was something he at one time had been half disposed to buy. Sweating and trembling as he was from hand to foot, he could not keep these thoughts out of his mind.

The slim, white arm advanced, the slender fingers, with the nails of pearl were almost on his foot, the waving light made circles of flame in the shadows, he could see the gleaming eyes of the terrified rats. He could see, too, the dark slime on the floor. Then the trap-door opened wider, and there was a sudden crash. Something was going to happen now.

But there was nothing to be desperately afraid of, after all. A big slice of the wall seemed to fall away, and behind the light of an electric torch Gilray could discern the outline of a slender figure. There was about it something pathetic and appealing—something that seemed to bring back Gilray's manhood again. He could not but see that the girl was in some trouble, and the idea flashed across him that her trouble had arisen because she had gone out of her way to assist him. She was gathering courage now. "You—you are Dr. Gilray?" she whispered.

Gilray replied hoarsely that he was. He wished that he could see his companion a little more plainly. As if in answer to his desire, the girl placed the torch on a ledge above her head, and stood out in the gleaming rays of it. And then, just for a moment, Gilray forgot his fear, forgot all his troubles and misfortunes, in the contemplation of that perfect face.

He was conscious of the exquisite chiselling of her features, the creamy ivory tint of her skin, and the clear lucent ruby of the pathetic lips. He saw the glint of gold and amber in the piled up masses of her hair, the violet grey eyes all heavy with unshed tears.

The girl was in trouble beyond all doubt, but the lines of sorrow on her face only added to her beauty, She was wrapped from head to foot in some soft clinging black drapery, but a wisp of fine old lace rippled about the white column of her throat, and another filmy wave was visible above her tiny ankles. Gilray's artistic eye apprised the value of the gossamer lace and the lovely old paste buckles on her shoes. Here was a mean, rat-haunted house in a mean and noisome neighbourhood allied with the beautiful and the costly in the strangest possible fashion, and Gilray would have given a good deal to know the meaning of it all.

"I came for you," the girl, explained. "I am sorry that you should have been left here so long."

She spoke as he had expected, in a voice low, sweet, and refined, yet just a little haughty. There was, too, a faint suggestion of hauteur about the face and in the carriage of the dainty head.

"It is nothing," Gilray hastened to explain. "I came here professionally, you understand. I knew it was an unconventional visit, so I was prepared to find an unconventional reception."

"So I understood. Will you come this way, please?"

"Might I not ask," Gilray stammered, "would it not be just as well for me to know where I am and the name of the people here? For instance; you are—"

The girl's face grew cold and hard.

"Does it in the least matter?" she asked. "I believe that the situation was made quite plain to you. It really was good of you to come, and Dr. Vorley is grateful. But as we are never likely to meet again my name can be nothing to you."

Gilray stammered some kind of apology. But he would have been something more than human not to have expressed some curiosity anent the situation in which he found himself. Beautiful women, were no strangers to him; he had seen beauty day by day in the most perfect, the most exquisite settings. But never before had he met a woman who moved him as this one did. He would have to marry some day, of course, he had always told himself that. Moreover, it was imperatively necessary that he should marry money. He could not forget the latter fact even in the midst of his surprises. Perhaps the girl was a heiress in her way, despite her sordid surroundings. Were there not those rings, that priceless lace, the old paste buckles to be accounted for?

"I am very sorry," he stammered. "You see, I sometimes have patients who wish to remain anonymous. I always decline to advise them. I had forgotten that to-night's business was exceptional. Is it not time that I saw my possible patient?"

The girl murmured that she had come to bring him to the patient, and without further ado led the way up a flight of steps into a corridor the walls of which were dark with age and grime. The floor apparently had not been scrubbed for years, yet here and there were scattered Persian prayer rugs that would attract admiration in Regent or Bond street. A picture or two, panels in oils, whose value could be seen at a glance, hung carelessly and crookedly on the dingy walls. Gilray took in all this with amazement, feeling more and more bewildered as he walked along. Presently he and his guide reached a square hall in which glowed a solitary electric lamp. It was strange to find electricity installed in so remote and sordid a house as this. Yet the hall was large and lofty, and had apparently at one time been richly decorated, for along the cornice Gilray could see peeling flakes of tarnished gold, and on the ceiling the faint remains of an allegorical painting. He remembered now what Vorley had said as to the time when this fragrant district had boasted fields and fair houses, houses wherein more than one chapter of past history had been made.

Down a flight of oaken stairs, rich with carved rails and balusters, Vorley came noiselessly. His coat was torn, his face was dirty, and one eye was partially closed. He had a bloodstained handkerchief across his forehead. It was then that Gilray, looking about him, noticed evidence of a struggle. A table and a couple of chairs had been overturned, and on the bare floor was a horribly suggestive dim red patch. With a shudder he remembered the din and confusion he had heard above him while imprisoned in the hideous darkness of the basement vault.

"Sorry to keep you so long waiting," Vorley said. "Did you hear anything?"

"It certainly seemed to me at one time as if some disturbance was going on. I also heard somebody singing most divinely. Probably I have to thank the young lady here for—"

"You are quite mistaken," the girl said coldly. "Are you not wasting time?"

She bowed and vanished into one of the unlighted rooms leading from the hall. As she closed the door behind her Gilray heard the click of a switch.

"What an exquisite creature!" he remarked involuntarily.

"Pretty girl, isn't she?" Vorley said carelessly. "You didn't get much out of her, I expect. Did she by any chance tell you her name?"

"She did not. She promptly checked all curiosity on the point."

"Umph, I thought so! As you will never see her again, probably it doesn't matter. We had a little bit of a scrimmage here, as you heard. It's a queer household, Lord knows how queer. But we're not poor, we can afford to pay for our little fancies. Still, come this way—your patient is upstairs. And a nice handful he is."

In one of the bare oak-beamed upper rooms the patient lay upon a plain iron bedstead. Vorley had rigged up an apology for an operating table, and by an ingenious arrangement of incandescent lamps and reflectors a powerful light was thrown directly upon it. Here, too, were all the necessary appliances for the administration of an anaesthetic, and it needed no second glance to see that Vorley had made no false boast when he claimed to understand this side of the business.

On the bed lay a big, heavy man, with luxuriant beard and whiskers. Between his frequent groans he was cursing in some language that sounded like German. A silk handkerchief was tied across his eyes. It was a queer pattern, in which orange spots predominated, and the design impressed itself upon Gilray's memory.

"It's all right, old man," Vorley said cheerfully to the man on the bed. "The oculist is here. No need to mention names, no need to do so on either side for that matter, but I've got the best that Harley-street can produce. Let's get that bandage off and see what really is the matter."

The bearded man muttered something that might have been gratitude. As Gilray removed the bandage he saw that the face was all raw and bleeding. Here and there were tiny punctures with raised edges, and the whole appearance went to show that the man had been wounded at long range by a charge of small shot. Both eyelids were granulated and suppurating and the inflammation was intense, making it plain that the sufferer was then quite blind, even if his sight was not lost for ever.

"Get him on the table and give him a whiff of ether," Gilray commanded.

With some trouble this was accomplished, and at last the patient lay inert and unconscious, ready for the operator. Directly Gilray had his instrument in his hands everything else was forgotten. He was no longer a stranger in a house of fear, he was the born genius with science on his side fighting for a man's sight. For an hour or more with his marvellously delicate touch he worked at the injured eyes, the grim rigidity of his face slowly relaxing as he moved on inch by inch towards victory.

He tossed the last bit of sponge aside, and wiped his face. Vorley was gazing at him with undisguised anxiety.

"Well?" he asked. "Are you satisfied?"

"Quite," Gilray said. "It was a very near thing, but I've managed it. The man has escaped total blindness by a sheer miracle. But he will get right again. All that's needed now is scrupulous care. A good, non-irritating antiseptic for washing purposes must be applied frequently and the eyes rebandaged closely after every application. Keep this going for a week, and then let the patient have light gradually; follow my directions carefully, and you'll not need me any more. And now we had better be going."

"Isn't there something to be done first?" Vorley asked.

"So far as I am concerned, nothing except the fee. I think you suggested that I could have this in cash, if necessary. A cheque in the circumstances might be difficult to negotiate. If the money is handy—"

Vorley chuckled, as if amused.

"Oh, you can have the hard gold if you prefer it," he said. "You will have to see the old man. Never mind what his name is. He's waiting for you in the room at the end of the corridor downstairs. Walk in, assure him of the success of the operation, and the money is yours. I'll wait for you and see you part of the way home."

Gilray followed the directions. He knocked at the door but no reply came, so he walked in and looked about him. He saw a desk with a swinging light over it, a desk piled high with gold, hundreds and hundreds of sovereigns, and stacks of bank notes. Behind the desk was a huge fire-proof safe full of books and papers that looked like securities.

Gilray fairly gasped at the evidence of all this wealth; he was gasping still as a door on the far side opened, and an old man came in. With a snarling cry of anger he banged down the top of his desk and turned to the intruder with raised hand. On the finger of the hand Gilray could see a Sard Intaglio, magnificent, and priceless.

"Who are you, and what do you want here?" the old man demanded. "Speak, or I'll—I'll kill you."

CHAPTER IV

THE THREE COSWAYS

Gilray shrugged his shoulders almost indifferently. He was getting accustomed to these dramatic episodes. Besides, he had nothing to be afraid of. Let him only get his money and he would not trouble this amazing household again. All the same, there was something exceedingly striking about this remarkable old man. He might have come straight from a stage setting, so strange was his aspect.

He was 'Gaspard' and 'Shylock' in one—tall and lean, and high of forehead from which the leonine grey hair was tossed carelessly back; he had thin, dark, hatchet-like features, and eyes that glowed like stars behind his gold-rimmed glasses. His keen, clever face was lined and wrinkled, his skin the colour of old parchment. To strengthen the likeness to the classical example of miserliness, he wore a kind of dressing-gown of velvet, and on his head was a skull-cap of the same material.

Surely he must be part and parcel of some stage production, Gilray thought. The room was almost the exact counterpart of the scene where Gaspard gloats over his treasures. The walls were almost bare, the carpet was thick with dust, there was a table and two kitchen chairs beside the great desk that stood under one of the windows. But the walls were not quite bare, for here and there a picture had been hung, and on the far side was a genuine Commonwealth chair or two. That the pictures were things of price Gilray knew at a glance—there were very few frequenters of Christies' rooms who were better judges than he.

"What are you doing here?" the old man asked again. "Who are you, and what do you want? How did you get into the house? And who let you in? And how much?"

"Three hundred pounds in gold."

"Too much. Far too much. My good man, where am I to get it from? I am poor, miserably, hopelessly poor. The fools outside think I'm rich. They grumble when I ask for my interest, they treat me violently. You know that I am poor."

He asked the question in a voice that was almost pleading. His keen eyes seemed to flicker over Gilray's face. There was a cunning here nearly allied to madness. Beyond question this old man was enormously rich. He was a miser, the garnering of gold was a mania with him. Obviously the type of madman to be humoured.

"There is some mistake," Gilray said. "I am an oculist. I practise in Hurley-street. The name of Gilray may be known to you. I came here to-night with Dr. Vorley to see a patient. I was," he said, "to have a fee of three hundred guineas—"

"Pounds curse him," the old man snarled. "He has no consideration for my poverty. And three hundred pounds is a deal of money. I am a poor old man, sir, a miserable old man—"

"I do not doubt it for a moment," Gilray said, curtly. "That is not the point. I came here on a distinct understanding, and I have done my work. I may say without boasting that I have been perfectly successful. Dr. Vorley sent me here to get my fee. Where is it?"

The old man's eye blazed dangerously. He shook with the passion that possessed him.

"Have a care, have a care," he said hoarsely. "I know you, Dr. Gilray. Bills, bills, and yet more bills. Papers in the hands of the Jews renewed over and over again. Betting and gambling. Cigars at six pounds the hundred, and champagne at a guinea a bottle. And yet representing one of the most Puritan consequences in England. Pah! I could ruin you to-morrow."

"Still, I have earned my money," Gilray protested.

"True, true! I take your word for it. You have done a great service, and you shall have your money. But it's a great wrench, a very great wrench."

The old man raised the flap of his desk as if there were something inside it struggling to escape from him and groped for a wash-leather bag. With a longing look, the look of a mother saying farewell to a child, he handed the round leather bag heavy with gold to Gilray.

"You will find the contents quite correct," he said. "If you like to count them—"

With a wave of his hand Gilray dropped the bag into his pocket. The old man chuckled. Then he frowned as he saw Gilray looking intently at a triangular object on the table.

It was a frame in gold and rubies in three panels, each panel containing a miniature portrait of some beautiful woman. There was no need for Gilray to ask whose work it was—the softness, the velvety smoothness and exquisite colouring proclaimed the artist to the connoisseur.

"You are interested in these pretty toys?" the old man asked carelessly.

"I cannot resist them," Gilray admitted, "It is one of my vices. And Cosway's work specially appeals to me. May I look at these?"

The old man gave a grudging consent. He might be a moneylender or a pawnbroker, as probably he was, but he loved these things for their own sake.

"Gon on," he said. "Examine what you like and keep your silence after. Those are not my things. They come to me in the way of business. They are security for borrowed money. Not my money, please understand, but the money of the capitalist who employs me. For I have nothing."

"And you are not afraid of keeping things here? Burglars?"

The old man chuckled again.

"'No burglars could come here," he said. "They know better than put their wits against those of Daniel Harley—"

Gilray made a mental note of the name.

"Because I am ready for them. Not that they know or guess. But my electrical alarms are perfect—the man who tries to get in here is held a prisoner till the police come. Geoffrey Herepath worked it all out for me. A young man, that, who will be a Kelvin some of these days. You know him—you are on a commission before which he gave evidence the other day. He knows that which before long will revolutionise the traffic of the world. You see, I read the papers, I keep myself abreast of the times."

But Gilray was barely listening. He knew Herepath by name, of course; they had met more than once lately, and there was no great love lost between them. Still, Herepath was a long way from Gilray's thoughts just now. He was engrossed upon these exquisite miniatures.

"The three Miss Hessingdales, are they not?" he asked.

The old man's brow clouded; he was growing hard and suspicious again.

"You know too much," he said. "Let me show you something now not quite so famous."

Daniel Harley laid his hand on the bell, and the door opened to admit the girl whom Gilray had seen earlier in the evening. She had discarded the black wrap now, she stood there all in white. Her grace and beauty seemed strangely out of place in that bare, desolate room, her fair face flushed as she saw that the old man was not alone.

"My second keys," he said. "Oh, they are here by my side all the time. My dear, this is Dr. Gilray. My daughter Enid, sir."

The girl flashed an imploring glance at Gilray. He rightly interpreted the look to mean that he was to meet her as a stranger. He bowed as he took the slender pink fingers in his, he thrilled at the contact of her warm flesh. The man was touched as he had never been touched before, moved to his soul. A wife like that, to call that exquisite creature his own! The rich wife that was a necessity to him. And to love her as well, to have his arm around that slender waist, to feel his lips pressed to that little scarlet mouth! His senses reeled as he thought of it. And there was nobody in the way, no rival in the field.

He was still pondering the matter after Harley had dismissed him with no suggestion that he should come there again. Still, he had a good excuse, he could almost demand a further inspection of the man upon whom he had just operated. Side by side with Vorley he walked the silent streets till the Tower Bridge was passed. Here Vorley paused, and called for a taxi from the rank.

"We had better part here," he said. "Goodbye, and many thanks."

"I might have to see my patient again," Gilray suggested.

"I think not," said Vorley drily. "Put him out of your mind. You said there would be no further occasion for you to come again. Oh, yes, Miss Harley is a lovely girl, and no lover comes her way, but all the same, keep your hands from the fire, or you will get burnt. Good-night."

Vorley turned on his heel and departed without another word.

Gilray, as he lounged back in the taxi, smiled to himself. He would be able to find his way back to that house of mystery with but little trouble, he told himself. He would first make a few inquiries, and quite satisfy himself as to the girl's prospects. But for his own folly and prodigal life, he would not have needed to have given money a thought. Had all been well with him, he would gladly have taken Enid without a penny.

He was thinking of the girl and her exquisite beauty as he got into bed; she disturbed his dreams throughout a restless night. Still, now that he had the money to meet that pressing claim, he could wholeheartedly give his attention to his morning's work until the stress was over and luncheon came. With that meal he picked up his 'Daily Messenger,' and tried to forget his professional labours. Then his knife and fork clattered on his plate as his eye met a paragraph that caused his heart to beat rapidly—

"Robbery in Park Lane. Van der Knoot treasures missing. A mysterious robbery took place last night in Park-lane, at the residence of Mr. Isidore Van der Knoot, the famous collector and dealer. It appears that the family were away from home, the servants are at the house in Scotland, and the premises are in charge of a trusted caretaker, who has been in Mr. Van der Knoot's employ for years.

"Just as it was getting dark, Walker, the caretaker, noticed a suspicious noise in the front drawing-room. On his going to see the cause he was attacked by a strange man, and a desperate struggle took place. Walker defended himself with a pistol charged with shot, and avows that he left his mark on the thief. He was overpowered, and rendered insensible, and when he came to himself found that nothing was missing save a three-panelled frame containing Cosway miniatures, presumably the portraits of the famous Misses Hessingdale.

"Probably the intruder, fearing the pistol shot would cause a general alarm, decamped without attempting to remove any of the numerous other treasures in the apartment. So far there is no clue to the thief, for the attack he made when disturbed was so fierce and sudden that Walker declares his utter inability to give any description of his assailant. The police, however, have the matter in hand, and are using every endeavour to trace the daring thief."

Gilray threw the paper on one side, and paced up and down the room. There was no doubt in his mind as to what had become of the missing Cosways. He had had them in his hand not many hours before. They had been stolen, and old Daniel Harley must have known it. But if so, why had he paraded the treasures in such an open fashion? He must have known that he was running a risk, under the eyes of a total stranger. Was the man he had attended, the thief? Was the picturesque old miser, Daniel Harley, a mere vulgar receiver? And did that exquisite girl with the face that recalled the pure features of a Madonna know?

Bah! The suggestion was ridiculous, incredible, impossible of belief. There must be some proper common-sense explanation of the mystery. There might be some—

Gilray's reflections were suddenly broken by the opening of the room door and the entrance of his neat and quiet body servant.

"You are wanted on the telephone, sir," said the man. "Mr. Geoffrey Herepath would like to speak to you. A matter that admits of no delay, sir."

CHAPTER V

Gilray nodded and walked as far as the inner consulting-room, where the telephone was placed. He was vaguely asking himself who this Herepath was who wished to speak to him so urgently. The name was oddly familiar, and yet for the moment he could not recall where he had heard it. It seemed in some way to be directly concerned with the stirring events of the past few hours. But then there had been so much to think about and, in any case, what did it really matter? Probably Herepath was no more than a casual patient who would see him to-day and would be gone to-morrow. There were hundreds of such, each regarding his or her own particular case as being of the first importance. And yet Gilray was annoyed because for the moment he could not place the name.

He took off the receiver and made the usual signal that he was there.

"Is that Doctor Everard Gilray?" a voice asked. "Oh, yes, I am Mr. Geoffrey Herepath speaking. We have met before at one or two scientific gatherings. I am an engineer—an electrical engineer."

"I begin to remember," Gilray said with practical professional glibness. "Oh, yes, Mr. Herepath, to be sure. Is there anything I can have the pleasure of doing for you?"

"Yes, you can give me an appointment," the voice at the other end of the line said. "I am sorry to say that I have been burning the candle at both ends, doctor. You see, I am an inventor as well as an engineer, and I prefer to do my own drawings. I dare not trust the secret of the process I have on hand now to anybody else. I once had a valuable set of drawings copied by a dishonest assistant who is now living on his own estate and motoring in a Rolls Royce car.

"There are scores and scores of minute lines on my plans, and I have to sit up half the night over them as I cannot find the time during the day. Lately I have experienced great difficulty in doing the work, and last night my sight failed me altogether. For some little time I could see nothing whatever. I went to my own doctor this morning early and he sent me to you. He took quite a serious view of the case and told me I must not lose a minute. Can you see me to-day?"

"I'll see you to-day with pleasure," Gilray said. "Hold a moment whilst I consult my appointment book...Are you there? Oh, yes, I can manage it. Say half-past one."

The voice at the other end of the 'phone murmured thanks, and the conversation ended. Gilray went back to his consulting-room, still somewhat puzzled. He did not recollect the man Herepath, and yet the name seemed quite familiar to him. He was sure that he had heard it quite lately, sure that he knew the man.

"Upon my word, I believe I have it," Gilray suddenly exclaimed. "Herepath was the name that queer old man down by the Docks spoke of last night. Herepath was the man who fitted up all those boasted burglar alarms in that mysterious house. Evidently a friend of the family. Very odd that I should so soon come in contact again with that queer crowd. Looks rather like fate. Anyway, it should give me a chance of following up my acquaintance with the beautiful Enid Harley. What a face, what a figure, what a voice. And probably rich into the bargain. It's any odds that the old miser is a Croesus. Never was there such a chance for a poor devil situated as I am. I'd willingly marry the girl if she hadn't a penny—if I only dared. But I must—I must—find a wife with money."

The old troubles came swooping down upon him again. True he had found the money to pay out that threatened attachment; he had already spoken to his solicitor on the telephone and despatched the money by special messenger. So far that ghost had been laid. But there were many other ghosts gibbering and mocking him, a veritable crowd of blue devils in the form of azure envelopes, littering his desk. He might manage to put off the great catastrophe for a week or two longer, but the end was inevitable unless some miracle happened, unless, for instance, he could prove to his creditors that he had a rich marriage in prospect.

He must find out all about Enid Harley and her father, and it seemed as if good fortune had tossed the opportunity into his lap in the shape of Herepath.

He had no appointment for an hour or two yet; he was tired of his own melancholy thoughts. To distract his attention he took up a newspaper and began to read mechanically. Apparently the 'Herald' was more enterprising than the 'Messenger,' and had much more to tell than its contemporary had about the mysterious outrage at Van der Knoot's place in Park-lane.

"Strange how everything keeps working in one line," Gilray muttered. "Here we are back to it again. I'm no judge of such things, if I did not see the missing miniatures of the beautiful Misses Hessingdale in the mysterious house by the river last night. Now what possible connection can there be between a millionaire collector who lives in Park-lane and a grasping old miser who has a house in the East End of London? Is Harley the head of a clever gang of international thieves who make a speciality of robbing people of valuable works of art? If so, it did not seem to worry him much when I spotted those priceless miniatures last night. And if he is a thief, what is Enid Harley? But, no—a girl with a face like her's could be nothing but good and pure. I wonder if I shall find any further information here."

As a matter of fact, there were several little points in the case the 'Messenger' man had missed. For instance, the 'Herald' stated that Mr. Van der Knoot's man Walker had been partially blinded by having snuff or pepper dashed into his eyes, and that there was a clue in the shape of a portion of a tie that Walker had torn from the throat of his assailant. The clue was in the possession of the police, and they, of course, had sanguine hopes that it would quickly lead them to the thief. Gilray smiled as he read.

"How, these newspapers help the criminal," he muttered. "Here is the thief, presumably by the very nature of his occupation a close student of the daily press, made a present of the information that the police possess a goodly portion of the tie he was wearing at the time he committed the outrage. Of course, the part of the tie he retained is in the fire by this time."

Gilray's immaculate butler broke in upon his master's meditation with, the information that if he was not engaged, Inspector Gillespie, of Scotland Yard, and another person would like to see him at once. Gilray fairly started. Had he been traced to the Docks last night? Was he about to be dragged into some sensational case? Well, if so, this was only one more straw added to the burden.

"I'll see the Inspector at once," he said. "Show him into the consulting-room."

Inspector Gillespie was sorry to trouble Doctor Gilray, but his business was urgent. Possibly the doctor had heard of the mysterious affair in Park Lane the night before. Perhaps he had read something of it in the papers.

Gilray breathed a little more freely. Evidently this affair had nothing to do with the equally mysterious house at Poplar. A glance at Inspector Gillespie's companion strengthened his impression. The man looked something between a gentleman's servant and a policeman in plain clothes, and he had a bandage over his eyes.

"I have just been reading the story," Gilray said. "Most interesting, I am sure."

"Very puzzling, too, sir," the inspector proceeded to explain. "We have no clue except that of a torn scarf. My companion is Walker. At the moment he told us all he could in his shaken up condition; since then he has been able to recall things a bit and has given us a closer description of the thief. But the poor fellow is badly handicapped by the injury to his eyes. For the moment, at any rate, he is practically blind, and if we did make an arrest couldn't help us much. His own doctor had done what he can, and says his sight will improve with time. But to us time is everything, and you can see how we are hampered by Walker's loss of sight. His medical man suggested that a specialist might expedite a cure. That is why I came to you, sir."

Gilray professed himself, with truth, ready to do anything to help. Apart from the professional side, he was now deeply interested in this business; he seemed to see that here was fate playing into his hands. He put his patient on a couch and removed the bandage from his eyes. He was the brilliant oculist now, and could think of nothing but his work. Nor did it take him long to get to the bottom of the mischief. He worked with a hand as steady as a rock, worked with the delicate instruments and brushes as fine as the point of a needle. Finally he applied some soothing fluid and replaced the bandage.

"There," he said, "that will be all right. You feel better already?"

"Thank you very much, sir, I do indeed," the grateful patient murmured. "The smarting has all gone and my eyes don't run any more. How long shall I be, sir, before—"

"Two days," Gilray said quietly. "The lotion night and morning. Take the bandage off this evening. Eight and forty hours hence you will see as well as ever."

"I should have liked him to have seen this first," the inspector said as he produced a fragment of torn silk from his pocket. "This is a piece of the thief's scarf, doctor. The only clue we possess."

Gilray put out his hand for the thing. As he looked at it he had some difficulty in repressing a cry. For the particular green ground and the queer arrangement of orange dots and splashes on it were quite familiar to him. It was the very pattern of the scarf he had seen bandaged over the eyes of his midnight patient at the house by the dock side.

But for his professional restraint and training he would assuredly have betrayed himself.

"Very interesting," he said coolly, "but rather fragmentary. And now, Inspector, if there is nothing else—"

Gillespie took the hint and departed with Walker in his train. All the rest of the morning patients came and went, and, though Gilray performed his tasks with amazing skill and assurance his mind was far away. He was wondering what all this was to lead to, and how it was destined to bear upon his fortunes. He was still brooding upon it when Geoffrey Herepath was announced.

He saw a tall, fair man, with a handsome, clever face, shrewd eyes, and a mouth relieved from hardness by a humorous, rather tender droop at the corners. He saw a man with power and intelligence written all over him. Then a flash of recognition came into his eyes.

"Your name puzzled me," he said. "I could not place you, though it was quite familiar. Why you were connected with me in that Clarges case some two years ago. I mean to take it up again when I have time. I am still convinced that there is money in it, and that we are the victims of a conspiracy."

"Certain," Herepath said. "I, too, am biding my time. But I have plenty of troubles of my own on hand just now, doctor. I think I explained everything to you on the telephone. I am anxious for your verdict."

"Quite right," Gilray replied. "I like to hear a man speak like that. Take off your coat and vest—and shirt. It is a theory of mine, based on one or two small successes, that these eye troubles are sometimes merely muscular...Yes, that will do nicely...Now I am going to put something in your eyes. No, not belladonna; I have a far better preparation than that, and one that causes no after inconvenience."

As Gilray bent in examination over his patient, he could see that Herepath had round his neck a slender gold chain to which a medallion was attached—an oval medallion containing a portrait which looked like a photograph on vellum or celluloid coloured by hand. He could see that this was the likeness of a girl, as he looked again his whole frame stiffened.

It was the photograph of Enid Harley.

Gilray opened his lips to speak, but not sound came. It was some little time before he could control himself sufficiently to say—

"That will do for the present. Let me bathe your eyes with this lotion...Yes, you can see quite as well as ever, I mean as well as you could when you came here."

"As well as I could when I came here, doctor, that sounds ominous. What is the—"

Herepath paused and Gilray passed his hand across a damp forehead.

"I—I can't tell you yet," he said. "It is far too early. You will have to come to me again in a week. In the meantime don't do any night work, and keep your eyes off those plans. Come again at this time next Thursday."

Gilray was alone again, alone and struggling with a fierce temptation. So that was the man who had robbed him of the girl, and her fortune. Her father who...it was preposterous. And it was so easy, so very easy to...

Gilray dropped into a chair, trembling from head to foot.

"I see my way, I see my way," he whispered hoarsely. "And, by heavens, I'll do it."

CHAPTER VI

MADAME NINON DESTERRE

Most of the houses in Park Gardens are small, and possess no gardens in the true sense of the word, but Number 4 differs from the rest, inasmuch as it stands in its own compact grounds overlooking Regent's Park, and therefore in summer presents an outlook reminiscent of sylvan shades in the heart of a peaceful woodland country. At one time the house had belonged to a famous artist, with an income equal to his refined extravagances, and the whole place had been remodelled according to his designs.

At his death the house, with all decorations and furniture complete, had been offered for sale, and was promptly secured by the present owner, known to her friends as Madame Ninon Desterre. The sale had caused some sensation at the time, and certain of the papers had striven to learn something of the history of the fair purchaser.

They had little to show as the result of their labours beyond the fact that Ninon Desterre was the young widow of a wealthy French recluse of mature years, who had devoted his considerable fortune to the collection of pictures and various other works of art. Monsieur Desterre was a Frenchman beyond question, but for many years prior to his death he had lived in Brazil, to which country he had gone after a violent quarrel with some member of the Academie Francaise in connection with a disputed old master. There he was supposed to have married the young daughter of a noted painter, whose career had been cut short by malaria just as he saw before him the opportunity of making a great name.

All this was very interesting to a certain class, and all of it was gravely absorbed as authentic. So far as the work-a-day world was concerned, it took little or no interest in the new owner of 4, Park Gardens. She was young, rich, and very beautiful, and a perfect hostess, who gave most charming and delightful entertainments. The result was that Ninon Desterre had become quite a prominent figure in society. Really it did not matter in the least where she came from so long as she gave those recherche lunches and dinners—little dinners to which everybody who was anybody looked eagerly forward. She was always beautifully dressed, and possessed a wit and bonhomie really remarkable for one who could not be more than five-and-twenty at the outside.

She sat in her own pink and gold boudoir with the wonderful Lelys and Watteaus on the walls, and those marvellous Persian carpets at her dainty feet. This was the delight and wonder of her intimates. It was never the same for seven days together.

There would be fresh pictures and carpets and Louis Seize furniture week by week, and all of the same matchless quality. It was as if Madame had somewhat a vast museum of artistic treasures, from which it was her mood to remodel and refurnish her sanctum at regular intervals.

She lay back with a tiny scented cigarette between her lips, in a wonderful carved chair, upholstered in silk tapestry.

Gowned for the evening in some diaphanous material, shell-pink in tint, she looked like some exquisite exotic flower. The red gold of her hair glittered in the firelight, and the glow was reflected in her clear, innocent amber-brown eyes. There was neither crease nor wrinkle on her face, nor did she owe one single charm to art. All that kind of thing Ninon Desterre despised. There would be plenty of time for that twenty years hence.

She was not alone. On the other side of the fireplace stood a tall, dark, good-looking man. He would have been still more striking looking but for a disfiguring scar on one cheek and a lameness in one leg. There was some suggestion of the soldier about him, and he had the air of a man who had travelled widely. At the same time his big slender hands bespoke the artist.

"Did you manage it all right, Hector?" Ninon asked.

"I'm not quite sure," the man responded "It was touch and go at one time. How much longer is this to go on, Ninon? Is there any real occasion for it?"

The girl's face changed for a moment. The fascinating smile vanished, the little red mouth grew hard.

"You seem to forget Daniel Harley," she said. "So long as he lives to trouble us, we must go on. Oh, you are a brave, strong man, and I am as little afraid of trouble as most women, but our master is there. We cannot defy him; without him we cannot move hand or foot. He was here a day or two ago, and some very plain words passed between us. He wants to know why it is I am dissatisfied. He pointed out that I was taking no risks that nothing could bring me, or you for that matter, within the grip of the law. He looks upon his cunning scheme as perfect."

"To give the devil his due, it is," Hector Marsail said grudgingly.

"Oh yes, I suppose so. But I am getting tired of it, all the same, old boy. I know I have heaps of money to spend, and that every tradesman in London would black my boots if I asked him to do so. Some of the best people in England come here as my friends. And I have carte blanche to spend what I like with Paquin and Worth. But, it is the lie that galls me, the sense of being a slave. To be in the power of that old man. But what is the use of talking? So long as he is alive—"

Marsail nodded moodily. He, too, could feel the gall of the chain about his neck.

"We must go on," he said. "Why did I ever go near that rascally old man? I could have borrowed money from a score of other sharks. And yet his terms looked so easy. Oh, confound it, what use is there in moralising? That hoary-headed old rascal could drive me out of society by holding up his hand. Some day I shall lose my temper and kill him. Why, he wasn't a bit grateful over that Park Lane affair, though he is pretty certain to make ten thousand out of Van der Knoot over the transaction."

"That was very neatly done, Hector," Ninon smiled. "And what an advertisement for the Dutch financier who was the happy possessor of Cosway's Three Miss Hessingdales. But I did not ask you to come here earlier than my other guests to talk of what has happened. Old Harley gave me a message for you. I was simply to say that Lady Stratton's diamond necklace is a fraud. I mean the one her husband purchased for her in Vienna when he floated his big company. He paid some twenty thousand pounds for it to Kreitzer, who sold it to him as having been once in the possession of the Catherine of Russia. It was a downright swindle, of course, and I believe that Harley was in it. Anyway, the stones are not worth more than a fifth of what they cost Stratton, and the history of the necklace is pure fake."

"The genuine Catherine necklace exists, of course, Ninon."

"Oh yes. Harley knows who has it, but he declines to say. Trust the old fox for keeping a piece of information like that to himself. As a matter of fact, I detected the fraud at the Duchess of Blanton's the other night. I could see that the diamonds were all right, but as soon as I caught sight of the settings I had my doubts as to the necklace being historical. I pretended to admire the gems, and had them in my hand. Quite a casual inspection convinced me that I was right. I think I know the hand that set those stones."

"I feel quite sorry for the vulgar, good-natured old soul. And I was glad for my own sake, Hector—glad and sorry at the same time. You see Harley had been accusing me of neglecting his interests lately; in his coarse way he said I was not paying my expenses. I mollified him by telling him of Lady Stratton's necklace, and he told me to see you—"

Marsail muttered something under his breath. There was an ugly frown on his handsome face.

"Then the next act is up to me," he said. "Curse all of them, curse all dealers who lay themselves out to swindle fools who have made money. I suppose every man is a fool in some way. Here is Stratton, a man who has made his money in the City by gulling investors, a financier with no scruples, and who regards everybody else as a knave at heart. Yet he parts with a small fortune on the strength of a pretty little fairy tale told him by a dealer in Vienna. And now I am to put this right. Well, I suppose I must do it, as I always do anything you ask me."

Something like a sigh of relief escaped Ninon's lips as a knock was heard and a servant entered. She was afraid that Marsail was about to drop into some warm avowal. She dreaded such an outbreak—it was one of the few things she feared. The man would have given his soul for her, and she knew it. He was the one man in the world, too, who could make her heart beat faster. Some day his strength would overpower her and he would take her away from all this to the simple, healthy life he instinctively belonged to. Well, some day, perhaps, she would be willing enough to go. But not yet, not yet. It would be hard to give up all this wealth and luxury, this possession of so much that the heart of a woman naturally longs for.

"Your guests are arriving, Madame," the servant murmured.

"I'll come down at once," Ninon replied. "Don't frown, Hector. I know you expected to have me all to yourself this evening. But I have a musical prodigy coming—a new tenor. Before long everybody will be talking about him. I have fifty or sixty people coming to hear him to-night."

Marsail smiled with the air of a man who makes the best of it.

Down below the beautiful rooms were rapidly filling with Ninon's guests. They were distinguished people, for the most part ready and eager to come to Park Gardens, despite the fact that they expected to be politely bored by the new tenor. There was a chatter of voices, and a ripple of laughter as Ninon came forward. She had an appropriate word and jest for everybody there, and she made no mistakes as to the names.

"This is quite an unexpected honour, Dr. Gilray," she said as the latter stepped forward. "I began to be afraid that you had turned your back on society altogether."

Gilray murmured some polite nothing, as Ninon turned away to greet some newcomer. He was somewhat cynically asking himself why he had come at all. It would have been better perhaps if he had turned his back on society long before. In that case he would not have been harassed as he was. What a set of chattering fools these people were! And what was the sense of getting into debt for the mere sake of a lot of other people who cared nothing about you? Here was Hector Marsail, for instance. What was an athlete and a sportsman like Marsail doing at this gathering?

"Bored to death, and so am I," Gilray told himself. "Hullo! What's this?"

He paused and looked at Marsail in astonishment. The rooms were a trifle overheated and the night was warm. The athlete had taken from his pocket a small silk handkerchief and passed it over his face. In the gleam of the electric lights Gilray plainly saw the pattern. It had a peculiar pale green ground and on it the dots and splashes of orange that Gilray had seen on the handkerchief over the eyes of his Poplar patient and on the ragged piece of scarf shown him by Inspector Gillespie.

"I seemed destined to come in contact with this amazing brotherhood," he mused. "But it's a far cry from a rascal in a riverside house to a man like Marsail. Am I in contact with something criminal, or is it merely a coincidence?"

Gilray looked up and gave an amazed start, as he found himself almost face to face with Enid Harley. She was dressed in white, and her face was pale as her dress. She looked strangely out of place there with her unhappy air and the patient suffering in her eyes.

Gilray made a step forward, but his hostess was before him. Never mind, he would get a chance to speak to her presently. He looked upon this as a happy omen. He told himself with exultation that he held all the cards, that he need be afraid of no man, least of all of Geoffrey Herepath. He could see the smile on Ninon Desterre's face and hear the light laughter from her lips. But he could not hear what she was saying to Enid.

"My dear," she whispered. "I'm so glad you came. But your face! You might be attending your own funeral. Go up to my room at once and wait for me. At once, I say. I have something to say to you that cannot be delayed."

CHAPTER VII

A COMPACT

Gilray pressed a little closer to the two women, he was anxious to hear what was passing between them. He was doing now what he would have scorned to do a year or so ago. His debts and his desperate troubles were sapping the moral fibre of the man. He was so nervously eager to get to the bottom of this mystery that his gentlemanly instincts were crushed out. Apparently he stood raptly contemplating one of the pictures on the wall. Ever and again words came to him, but he could make very little of them! Then he started.

Ninon Desterre was talking. Just for a moment she seemed to forget herself, for her voice was raised eagerly.

"Your esteemed father will never have enough," she exclaimed. "It is a growing disease, this money making. He told me that when he had made a million...more than that was...a profit of fifty thousand a year! If some of my pretty boys only knew, my dear. They would not go to America to look for a rich wife. Why, if you cared to, you might be a duchess...Very well, I won't."

Gilray edged away. He had learnt all that he required for the moment. So the dainty little white beauty with the innocent face and beautiful eyes was heiress to a million. The miser of Poplar was worth that and more! It looked as if the stars in their courses were fighting on his side now.

True, there was a rival in the path, but Gilray would know how to get rid of him. He had the weapon ready to his hand, and he would not hesitate to strike when the proper time came. And nobody would know; nobody would be any the wiser. He did not see how the crime he contemplated could possibly be brought home to him.

He moved on a little further until he came to a group of people whom he recognised. A popular novelist was fighting a battle of wits with a sculptor of repute, and others stood round listening to the merry duel. Gilray put aside all his troubles for the moment and became as interested as the others.

He did not know that Ninon had watched him as he had moved off.

"That man was listening," she said. "I felt it in my bones. Now, why was he listening. What have we to do with a fashionable oculist? Does he know you?"

"Well, he does, and he does not," Enid replied. "I was rather startled when I saw him here. I thought he failed to recognise me, and I was thankful for it. Are you sure he was listening, Madame Desterre? It makes me uncomfortable to think of such a thing."

"Certain of it, little one, certain of it. I never make mistakes of that kind. But why should it make you uncomfortable?"

"Well, Dr. Gilray came to our house last night. A friend of my father's brought him. We have a— gentleman staying with us who met with an accident to his eyes. Oh, don't ask me anything about how it happened, for I don't know. I live in queer surroundings. Sometimes I feel that things are being done that will reach the ears of the police some day. I am not consulted, I have only to fetch and carry, and do as I am told without asking questions. This man with the injured eyes is lying in our house. How and when he came I don't know. I am not surprised now at anything that takes place at home. All I know is that it was necessary to have an eye specialist at once, and one was fetched near midnight. I had to see him first, for we were not quite prepared for his visit. The man was Dr. Gilray. He was to ask no questions, and in return for his services he was to have a special fee. When the operation was over my father paid him three hundred guineas."

"Who would not be a popular surgeon?" Ninon said, smilingly. "Go on."

"He took the money, and he asked no questions. He must have known that there was something strange and unusual in the circumstances. Had I been in his position I should have refused."

Again Ninon smiled. The story seemed vastly to amuse her.

"Had you been in Dr. Gilray's position you would have done nothing of the sort," she said. "On the contrary, you would have prayed for many other such unusual calls. But we must not talk any more here. Go to my room."

"Not yet," Enid pleaded. "Oh, not yet! There is somebody coming here I must see. If I were to miss him I should never forgive myself."

Ninon hesitated, against her better judgment. She had a soft spot in her heart for Enid Harley. There was danger in the delay she knew quite well, but she did not want to be hard.

"We women are never really business-like," she said. "Even the hardest of us sometimes allows her heart to get away with her head. And I never could resist a romance, Enid. Mr. Herepath is late, eh?"

"Yes, he is," Enid said innocently. Then she coloured up to the roots of her hair. "How—how did you guess?"

"Guess, my child. Guess! Am I so old a woman that I have no curiosity as to affairs of the heart? Have I not had my own little episodes? Oh, I know why that brilliant young man comes here. When his great invention is complete he will be rich, he will take you away from here, and a very good thing too. I give you another quarter of an hour. If the prince has not come by that time, you must go to my room, and wait for me there. Now, mind you have only a quarter of an hour."

There was a mock frown on Ninon's face as she flitted away in the direction of a group on the other side of the room. Someone was speaking in Enid's ear, she felt a pressure of her hand. Then she looked up into the eager, tender eyes of Geoffrey Herepath.

"Here's a fine piece of luck for me, darling," Herepath whispered.

"I heard that you were coming," Enid whispered. "And I had to be here in any case. I came on business for my father, and Madame Desterre has given me a quarter of an hour. After that I have something to give her, she has some instructions for me, and then back home I must go."

"Then my luck is not so great as I had expected," Herepath said. "A quarter of an hour? Let us not waste a precious minute of it. Let me show you the way."

The rosy flush was still on Enid's cheeks as she followed. It was not often fortune smiled on her like this. Here had been a strange romance, an hour stolen here and there, a gradual advance from mere liking to fervent love for Geoffrey Herepath even before she realised that he too cared for her.

Nobody besides Madame Desterre suspected the existence of this affection. This was not the first time she had given the lovers one of their golden opportunities. Doubtless she had found out that Enid was coming here tonight, doubtless also, she had known of it for some considerable time before Enid had been made aware that she was to pay her a visit. It was all very fortunate and pleasant, but at the same time disturbing.

The lovers were seated in the loggia, which they had all to themselves. In a dimly-lit cosy corner behind a bolt of palms they nestled side by side. Geoffrey's arm was about her waist, and her red-gold head drooped on his shoulder. The world was a long way off just then.

"You are silent to-night, dear," Herepath whispered.

"I generally am when I am happy," Enid answered softly. "It is so delightful to get away from that horrible old house of ours. You know it, you discovered all those electric appliances to keep burglars away. Not that any of them are in the least likely to visit us. My father poses as a poor man—"

"Don't you think that he may be a poor man, Enid? Men of his temperament have strange delusions."

"Possibly, Geoffrey. I don't know what to think. Madame Desterre says he is rich. They have a good many business transactions together. I have been here many times with art treasures. I have some to-night. I know my father better than most people, or at any rate as far as it is possible for anyone to really know him. And when he dies I have a feeling that he will leave nothing."

"Then I shall get a poor wife, after all," Geoffrey said banteringly.

"I think so. Will it make any difference, Geoffrey?"

Herepath took the pretty, inquiring face between his hands and kissed the red lips.

"Nothing could make any difference," he said. "You only ask the question because you know I should answer it in this way. As for money, I shall have enough for two."

"Then you are still prospering with the new invention, dear? But your eyes. Remember what you told me about them. Remember that you promised to get assistance with those drawings, that you would not work at night."

"Oh, yes, yes." Herepath said a trifle impatiently. "I know. I engaged an assistant who proved too clever for me. He took a too intelligent interest in his work. He was learning the heart of things. A little longer and my secret would have been his. He was a spy in the pay of a firm in the north. I managed to lead him into a kind of blind alley, and then dismissed him. My dearest girl I had to do my own work. And my eyes have been very queer lately."

"Geoffrey. You frighten me. You must go to some good oculist at once.

"My dearest little girl, I have already done so. I saw Gilray, who, by the way, is here tonight. I am to call upon him again in a day or two."

"And what did he say? Was he at all doubtful? Geoffrey, you don't know how anxious I am."

"Well, he pronounced no judgment. He said it was too early to be definite. But he told me that I was not to do any more drawing just now, and that I was to spare my eyes as much as possible till he saw me again. He did not say that there is really anything serious."

But Enid was not so easily satisfied. She was pondering over the matter after Herepath had gone. It occurred to her as strange that Geoffrey should have consulted Gilray. In a way Gilray was coming into her life. She seemed to be meeting him now at every turn. And, in some strange, uneasy fashion, she had a feeling that he was watching her. She felt an impulse to get out of his sight. Anyway she was anxious to finish her business now and get back home. She waited impatiently for the best part of half an hour in Madame Desterre's boudoir, but the mistress of the house did not come. Something was evidently detaining her. Surely Enid had not misunderstood her instructions. She crept timidly down into the hall again, where a little knot of people were discussing some subject with a good deal of interest. Enid could see that Gilray was one of the group.

A small man was speaking, a little man with a fat, flat face, out of which, on either side of an aggressively hooked nose, gleamed a black eye hard as a diamond. Gilray moved round and stood by Enid's side. His own eyes were only a shade less hard and brilliant than those of the man who was talking so rapidly.

"That is Mr. Van der Knoot," Gilray whispered. "The man whose house was burgled."

Gilray, as he spoke, was startled to see the colour fade from Enid's cheeks. Her hand went involuntarily to her side, her lips parted in a sudden gasp. She stood there white and rigid.

"There is no clue," the German financier was saying. "There never will be a clue. The police expect to do great things with that torn scarf, but I cannot see how they can use it. By this time it will be that the other part has been destroyed. I shall my miniatures see never again. And I paid—it was three thousand guineas for them."

"But what use can they be to anybody?" a guest asked eagerly. "Stolen property like that is so easily identified, it is property with a history—"

"Ah, my young friend," said the German sententiously, "you but little know of the hardened collector. He no honesty has when on his hobby, no moral sense. He anything would take, and gloat over it in secret. He would the price pay for his own private gratification, and never let a soul know what he had got. Why, there are collectors who to see my treasures come, well-known men and quite honourable in other ways, that I would not leave by themselves in my galleries for a single moment. No, no," he said regretfully, "I shall look upon my beautiful Cosways never any more."

"I am not so sure of that," Gilray said. "Now what would you give me if I could put you in the way of getting them back once more? If I told you exactly where they were—"

Gilray paused and glanced at Enid. He saw her hand once more go to her left side, he caught in her eyes a look of terror and entreaty. She was imploring him to be silent.

"Oh, you mock me, you make fun of my misfortune," sighed Van der Knoot. "It is to me, alas, a certainty, that I shall my treasures never see again."

Enid swayed a little and Gilray caught her hand in a firm grasp. None of the others seemed to notice them. They could not hear the girl's quivering whisper in Gilray's ear:

"It you are a gentleman you will say no more."

"It Is a compact," was Gilray's answer. "A compact between us. You shall give me my reward later on."

CHAPTER VIII

THE HIGH ROAD OF ADVENTURE

Here at last it appeared to Gilray was Fortune holding out both hands to him. He had formed a compact with Enid, showing that she was more or less under an obligation to him. It would have been a difficult matter to state precisely what that obligation was, but no doubt time would help him to give it some satisfactory definition. Anyway, Enid had been desperately afraid lest he should speak, lest he should say something that might put Van der Knoot on the track of his missing miniatures. Gilray had certainly seen the precious pictures in the hands of Daniel Harley. Whether they had been stolen or not it did not in the least matter—perhaps there was some strange story attached to their appearance in the queer dock-side house, some plausible explanation. Even the blackest evidence sometimes becomes commonplace when the witnesses for the defence enter the witness-box.

What did it matter? Suppose Daniel Harley was a thief, what then? At any rate he was a man of immense wealth and Enid was his only child. If there should be any scandal it would be an easy matter Gilray argued to himself, to shield her good name. People would be sorry for her, she would have the sympathy of everybody. It is not a difficult matter to extend the hand of friendship to a girl who has a million or so of her own. Folks would tell the story of the beautiful wife of the popular and fashionable Doctor Gilray—and envy her. Assuredly everything was going the right way now, his creditors would wait when they knew everything. And the girl was already more or less in his power. But he must not let her see that yet.

Enid had been watching Gilray as these thoughts rushed swiftly through his mind, with a look of appealing alarm upon her face. He noted her expression and turned to her again with gentle deference.

"You may rely on me implicitly," he whispered almost tenderly. "You have not the faintest cause for fear. Remember that a doctor regards the confidence of his patient as sacred. I have already forgotten what I saw in that old house of yours. But you won't forget me, Miss Harley. You will let me see you sometimes."

Gilray paused. It seemed to him that he had put the matter with great delicacy. Enid's lip quivered in a smile, her eyes were eloquent of her thanks, and yet she felt conscious of being in some sort of trap, although she could not see the bars.

"I very rarely come here, Dr. Gilray," she said. "You have been very kind, perhaps more kind than you know. Oh, how all this mystery worries me."

Enid spoke the last few words impulsively, and then, as if, suddenly conscious that she was saying too much, pulled herself up short and with another murmur of thanks slipped from Gilray's side and moved towards the door.

He made no attempt to detain her, he was perfectly satisfied with the progress of affairs so far. So he leisurely turned to listen to the woes of the unfortunate rich, as expounded by the disconsolate Van der Knoot who, the centre of a knot of sympathisers, was still bitterly lamenting his misfortune.

"I am only one of many," he fumed. "Look you at the scores of thievings of this kind that have in London happened lately. Always it is the small things worth the most that go from us. What is it the police are doing? They have, it would seem, no way to check this kind of thing. It is for my wife I am more sorry than for myself. You see, it was to her that the stolen miniatures belonged really."

Mrs. Van der Knoot fidgeted uneasily. There was a deep flush on her dark, handsome face.

Already she had made more than one attempt to change the conversation. She seemed to suggest an aloofness from her husband's somewhat vulgar ostentation. As the daughter of an impoverished Irish peer the Honourable Mrs. Van der Knoot despised the wealthy Teuton plebeian she had wedded for his money. So long as she was free to indulge in her bridge, her turf, and her stock Exchange gambles unmolested she was prepared to tolerate his coarse city friends, but this was no place for the manners of Throgmorton-street.

"You are boring these good people here," she said coldly. "Really, anyone would think that it was a serious matter. And, anyway the loss is mine, not yours. You brought me those pretty miniatures, because I took a fancy to them, and now they are stolen. My dear Ninon, are we to be permitted any bridge to-night?"

Ninon's dancing, mischievous eyes suddenly grew steady. She had been watching the whole scene with infinite amusement, nothing had escaped her. From behind her mask of frivolity and inconsequence she saw into the heart of things as few around her did.

"I am desolated, ma cherie," she cried. "It cuts me to the soul to disappoint you. But alas! this evening it cannot be. You have sat in the music room and listened enraptured to my wonderful tenor, and for to-night that must suffice. On the stroke of 12 I shall have to turn you all out, for I have to go further. Behold the Peris outside the gates of Paradise. I blush for my hard, cold inhospitality."

She flitted like a butterfly to another group of guests, but left them almost as quickly as she came, and caught Enid in the doorway. Here, in a flash, she became another woman, cold and persistent, with the light of a great determination gleaming in her eyes.

"I love the life of a kaleidoscope," she said rapidly. "My foi, how things develop in the course of a few seconds; I have had to rearrange all my plans, little Enid. I have to go out when but a little time ago I was hoping to retire early. There is no occasion for our conference after all. Still, I have a few questions to ask, and you must reply to them freely. What was Dr. Gilray saying to you, and what reason have you to be afraid of him?"

"Oh, if I only knew," Enid said passionately. "Take me somewhere so that I can speak to you without fear of interruption....Yes, this will do. You asked me a question—let me reply by asking you one in my turn. What is the meaning of all this mystery? Why am I treated as if I were some child, some baby who cannot understand? Why am I a mere puppet in the strange transactions that take place between my father and you and that drunken, good natured Doctor Horace Vorley?"

"My dear child, let business matters alone. They are not for you to worry about. Be content with your life as it is. I want you to believe me when I say that I am your friend. I asked you a question. And I asked it with a sincere desire for your own welfare. Are you in that man's power?"

"I don't know," Enid said helplessly. "I don't know. He forced me to make a kind of friendly compact with him. He spoke nicely enough, and yet there was something in his voice that made me hate him. He—he knows that I have the Hessingdale miniatures here in my possession."

Ninon Desterre's face grew hard, and her eyes gleamed wickedly.

"Oh, indeed," she said. "So our brilliant Gilray guessed so much, did he? He has nosed out, has he, that you came here tonight bringing a parcel purporting—only purporting, mind—to contain the missing miniatures?"

"But, my dear Madame, it does not contain the missing miniatures. And they belong to Mrs. Van der Knoot."

"They don't, you silly little cabbage. I give you my word of honour they don't. I cannot explain, but you can accept my statement implicitly. It is all a most complicated business matter, child, that you could never understand. And Gilray thinks he has found something out. My dear child, why did you clasp your hand to the place where the parcel is in that dramatic manner? I was watching you. Of course you made the Doctor think you had something hidden. He's a very clever man, is Dr. Gilray."

"But he knew about the miniatures before. He was at our river-side house last night. I told you he came down to see a patient who is, well, hiding I call it, with us. The miniatures were on the table in my father's room and Dr. Gilray saw them. He had them in his hand. Had he chosen to open his lips to-night he could have ruined me, and all of us. Cannot you see the danger?"

"Oh, yes," Ninon said gravely. "I can see danger of a sort, mark you. It was a good thing, a very good thing, that our friend the doctor did not speak—especially for him. He came here to spy out the land, no doubt, and he has put two and two together and made them five. I think I see his motive. You are young and lovely, Enid, and some of these days you will be the happy possessor of great wealth. On the other hand, Gilray is poor and ambitious. No wonder that he artfully managed to make a compact with you, that he took advantage of your position. But do not be afraid. I shall know how to deal with the ambitious doctor when the time comes. Now just go quietly home, and don't let this stupid affair trouble you any more. The compact, if you chose to think it as such, will not be very troublesome after all."

Enid smiled gratefully. She was wonderfully comforted by Ninon's assurance. She was beginning to realise that there was some strange power and force behind this brilliant society butterfly; that she had a purpose in posing as a woman of whom nothing mattered in the world besides gaiety and self-indulgence. At the same time Enid still resented being treated as a child whose thoughts and opinions were of no consequence.

"I should like to feel sure," she began timidly, "that what you say as to the miniatures—"

"Is true," Ninon interrupted shortly. "Of course it is. We are exceedingly clever business people, my dear, so clever that we do nothing to bring us within the grip of the law. We believe in the truth of the saying that there is a fool born every minute, and some fools are very rich, and we arrange our business accordingly, my dear, that is all. And now, if you like, I will call Mrs. Van der Knoot here, and she shall tell you herself that the Cosway miniatures no longer belong to her. She shall even give you information that would afford some folks a good income for life. But, thank goodness, you don't belong to that class, Enid. Now, shall I call Mrs. Van der Knoot?"

Enid smiled in spite of herself. All that Ninon was saying sounded ridiculously wild and extravagant, but her manner gave the impression that she was quite in earnest.

"No, no, do not call her. I could not speak to her on such a matter. The mere idea frightens me," said Enid, quickly. "Only I am getting so tired and weary of this nightmare existence. How much longer am I to live in it?"

"Not much longer, dearie. Have patience. It is only young people who cannot wait for anything. The older one gets the less time seems to matter. Now go back to your taxi and don't come here again until I send for you. Good night, my dear, and pleasant dreams."

The guests were dropping away one by one, the beautiful rooms were being gradually deserted. One of the last to go was Gilray. He stood for a moment bending over the hand of his hostess. He had something easy and pleasant to say as usual, for his compliments were always well turned.

"It is always such a pleasure to come here," he murmured. "You strike an original note. There is no salon in London quite like yours, Madame Desterre. May I come again soon?"

"As soon as to-morrow night," Ninon said with one of her fascinating smiles. "Come and dine with me at 9 o'clock. I shall be quite alone for once. I will show you a way out of your troubles. Only it will not be by means of a marriage, at least not the marriage you are at present contemplating, my dear doctor. Now I have warned you."

"Are my troubles public property?" Gilray asked, a trifle coldly. "Am I to be told that?"

"You will be told what I choose to tell you," Ninon said coolly. "My dear, clever doctor, when you know me better you will find that I always get my own way. And it is quite dangerous for people to interfere with me. If you are only sensible you will be happy and prosperous yet. Good-night, and mind you are punctual to-morrow evening."

Gilray went away conscious of a vague sense of defeat. What did the woman mean? Why had she spoken in that frankly impertinent way of his affairs? Was there a hand of steel under that exquisite little velvet glove? Gilray was asking himself these questions as he passed down the garden to the road. From somewhere in the background he caught the flash of a lamp, he could hear the purring of a motor engine. The car swept by him a moment or two later, the light gleaming inside. As he looked he caught sight of Madame Desterre, a companion by her side. It was only for a moment, but that moment sufficed to disclose the dissipated features of Horace Vorley.

In a flash Gilray hailed a passing taxi cab.

"Keep that motor in sight," he commanded. "Follow it to the end of the world if necessary. Here's a sovereign on account of your fare. Now then, get a move on you or you'll be too late."

CHAPTER IX

ALONG THE ROAD

It was done rashly and on the spur of the moment. Exactly what he was going to discover Gilray had not the faintest notion. It seemed a ridiculous thing for a prominent Harley-street specialist to be setting out on a wild, midnight adventure like this with no logical excuse, and no notion where the escapade might lead him. Madame Desterre had annoyed and piqued him. She had spoken of his private affairs with thinly-veiled insolence, and she had, moreover, threatened him. Who was this giddy, glittering society butterfly who ventured to pit her wits against his? He would show her that this sort of thing was not to be tolerated.

Gilray's blood was up now, and he was determined to see the matter through. The more knowledge he gained the better armed would he be for the fray, if fray there was eventually to be. He had been warned to make no further advances towards Enid Harley: he had been threatened with serious consequences if he did so. Indeed, it seemed to him that Madame Desterre had almost gone so far as to offer him a bribe. She had certainly given him a hint to the effect that his troubles would be at an end if he did as he was told. Assuredly his financial embarrassments must be quite well known to the beautiful and fascinating Frenchwoman.

But was she quite the frivolous, featherheaded, little creature he took her to be? Of course, she was witty and intellectual, and she had a profound knowledge of artistic things. This latter, no doubt, she had acquired from her late husband. But she was something more than a wealthy widow whose sole ambition it was to make the most of life. In the first place, she evidently knew all about the mystery surrounding the strange old house amongst the crumbling wharves. She, it was clear, was personally acquainted with the dissipated and eccentric Vorley. She could, no doubt, have told the police all about the disappearance of those miniatures from Park Lane. And Enid had been at Park Gardens that night with those very missing Cosways on her person. Why? And why, also, had Mrs. Van der Knoot been so indifferent over her loss?

It was a little disturbing to reflect how easily Madame Desterre had read his intentions with regard to Enid Harley. Still, it did not much matter—he was going on all the same. The woman had learnt a great deal about him, and if in return he could learn a little of her queer movements, then so much the better.

Probably the car was not going very far, possibly to the place near the Docks. No doubt an hour or so would see the end of the night's adventure.

Thus thought Gilray in his self-conceit; but he began to grow uneasy when the car and taxi sped on from crowded streets to suburbs where the houses grew more and more scattered, and at last ran into the open country. Here it was not policy to get too near the car, so the taxi kept the best part of half a mile behind. Gilray put his head out of the window and addressed the driver.

"Where are we?" he asked. "How far from town?"

"A good ten or fifteen miles I should say, sir," the man replied. "Getting towards Sevenoaks, if I'm any judge."

"The car in front does not seem to be a very speedy one."

"Well, that's where I'm a bit puzzled, sir," said the driver. "She's a fifty to sixty Gainsborough, that car is, and she could leave us standing if she liked. It's no business of mine, of course, sir, but it looks to me as if them parties in front have tumbled to it as we're a following 'em and are having a bit of a game with us."

Gilray rejected the suggestion impatiently. Probably, he told himself, there was something wrong with the car. If they knew that he was in pursuit, they would have shaken him off long ago There would be no object in luring him into the country like this. Besides, how could Madame Desterre know that he was following her. The mere fact of a taxi in her wake would not arouse her suspicions.

For another half-hour or more the two vehicles sped along, the car in front gleaming like a star. Gilray could see the glow before him. The road in front stretched away straight and level, so that the tall light of the car was plain to the eye. Then suddenly it vanished as if it had been wiped out of existence altogether. The astonished taxi driver pulled up in amazement.

"Well, that's the funniest bloomin' thing I've ever struck," he muttered "Now where the dickens have they got to? Couldn't have met with an accident or we should have heard the smash."

"Get to the spot and see," Gilray cried angrily. "We'll fathom this thing."

The taxi pulled up so far as the driver could judge, exactly at the spot where the lights had vanished. Then, detaching a lamp, he and Gilray made a careful investigation of the road. They saw the freshly-indented marks of a corded tyre leading to the soft glassy side of the road, and there they vanished abruptly in a tangle of blackberry bushes. There were no further tyre marks, no sign of the car, and no traces of any accident. It was as if some giant hand had picked up the big Gainsborough and carried it away bodily.

"Drive on," said Gilray shortly. "These people have hit upon some clever dodge to hide their tracks. We shall pick them up again presently. For some reason or other they have put their lights out."

The taxi driver shrugged his shoulders. All roads were the same to him so long as he got his fare and his petrol held out. He sped along at his top speed till the road made a sharp drop into a long valley where, at the foot of the hill, a house loomed large by the roadside. At this moment there was a heavy report, like the crack of a heavy rifle and the taxi swayed dangerously. Then it came to a stop with a shudder like some wild creature mortally wounded.

"Here's a pretty go," exclaimed the driver. "I've busted a tyre. And, what's more, I ain't got never a spare one nor a 'Stepney' with me. We'll have to stay here the night, sir. Anyhow, we shan't be able to get away till I can raise another bloomin' tyre from somewhere."

Gilray swore under his breath. He cursed himself heartily for the insane folly and idle curiosity that had impelled him to take this foolish trip.

"What's the place opposite?" he asked. "It looks to me rather like a public-house. Can't I see a sign hanging over the door?"

"Somebody's been a-emptying a lot of scrap-iron here," the driver muttered. "Here's the jagged bit that did for my tyre. Cut it clean through an' through, it has. If I could put my dooks on the blasted fool as did this—Eh? Oh, beg your pardon, sir. Oh, yes, it's a pub all right. 'The Blue Anchor.' Looks like a decent kind of a place. Shall I knock 'em up, sir?"

Gilray nodded impatiently. He was thinking about his important appointments for the morrow. The taxi-driver hammered at the door of the inn, and presently an upper window was opened, a head was thrust out, and a surly voice demanded to know what all the noise was about. Then the head withdrew, and the door downstairs was opened.

"You can have a bed if you like," the innkeeper explained none too civilly. "There's a fire in the kitchen and some cold meat on the dresser. You'll find all you need there. I'll light the lamp and you can help yourself to what you want from the bar. No. 9 is the bedroom. My wife's away and the barmaid's away, and I'm supposed to be in bed with the 'flue. That's why you've got to help yourselves and make the best of it. There's a sofa in the kitchen where your man can sleep. Here's the lamp, and here's the matches, and now, good-night."

The surly landlord vanished without another word. It was not exactly a cordial greeting, but there was nothing to be gained by grumbling. Anyway, the kitchen fire was a good one, and the cold meat left little to be desired. As soon as he had finished his meal the tired chauffeur flung himself down on the couch.

"Excuse me, sir," he said. "First time I've rested for thirty hours."

He closed his eyes and was instantly fast asleep. There was no sound in the house besides the steady noise of his breathing. Gilray envied the man his ability to sleep. He would have given a good deal for the same gift. He was very tired and very disappointed, and yet he had never felt more disinclined for sleep in his life. He looked about him for something to distract his attention from his moody thoughts.

It was a fine old inn, evidently a survival of the old coaching days. The walls of the kitchen were lined with oak panelling of quaint design, the rafters were black with age. It seemed almost impossible to connect this place with trouble and strife. The whole house seemed to be steeped in a slumber as profound as that of Rip Van Winckle, and at the sudden bark of a dog in the distance Gilray fairly started.

He started again a moment later at a heavy footfall overhead. It seemed to him that he could hear somebody coming down the stairs. Then a door appeared to open somewhere, and from behind it came the sound of a laugh. It was a light, silvery laugh, and could only have come from a woman's lips.

Where had he heard that laugh before? It struck a familiar chord in Gilray's ear. He was absolutely certain that he had heard it before. Just for a moment he associated it with Madame Desterre. But that was quite impossible, for the volatile little Frenchwoman was miles behind or miles ahead—it was impossible to say which.

At any rate, Gilray was going to find out, if he could, the origin of that laugh. There was no reason, at all why he should not go to bed. He had his candle and a box of matches, and therefore ought to have no trouble in locating room No. 9 that the landlord had allotted him.

He lit the candle and made his way cautiously up the stairs. It was not quite as late as he had expected, for as he passed up, a grandfather clock on the landing proclaimed the hour of one. As he reached the big, square space from which the bedrooms branched off, he stopped suddenly and blew out the candle. He had the box of matches in his hand, so that he could light it again any moment that he chose. He could hear that laugh again distinctly, just as careless and gay as ever. It seemed to come from one of the rooms on the right, though it was impossible to locate the precise apartment. Over the doors were quaintly-carved numbers on small oak shields depending from brass studs. Here was No. 9 all right, as Gilray could see by striking a match. The door was closed, and he was about to open it when once more rang out that easy laugh. Behind the door next to his somebody was talking.

He bent down to listen, for it seemed to him that he was on the track now. He could only catch a word here and there, but they thrilled him to the core, set him tingling from head to foot with excitement and curiosity.

"Mrs. Van der Knoot...Oh, there was no mistake about the name, of course. Yes, you were quite successful...We'll give him a lesson."

"He's a dangerous chap," another, deeper, voice replied. "Clever and unscrupulous, and most desperately hard up. If you think that Gilray—"

He heard no more. It was maddening. And the worst of it was he had not the faintest idea as to who was taking his name in vain. Was this some cunning trap that he had been lured into? Well, if so, they should get nothing out of him. If it was a trap, then it was an extremely cunning one. If Madame Desterre had had anything to do with it, then it should go hard with her later. He would show her what it was to come between him and his plans.

He jumped back into the darkness as the door of the room opened suddenly, and a lance of light flashed across the landing. He would learn now who these people were.

CHAPTER X

IN THE DARK

Just for a little while Gilray could see nothing. True, the door was open, and he could hear a chatter of voices, but he had darted into the shadow that lay black on one side of the corridor so that only a glimpse into the bedroom was afforded him. He could make out a portion of the panelled wall with a picture or two upon it, there was the outline of a Chippendale cabinet full of old china. One of the pictures was undoubtedly a Millet, as Gilray's trained eye could see at a glance. These were unusual objects to encounter in a wayside inn, and at any other time he would have noted them with astonishment.

But so many amazing things had happened during that wonderful evening that it seemed to Gilray now that he was past all further astonishment. Otherwise he might have gasped aloud as a man emerged from the mysterious room carrying a candle in his hand. The candlestick was of old silver, but it was not this fact that specially attracted Gilray's attention. The man was the landlord of the Blue Anchor: the somewhat dishevelled individual whom he had seen but a little time before with tumbled hair and limbs encased in crude pyjamas.

The man was transformed. His hair now was sleek and well groomed, he was dressed in immaculate evening clothes. The cut of the coat and the set of the white vest spoke eloquently of Bond-street; the glossy linen and carefully tied bow left nothing to be desired. It was almost impossible to believe that it was the same man, but Gilray knew that his eyes did not deceive him.

The man with the candlestick made his way downstairs, humming some operatic snatch to himself as he went, and a minute or two later it seemed to Gilray that he could hear the faint hum of a car in the distance. But for the moment he was not curious on that score. The door of the room nearly opposite was wide open now, and he was going to make it his business to find out what was going on inside. He moved noiselessly across the corridor, and stood within the doorway of a bedroom exactly opposite.

Then he rubbed his eyes in astonishment. It was like some scene torn out of the pages of the Arabian Nights' Entertainment. The sitting-room was furnished to perfection, the old panelled walls were covered with pictures, there was silver and china and bronze of price, the table and chairs and cabinets were of Chippendale's best period. In the middle of the room was a gate-legged table on which a dainty supper was set out, the flowers were sprays of blue orchids like a cloud of butterflies, the candles were dimly shaded. Gilray could see the gleam of wine in the cut glass decanters, the bloom on the grapes, and the pink hue of the peaches.

There were three people in the room—Madame Desterre, just as Gilray had seen her an hour or so before, Vorley changed almost out of all knowledge, and as immaculately clad as the man who had just gone downstairs. The other guest was a tall, slender woman with dark eyes, clean-cut features, and a small head crowned with a magnificent mass of black hair. There were diamonds in her ears and a tiara of brilliants flashing and dazzling like stars across the sombre wonder of her hair.

"Good heavens, what does it all mean?" Gilray muttered to himself. "What sort of a public house have I tumbled upon? Landlords in Bond-street clothes carrying Queen Anne silver candlesticks, and sitting-rooms furnished by Chippendale! Moreover, if the dark woman yonder is not Princess Helena of Pau, then I am either mad or my eyes have failed me. Now, what on earth is that eccentric lady doing here?"

Just for the moment the most amazing Princess in Europe was smoking a cigarette. Gilray watched her in fascinated curiosity. He had met the Princess more than once, he had heard a great deal about her extravagances and her boundless generosity. She spent much of her time in England, and was persona grata everywhere. Somewhere in the background there was a complacent spouse, but he was seldom met with very far from Monte Carlo.

"Don't you think it is time we were on the move, Ninon, my dear?" the Princess suggested. "This is a very charming adventure and the supper was exquisite. The peaches were a dream. And I have positively fallen in love with this quaint old place; but business, carissime, business."

"You are a reproach to me, Princes," Ninon Desterre said, showing her teeth in a dazzling smile. "For the moment I had almost forgotten the serious side of the evening. But be content—everything counts to the one who knows how to wait."

The Princess tossed the end of her cigarette into the fire.

"Ah, that is never me," she sighed. "To me it is not capable to wait. It is a gift that none of my family possess. You see it is this money—I must have it. If the drama of the evening fails, positively, I shall be what you call broke to the world. My good friend the doctor Vorley smiles. He does not understand what I mean."

"Madame, it is the only thing in the world I do understand," Vorley said, gravely. "It has been my condition since the days when I was at school. There are rare intervals when the sun shines—metaphorically speaking, it is going to shine to-night, that is if you are patient. The scheme cannot fail. I am here to see that it does not."

The Princess smiled like a child who has been presented with a new toy. She laughed delightfully. Gilray, watching them, was wondering whether a tragedy, or a comedy was in progress. That some mischief was afoot he did not doubt for a moment. He was still turning the question over in his mind when the man, whom he knew only as the landlord of the inn, returned, looking as if something had displeased him.

"I'm very sorry, good people," he said, "but I cannot get the car to go. What are we going to do? It is quite a mile from here to the castle—"

"Walk," Ninon decided promptly. "It is fine night, fairly dry under foot, and I know that there is a good road to the castle. We can turn down the avenue by the stables and enter by the Monk's door. It would be far better for us to do that than to drive up to the front entrance and be properly announced. I did contemplate some such plan at the start. I've my overshoes in the car and the Princess already has hers on or she could not have got in so quietly as she did. For certain obvious reasons the Doctor brought his goloshes. I presume you have a pair?"

"Oh, I'm all right," the landlord responded. "Don't worry about me, Ninon. Perhaps it will be our best plan to walk after all. In which case we had better be off."

Gilray smiled grimly. Wherever these people were going he intended to follow. He also was equipped with goloshes, for he had originally intended to return from Park Gardens to Harley-street on foot when he saw the car that had led him into this wild and mysterious adventure.

"Then the expedition primitive sets out afoot," the Princess cried gaily. "In that case we must make a move at once, for there is no time to be lost. I fly to tidy myself. It is not longer than two little seconds that I keep you waiting."

"Keep to your word," Ninon said. "One of us must stay behind. I am very sorry for you, my dear landlord, but that fate must be yours. It is essential that the car should be ready to start the very minute we return. If I were you, I should muffle myself up and get that unfortunate taxi-driver in the kitchen to do the work. Then you can either follow us on to the Castle or stay here till we come back. I must fly and tidy myself, too."

The Princess had already vanished into her room, and Gilray deemed it prudent to seek his. Where these people went he would follow.

Possibly he would learn something that he could turn to advantage. Ninon Desterre had threatened him, and he was not the one to forget that kind of thing. Also she had promised him a way out of his troubles if he was wise enough not to thwart her wishes. Well, perhaps he might use her to advantage and get his own way at the same time. There was nothing criminal here as he had at first imagined—the presence of the Princess guaranteed that. Possibly the whole adventure was based on some political intrigue, and he was going to see to that.

He lit his candle cautiously and looked about his bedroom. It was furnished according to its needs, quite as handsomely and tastefully as the apartment on the other side of the wide corridor. Evidently it had recently been used by some lady of fashion as a dressing-room, for the dressing-table was littered with scent bottles and powder puffs and there was a pearl-mounted comb and a pair of ivory-backed brushes bearing a coronet in diamonds. They would do quite well for him, Gilray decided grimly. He would come back here very soon again and investigate this mysterious inn where the bedrooms were furnished in Chippendale and the guests used hair brushes with diamond coronets on the backs. It might pay him to do so.

He was quite ready now, even to his overcoat and goloshes, for his self-appointed spying mission. Very quietly he opened the door and listened for the movements of the conspirators. He could follow a whisper of voices and some laughter, then the stairs began to creak and afterwards was silence. Gilray cautiously locked his door and dropped the key in his pocket. He was taking no risks, he was not going to give that wonderfully well-dressed landlord the chance of prying into his room to see if he was sleeping. He stood at the top of the stairs looking down until he saw the last of the party vanish into the night, and was pleasantly surprised to see that the landlord accompanied them.

"I wonder what my patients would say if they could see me now," Gilray soliloquised. "I should not have a shred of reputation left. But I feel that some way there is a fortune in this queer night's business. It may give me the power to dictate terms to Madame Desterre. Anyway, I've got Enid Harley to fall back on—my salvation certainly lies there."

It was quite an easy matter to follow the party in front. The night was not very dark and there was no wind. The landlord had dropped out somewhere, for Gilray could distinctly make out that there were only three people in front of him. They turned off the high road presently and passed through a fine old gateway which brought them to a magnificent pile of buildings with lights a-gleam from quite a hundred windows.

What place was this, Gilray wondered? He had heard it spoken of as the Castle, but that had not conveyed much to him. Evidently it was some great country seat and obviously there was a big function going on within its walls.

Gilray pressed eagerly forward, for he had lost sight of those whom he was following for a moment. He was close to a door now, and he was examining carefully when he gave a savage exclamation.

Somebody had grasped him from behind in a grip that left him helpless. The door he had been scrutinising was flung open and he was fairly tossed inside as if he had been a feather. He scrambled to his feet with an oath, but he was too late. The door closed behind him; he heard the sharp click of its bolts as the key turned in the lock. They had tricked him again and he was a prisoner.

Then for a moment he lost his head. He fairly raced along the brilliantly-lighted corridor in which he found himself and turned like a hunted fox into a room where a man was seated. Mechanically he took off his coat—his hat was goodness knows where—and turned in a dazed way to the stranger.

"Don't you apologise," the latter said. "If you've come any distance, you are doing quite the right thing. I've been here before, so I know the ropes. You will find everything for the comfort of cold and thirsty humanity on the sideboard. Help yourself."

CHAPTER XI

A SOCIAL FUNCTION

Gilray was amazed at his reception, but he steadied himself with one hand upon the table. He must not betray himself before the stranger who so kindly took his presence for granted. There would be plenty of time for an explanation later on. It would be as well too, if he followed the other man's suggestion. He was feeling jumpy and nervy, as well he might, when all the circumstances were taken into consideration. So he quietly helped himself to a whisky and soda, and gulped it down. The generous old cordial warmed his blood and restored his flagging spirit.

Where was he, and what was going on? That he would have to find out as quickly as possible. To try to explain his presence there by a bold recital of the plain truth was out of the question. His host or hostess, as the case might be, would rightly refuse to believe him. They would probably hand him over to the police, and then a ruinous scandal would be caused. He had no desire that his professional reputation should suffer.

He was evidently in a very large house, a house presumably in the occupation of some person of immense wealth. The place was humming like a hive; he could hear the chatter of voices in the distance, the sliding of feet over a floor; and the faint strains of a band. He wondered why and by whom he had been forced into his present position. It was just possible that the whole thing was an elaborate practical joke. "It seems to me that I have met you somewhere before," Gilray said, fighting cautiously for an opening. "Really, your face is very familiar. If you are one of the—er—family—"

"No such luck, Dr. Gilray," the other interposed laughingly. "Merely a family friend. It is not for me to call myself a relative of the Duke of Glenday, husband of the charming Duchess, nee Miss Pamela Dewitt, some time of Chicago, and the richest heiress in the States. Not that I am a pauper, but we can't all live at Glenday Castle."

Gilray smiled. He was getting on. The mere fact that this man recognized him was in his favour, but he was not thinking of that. He had contrived to clutch the fact that he was at Glenday Castle, the palatial residence of the Duke of Glenday, and his beautiful wife. He had heard something of this evenings' function; his lady patients had been chattering about it for days. Something like fifteen hundred guests had been invited to a dance and fancy fair. Every guest had been expected to pay a sum of five guineas for his or her ticket. It was one of the Duchess's brilliant ideas in aid of some of her pet charities. Gilray seemed to have heard it said that the tickets were transferable. He was beginning to feel a little easier in his mind. If this were true, there was no reason why he should not see the adventure through serenely. He would be tolerably certain to find scores of people here that he knew, and his presence would pass in the crowd. He no longer contemplated a lame apology for his intrusion and a speedy retreat after making it. Oh, dear, no. He rose buoyantly on his self-conceit.

"I suppose this is a very brilliant function, Mr.—er—Mr..." he began.

"Herries, Jack Herries, of the Rifle Brigade at your service," the other man said. "Brilliant—I believe you my boy. It is absolutely it. Nothing like it has ever been seen in the county before. There are two bands and two dancing floors, to begin with. There's a fancy fair in the royal suite, a music hall show in the gallery, pictures somewhere above, and a real imitation, if I may use the expression, of a country fair in the winter garden. Everybody's here, from Princess Helena of Pau downwards."

Gilray pricked up his ears. He was learning something.

"Is the Princess staying in the house?" he asked.

"Oh, yes, and about a hundred people besides. She's got all her family jewels here. I've never seen such a display of diamonds outside a drawing-room or on a gala night at the opera. Go and have a look at it for yourself. As a matter of fact, it is quite out of my line. Never did care for these swagger functions. Give me a quiet rubber of bridge, and I'm content. But don't let me keep you."

Gilray divested himself of his goloshes. A glance in a long gilt mirror convinced him that he was perfectly all right, and would pass muster anywhere. If somebody had played a practical joke upon him, they were not going to gain much by it.

"I've never been here before," he explained. "Apparently I was wrongly directed, for I came in by a side door. Which turning do I take?"

The man called Herries gave the necessary directions. A sudden turn at the end of the corridor brought Gilray into the centre of the festivities. He had attended some brilliant gatherings in his time, but never such a one as this.

A magnificent space, some three hundred feet square, paved with mosaic, and covered by a lofty lantern roof, lay before him. The whole area was dotted with groups of palms and ferns and brilliant banks of tropical flowers. The place was heated almost unpleasantly, but in that warm, rather moist, atmosphere, the red and gold and azure orchids flourished, and the creeping plants rose to the roof. Cunningly hidden here and there amongst the luxuriant leafage were clusters of electric lights gleaming out like shafts of sunshine. Under the waving branches of the trees rows of tents had been erected, and each of them contained some extravagantly advertised show, after the manner of a country pleasure fair. The charge for admission to each had been fixed at five shillings, and it was held to be a point of honour that every guest should do the fair honestly and thoroughly.

Nothing was wanting even to the tent of the fortune-teller, a swarthy bearded Indian, carefully made up for the part, and now for a moment relaxing his Delphic labours, and smoking a cigarette in the opening of his tent. A constant laughing stream of well-dressed men and women moved along, talking at the top of their voices, for the proprietors of the various shows were vociferously insistent, and advertised their attractions in stentorian tones.

For a moment Gilray had an impulse to put aside his curiosity, to forget the errand that had brought him there, and abandon himself to the gaiety of the hour. He was feeling more at home now; there were plenty of acquaintances present; and he had already acknowledged the smiles and bows of a score of people he knew. At the same time, it was just as well to remember that he was not there for amusement only. In the distance he could see Madame Desterre laughing and talking to a little group of her intimates, with Vorley hanging watchfully in the background.

Gilray made his way towards them, and presently found himself by the side of the beautiful volatile Frenchwoman.

She arched her eyebrows with a pretty gesture of surprise. There was not the faintest suggestion of embarrassment in her manner as she came forward, and Gilray looked in vain for any trace of mischief or amusement.

"So we are determined to meet twice in the same night," she said. "Now why did you not tell me last evening that you were coming here later?"

"I did not know myself when I left your house," Gilray said. "It was quite early when you dismissed us so cruelly, and it seemed a pity to go home."

"Oh, yes, perhaps. And how did you get here?"

"I took a taxi-cab. It was the quickest, and, in fact, the only way."

"Extravagant man! I am afraid you do not properly appreciate the value of money, my dear doctor. You will be sorry for it some of these days."

Gilray shot a quick glance at his companion. He was wondering if she meant anything by that remark, if there was some hidden threat or sting in it. But Ninon was innocently smiling, as apparently in rapt admiration she contemplated the bewildering tangle of gold and crimson orchids bowered overhead.

"I am no miser," he said coldly, "and besides I have only myself to consider."

"For the moment, yes. But you will not remain a bachelor all your life, doctor. There will come a time when you will meet the right woman. Perhaps you imagine that already you have met the right woman. Am I not curious, doctor, dear?"

Gilray set his teeth together. Under all this lightness, and behind that dazzling smile, the woman was again warning him, again defying him to go his own way. She must be made to understand.

"Curiosity is at once a weakness and charm of your sex," he said. "Who could resist Madame Desterre when she invites one's confidences so prettily. Yes, I fancy I have found the fair one. Your young friend, Miss Enid Harley, is very beautiful."

"Lovely," Ninon murmured. "Oh, yes, I understand your meaning. You pay me a great compliment in thus giving me your secret. A case of love at first sight, eh? Well, I have read of such things, I am prepared to believe that there may be authentic cases. But then, such sudden affection must be mutual to render the little romance complete."

"It generally lies in the hands of the man, Madame. If the man is clever and capable. If he has a fair conceit of himself, he can soon inspire the object of his regard with love."

"Yes, yes. But if there is another lion in the path? What then, Monsieur?"

Ninon looked up swiftly as she spoke. She saw the sombre gleam in Gilray's eyes, she caught the savage knitted frown on his forehead.

"There are ways and means," he said. "All is fair in love and war, Madame Desterre. I hope you will realise that I am not the man to—"

Gilray hesitated, conscious of the fact that he was going too far.

"To stick at trifles," Ninon finished the speech for him. "No, I don't think you are. But unfortunately for you, I have other views for my charming little Enid. And when I make up my mind to do a thing, doctor, I usually contrive to see it done. Now I could find a wife for you equally charming and equally rich. Let me introduce you to her—she is under this very roof at the present moment."

"Madame, an Englishman's affections are not like those of a Frenchman, made to order. Pardon me, if I decline your offer."

"Then you defy me," Ninon made no pretence of politeness now. "It is to be a duel a la morte? Good. Then I warn you that the time is not far distant when you will bitterly rue the day you crossed my path. Turn back before it is too late, I implore you. Ah, you laugh."

Gilray smiled at this exhibition of passion. Yet there was a note in Ninon's voice that told him she was not playing, but meant every word she said.

But he would treat it as a play nevertheless, so with a shrug of the shoulders, he said—

"Now we come to the melodrama. Woman, I defy you. You shall not come between me and the dream of my lifetime. Do your worst."

Ninon met his forced raillery with a similar weapon.

"Oh, I shall," she said, and laughed merrily. "It is just as well, sir, that you and I should thoroughly understand each other. There is yet a chance for you to see the error of your ways. If you will not be warned by me, then perhaps you will listen to the mysterious being yonder who reads humanity's fortune in the stars. I mean the Indian person opposite who looks into the future for a fee. Come and spend five shillings on him. It may save you from a fate so terrible that I shudder at the mere contemplation of it. Do come."

CHAPTER XII

THE FORTUNE-TELLER

Gilray smiled. After all it was a difficult matter to be angry long with Ninon Desterre.

"I know my fortune already," he said. "Most men of ambition do. We make our own, Madame Desterre. It is a mere matter of selection."

"Really! But is there not a popular saying to the effect that nothing happens but the unexpected? Man may propose, you know, but the power of disposing lies elsewhere. Ah, you are ambitious for political honours and a seat in the Cabinet. To reach that goal you must give all your time to the game, and be independent of your profession. Therefore, you follow the lines of the least resistance and look for a rich wife—"

Gilray smiled again. He was not going to be drawn any more. On the contrary, he was here to find out what Ninon Desterre was doing. It amused and flattered his egregious self-conceit to imagine that he had utterly deceived the pretty Frenchwoman, and that she was in blissful ignorance of the fact that he had tracked her every step of the way from London. If there was some clever moneymaking scheme afoot well then he might as well share it. If he could force himself into the conspirators' ring he could demand his price. And a few thousands pounds just now would mean salvation. Perhaps it might help him if he could manage to get an introduction to the Princess.

He had seen her as the thought came to him, and in another moment she came up. She fairly glittered with the diamonds she was wearing. It seemed to Gilray that she was adorned far more extravagantly now than she had been at the time she left the old inn.

"Let me present Dr. Gilray, Princess," Ninon said. "Dr. Gilray is one of the leading authorities on the eye. He is an autocrat in his profession. Whenever he issues his commands there is nothing for us but to obey."

The Princess smiled dreamily. She extended her hand with a charming frankness that was all her own. Her dark beauty was positively dazzling.

"I have heard of you," she said. "My uncle the Duc de Medoni was a patient of yours. He says that you gave him new sight. Ah, well, it is a dreadful thing to have trouble with the eyes. Fancy not being able to witness so charming and delightful a scene as this. Not to see the colours and the lovely flowers."

"You came over on purpose, Princess," Gilray hazarded.

"Well, not quite. You see, I am a guest of the Duchess. I have been staying in this delightful house for days. Positively it is an asylum for me, Dr. Gilray. I am so poor that it is to me impossible to stay in one of your London hotels."

Gilray murmured his condolences. He was perfectly grave and sympathetic. But he spoke with his tongue in his check all the same. It seemed impossible to associate this brilliant dark beauty with poverty. Her dress was the latest and daintiest costly frivol from Paris; she stood there pleading impecuniosity with twenty thousand pounds' worth of diamonds flashing in her hair and glistening on her corsage.

"It is a terrible thing to be poor," Gilray said, gravely. "I speak from experience. It makes us dread the future."

"Is that why you are afraid to have your fortune told?" Ninon Desterre asked coldly. "Princess, I have challenged the doctor to have his fortune told. He puts me off by saying that an ambitious man knows his own fortune. All the same, I am quite sure that he is moved by some silly, superstitious fear."

"I love it," the Princess cried. "There is nothing I enjoy better than the telling of one's fortune. I am so poor that nothing the seers reveal to me can be worse than the reality."

"And you are going to try your fate again, Princess?" Gilray asked.

"Positively, yes. You shall go and pave the way for me. Never let it be said that a man is afraid to hear the truth—I will wait for you here."

Gilray hesitated a moment, suspecting a trap. Possibly these people after all suspected that he was watching them and had planned to get him out of the way. Yet there was no eagerness in the Princess's manner. It was very difficult to connect her with anything definitely wrong. It was also very difficult to refuse a request so charmingly and winningly made.

"You have only to command me and I obey," he smiled. "When the tent is empty—"

"Which is now," Ninon exclaimed. "See, Lady Blessinglay is just leaving. Go in at once and we will wait and hear what the seer has to say. I'm told he is wonderful."

It was quite dark within the tent. Gilray found himself gripped by the hand, and quietly but firmly led to a seat. Then a dim light appeared from somewhere, and Gilray could just make out the outline of a tall figure wrapped in some clinging gown. The seer bent over his hand, just visible in the dim light, and examined it gravely.

"You regard this thing as nonsense?" the seer asked gravely.

"Not for you," Gilray retorted. "There is a business side to everything. Hand-reading will ever remain popular whilst a fool is born every minute.

"We shall see," the seer went on importantly. "You are Dr. Gilray, of Harley-street, the man who looks to the eyes of the fashionable world. Nothing wonderful in my knowing all about that, you may say. You have a large practice, you are young and popular, and you have already made something of a name for yourself in the House of Commons, and yet with it all you are not a happy man, Dr. Gilray."

"Can anyone lay claim to be entirely happy?" Gilray asked indifferently.

"True. Happiness is a relative quality. You can make some people happy with a slice of suet pudding. Another is miserable though his head carries a crown. But you are not happy, and all the more miserable because your misfortunes are your own fault."

"I am not denying it, magician. If the average man could only analyse himself candidly, he would find that his misfortunes were usually of his own making."

"That is exactly what I expected you to say. With some the curse of drink, with others merely ostentation. There is no more fruitful source of misery than ostentation. It is the curse of our ruling classes, and it is rotting the backbone of England. And that is your trouble. You must have a house in Harley-street, even if you have to go to the Jews for the money to pay for the lease and the furniture. Then everything must be on the most lavish scale. At this moment you are up to your ears in debt; you don't know which way to turn for money. It only needs a feather on the wrong side of the scale to put the balance in favour of disaster."

"Truly you are a wonderful man," Gilray said sardonically. "Go on. I neither admit nor deny a word you say. If this is blackmail—"

"Do you want me to throw you out of the tent? Do you want me to break every bone in your miserable body? If so, kindly repeat that remark again, Dr. Gilray. I am here to save you from yourself. You are meditating a crime, sir."

"A crime!" Gilray started. He was moved from his attitude of cold contempt at last. "Since you know so much, what is this crime you speak of?"

"Oh, so you begin to understand me," the seer said quietly. "You give me credit after all for some little foresight. The crime you have in your mind is one that may never be found out. It will inflict cruel injury on one who is powerless to retort; it may mean the ruin of two lives. But you will not care for that. The ground will be clear for you, and you will flatter yourself that you are on the way to safety."

"All this is Greek to me," Gilray said in a voice that was none too firm. "If your desire is to impress me, you have gone quite the wrong way about it. I suppose you go on the principle of firing blindly in all directions in the hope of hitting a stray bird somewhere. But you have missed the mark this time."

"My bullet has gone to the centre of the target, Dr. Gilray. I have warned you, so look to yourself if you refuse to heed that warning. The rich marriage you picture in your mind will never be yours; persistence in the course you contemplate will end in ruin and disgrace. There is no bride coming out of the East for you."

"In that case I am wasting my time," Gilray said as he rose to his feet. "I can only conclude that you are somebody who knows me, and that the seance is an elaborate jest. Let me compliment you on it and wish you good night."

The seer merely bowed in silence, and made no effort to detain the visitor. There was a smile on Gilray's lips as he emerged from the tent into the glitter of lights and the movement of the brilliant throng; but the smile was not in his heart. Indeed, he was more shaken and disturbed than he cared to admit. As he had suggested, the fortune-telling might have been no more than admirable fooling, but the arrow had gone very near the mark. He was not particularly pleased to find the Princess and Ninon Desterre awaiting him.

"You look like a man who has seen a ghost," the latter declared.

Gilray muttered something under his breath. The Princess moved forward in the direction of the tent. She seemed childishly eager for her turn to peep at Fate.

"I hope the magician will be less candid with the Princess than he was with me," Gilray said. "Upon my word, there is no limit to the impudence of this sort of people. I presume they make it their business to hang about the areas of West End houses and pick up the gossip of the kitchen. Really—"

He saw the mischievous gleam in Ninon's eyes and stopped suddenly. He had an uneasy feeling that she could throw some light on the seer's knowledge of his affairs. But she chattered away in the most inconsequential manner, making such shrewd remarks on passing guests that, in spite of himself, Gilray was interested. It seemed hard to believe that this vivacious little Frenchwoman could really be serious even for a moment. She was still laughing when the door of the tent opened, and Princess Helena came out.

"The most wonderful man," the Princess exclaimed. "Positively he thrilled me. I am amazed that I did not fall fainting at his feet. My dear, when I tell you—"

"Tell me something else first," Ninon interrupted quietly. "Princess, will you please tell me what has become of your diamonds? Positively you have not one left."

CHAPTER XIII

"STOP THIEF!"

For a moment Princess Helena made no reply. It struck Gilray that she looked a little pale and distrait, much as if she had been suddenly aroused from sleep. The pupils of her eyes were dilated, and Gilray suspected drugs. As a fashionable doctor, he knew the symptoms.

Certainly the Princess had disappeared into the fortune-teller's tent a few minutes before in full possession of all her faculties, and wearing all those magnificent jewels. And here she was now with not a single stone in her hair or on her corsage. It was no time to stand on ceremony. Gilray laid his hand on the Princess' shoulder, and shook her sharply.

"Tell what has happened," he demanded. "It may be nothing but a joke, but it is possible to carry such jokes too far. Where are your diamonds?"

The Princess lifted her hands to her head, then rapidly felt her neck and breast. It was as if she were trying to struggle back to recollection of things. Certainly she was behaving exactly like one just recovering from the effects of some powerful drug. And yet she appeared lively enough as she had emerged from the tent. She must be roused anyway. Gilray spoke again, very sharply this time. Then he could see intelligence returning.

"My diamonds?" the Princess whispered. "What about my diamonds?"

She was awake and in earnest now. She took a step forward, clutching at her breast.

"What has happened?" she demanded. "All at once I felt quite faint. Why—yes, yes, my jewels have gone—somebody has stolen them!"

Gilray waited to hear no more. He was quite convinced that this was no jest. Even in the fun and excitement of a fancy fair under such a roof as that no guest would so far forget good manners as to take for a joke the jewels of a Princess. There were limits even where the 'smart set' was concerned, and the Duchess of Glenday would assuredly not be pleased to be considered one of that coterie. Beyond all question the Princess had been the victim of an audacious robbery.

There was no time to be lost. The magician must be still in the tent; indeed, he could not have left without being seen, for it was only three or four yards away. Without further hesitation Gilray darted forward and lifted up the canvas flap. He intended to get to the bottom of this.

"Here, you there," he commanded, "what is the meaning of this? What have you done with the Princess Helena's diamonds?"

No reply came from the dim recesses of the tent. There was no sound of any movement. Gilray had an uneasy feeling that he was alone there. He fumbled nervously at his watch chain for his match-box, and struck a vesta. As the flame brightened he looked anxiously around for any sign of the magician.

The tent was empty, its late occupant had vanished like a dream.

This startling discovery for a moment deprived Gilray of the power of thought. Where on earth had the fellow gone to? He was certainly there but a few minutes before. It was equally certain that he had not come out by way of the tent door. Gilray struck another match, and made a more careful search.

Ah, there it was—he had found it. A long clean slit on the far side of the tent explained the rascal's unnoticed escape. Gilray eagerly pushed his way out. Right in front of him was an avenue of palms and orchids, and at the end of it, not many yards away, was a door leading to the garden. By this door lay a long black gown, and by the side of it a black wig and beard. It was now beyond all question that the Princess had been made the victim of a bold and carefully planned conspiracy.

Gilray rushed back to the spot where he had left the Princess and Madame Desterre. He found them no longer alone, but the centre of an eager and excited crowd of guests. The coolest and most collected person there was the Princess herself.

"I cannot explain," she said. "I do not profess to know. Like so many of you, I go in to see the magician. He bids me to take a seat, and he tells me things. He tells me the most amazing things connected with my past life. I am so upset that I feel quite queer. Then he gives me a handkerchief saturated with some scented stuff, and bathes my face with it. Then for a moment or two I remember nothing. When I come out I feel faint, and my good friend, Ninon Desterre, cries out that my diamonds are gone. And they are gone. Some thief has stolen them."

The tall figure of the Duke of Glenday pushed through the excited mob of guests.

"This is very distressing, Princess," he said. "When someone came running to me to tell me what had happened I could hardly credit my own ears. That such a thing could happen under my roof grieves me beyond measure. You are quite sure that it is not some jest?"

"There Is no jest about it, your Grace," Gilray interrupted. "A short time ago I had a personal interview with the alleged magician. When I came out of the tent the Princess went in. I stood chatting with Madame Desterre till her Highness came back. She was then without the jewels she was wearing when she entered the tent so short a time before."

"Whereupon you raised an alarm, sir?" the Duke asked.

"No, I didn't. I was so staggered for a minute or two by the discovery that I was not capable of thinking of anything else. It seemed such an amazing thing to happen in a house like this. Directly I recovered my presence of mind I dashed into the tent to challenge the occupant. But no occupant was there. I was certain he had not left by the ordinary exit, and making a quick search I found a long slit cut in the back of the tent by which he had escaped. He had evidently hurried along a corridor at the back of the tent, and escaped to a door leading to the garden. By that door you will find a black cloak and a beard and wig thrown off by the thief as he left the house. The police should be telephoned for."

An excited murmur followed this statement. Many pretty, daintily-dressed women had been under the spell of the magician during the evening, but none of them had lost as much as an earring. Evidently the rascal had coolly waited the chance of a big haul.

"Let the police be telephoned for at once," the Duke said, "it is just as well perhaps that nothing worse happened. That ruffian might have caused serious consequences by his reckless use of chloroform. I suppose it was chloroform."

"I am quite certain of it," Gilray said. "As an operating surgeon who uses anaesthetics every day, I should know, your Grace."

"Oh, so you are a doctor. Pardon me, but I do not recognise your face. But probably you are one of my wife's guests. At a moment like this...you understand."

Gilray flushed a little. He knew perfectly well what the Duke meant. He was putting it as politely as possible, but all the same he was asking for his unknown guest's credentials, how he got there, and whence came his invitation. The inquiry if pressed home might land Gilray in a very awkward predicament.

Madame Desterre gracefully and easily came to the rescue.

"Dr. Gilray," she said sweetly, "who belongs to my party. Her Grace told me—"

"Not another word, please," the Duke interrupted. "I apologise to Dr. Gilray. Nay, more, I have to thank him heartily for the great services he has performed. You think the Princess was drugged, doctor? Yes? Ah, here is Mr. Lascelles, my secretary. You have heard everything, Lascelles? Do you know anything about this fortune-teller? Who engaged him?"

"I am responsible, Duke," the smooth haired secretary replied. "I engaged the few professionals we have here this evening. Of course, to produce a better effect it was necessary to change the names of some of them. The magician was Zana, of Bond-street."

"Ah, yes. Quite a well-known man, Lascelles. The fashionable charlatan most of our best women consult. It's all arrant nonsense, of course, but Zana has a good reputation. They tell me he makes thousands a year, that he keeps a motor, and belongs to some good clubs. It seems very strange a man like that should run the risk of arrest in this way. It is any odds on his being caught. The man must be mad."

"I can't make it out at all," the puzzled secretary replied. "All Zana stipulated for was that his name should not be disclosed, and that I should consent to his being disguised. As there was no objection to that, I consented. When I paid him his fee a day or two ago he told me he should motor down for his performance ready dressed, and I gave him directions as to the door to enter by. I am quite sure there is some mystery here that we have not yet fathomed."

For the moment at any rate there was nothing more to be said or done. No doubt the bold and daring thief was by this time miles away, for the man who could plan such a coup would assuredly have a motor waiting for him in some secluded spot close at hand.

Pending the arrival of the police the festivities of the evening were resumed, but all the gaiety had gone out of them. Everybody seemed worried and listless. The Princess behaved magnificently over her great loss. No doubt, so she affected to believe, the gems would be recovered in time. Meanwhile she had a rather distressing headache, and would be grateful if the Duchess would allow her to retire to her room.

Madame Desterre, with a strange, mocking smile upon her lips, turned to Gilray.

"You are in my debt," she said. "Ma foi! you might have been accused of the theft yourself. Was it not a bold thing to come here uninvited? May I ask why you did so?"

"I could put a few questions in my turn," Gilray retorted. "Meanwhile let me thank you. But all the same, we do not give our confidences to our enemies."

"No, but there are times when in reality those we regard as enemies are our dearest friends, Dr. Gilray. I beg you to cherish that remark, for I shall recall it to you again some day. So those silly young men have come back from the chase. They have done no more than ruin their pretty shoes, I fear."

Half a dozen of the younger men had burst suddenly into the garden, and were talking excitedly together. They had rushed off on the impulse of the moment with a vague hope of capturing the thief. For the last hour they had been ineffectively searching the grounds. Almost on their heels came another lot of excited young men, who seemed to be half carrying, half dragging, some struggling burden between them.

"Got him," one cried in tones of triumph. "Got him. Found him in the bottom of a ditch where he seems to have fallen. Rather shook him up, I fancy. Steady, old chap, you're not likely to get away again. Hand over those diamonds."

The captive struggled to his feet, protesting vigorously.

"Fetch Mr. Lascelles,'" he demanded. "Leave me alone, I say. A fine time I've had of it. This is an outrage. I'll make a police court matter of it as sure as my name is Zana."

CHAPTER XIV

A MISSING LINK

There was to be no interruption of the festivities, that, the Duke had insisted upon. But all the pleasure and healthy excitement had vanished. Already more than one guest had suddenly developed a thoughtfulness for his chauffeur—whose very existence he had previously forgotten. It was all very well for the bands to play, for the younger people to fling themselves into the pleasure of the dance, but the chill breath of suspicion lay over all, like an unexpected frost in a garden of flowers.

The police were expected now at any moment. Even in so brilliant a house as Glenday Castle it was impossible to feel gay and light-hearted with the advent of a detective force from Scotland Yard. Somehow the thought of their coming disturbed the Princess much more than the loss of her diamonds.

Meanwhile she was consoling herself with a cigarette before the cheery flickering of a wood fire in her bedroom. She lay back, with one hand thrown behind her dark head, listening to the lamentations of her hostess.

"My dear Pamela, why distress yourself," she asked. "I am not worrying. My only trouble is that I shall have to be at the beck and call of those dreadful police for goodness knows how long. They will dog me like my shadow. They will drag me from comfortable country houses to unpleasant police stations, and ask me to identify impossible thieves. In my opinion the whole affair is political."

"My dear Helena, you don't really mean that?"

"But I do," the Princess protested. "When that silly revolution broke out, and my brother was driven from his little tin principality, he took certain things with him. Amongst them were what the revolutionary party are pleased to call the Crown jewels. Pah, there never were any Crown jewels. All those ornaments that delightful boy of yours calls my 'war paint' belonged to our family absolutely. As my brother is a confirmed and hardened bachelor, and also as the dynasty is no more, he handed the jewels over to me. The Republicans were furious, and vowed to get them back. And, ma foi! dear Pamela, it looks to me as if they had succeeded."

"But you have not mentioned this matter to anybody. You did not tell my husband."

"Nor anybody else so far as that goes. I shall now, of course, be compelled to inform the police. But, beyond them, only to my intimates must this secret be known. It is not one of my ambitions to find myself the subject of many paragraphs in the society papers. For my part I should like to go to bed. But I suppose I shall have to wait till those stupid police have done with me. And I should like to see Ninon Desterre. There is nobody who amuses me as she does."

The Duchess took the hint, and rang the bell. She hoped that Ninon Desterre would prove an efficient remedy. Would the Princess mind if she slipped away and looked after her guests? Things had been unpleasant enough without giving people the chance to remark as to her absence.

Ninon Desterre came up to the bedroom presently, and closed the door carefully behind her. Apparently the unhappy affair had had no effect upon her brightness and gaiety. She made no kind of apology, nor did she allude to the robbery at all. The Princess smiled gratefully.

"You are always so tactful," she said. "So soothing to the nerves. Probably I shall have to engage you as companion at an enormous salary till people have forgotten my loss. I could refer any question on the subject to you, and thus avoid the inevitable mental collapse. Or at least I would do so if I had the money. I would like to see my husband's face when he hears what has happened."

The Princess rippled with laughter as she spoke. Her husband was notoriously as mean as he was wealthy. The Princess could have all the money she needed if she would only stay at home.

"And now I shall have to go back," she said with a dazzling smile. "I have nothing left, next year's allowance is mortgaged. Ah, what a true friend you are to me."

Just for a moment Ninon looked a little uneasy. Then the door burst open, and the Duchess literally flung herself into the bedroom.

"I should have knocked, of course," she gasped excitedly. "But my feelings got the better of me. They have caught the thief. Some of the young men got on his track, and ran him down in the grounds. He is downstairs at the present moment. I have not seen him, nor have I any details; but they have caught him all right. I felt that I must come up and tell you at once."

"Have they got my diamonds back?" the Princess asked.

"My dear Helena, I haven't the faintest notion. But I presume that as they have the thief your jewels are not very far off. I do hope it is going to be all right."

Ninon Desterre slipped quietly from the room. Apparently she had no intention of offering the Princess her congratulations until she was sure that they were justified. Downstairs in the scented garden she found an excited group gathered about a man in evening dress, a tall fair man, who at the first sight did not much resemble a professional thief. Nor was he displaying emotions that suggested guilt or dismay. On the contrary, he seemed to be exceedingly angry and astonished.

For a moment Ninon laid her hand on her heart, as if she had some little difficulty with her breathing. Then the radiant, easy smile came back to her lips.

"What is it, Zana!" she cried. "What are they doing with you?"

The man called Zana looked up as if he had suddenly recognised a friend.

"That is precisely what I am asking, Madame Desterre," he said with a bow. "I give my own professional name and nobody believes me. It is very good of you, Madame, to come to my assistance. Why have I been treated thus? What am I accused of?"

At that moment the Duke came forward accompanied by a bulky, official-looking man. A thrill ran through the assemblage. The police had arrived.

"Here is Inspector Gillispie," the Duke explained. "I have told him everything. It seems to me that the explanation of this person here should be made to the Inspector."

The audience crowded round eagerly. But there was no suggestion of fear on the prisoner's face. On the contrary, he greeted Gillispie with evident signs of pleasure.

"Now perhaps we shall get a little common sense," he exclaimed. "As far as I can gather, Inspector, there has been a jewel robbery, and I am accused of the theft. They say that I was engaged here to give a thought-reading and fortune-telling performance, and that the lady came to my tent. Then they say I robbed her, and made my way into the grounds, where I was pursued and caught in a ditch. As a matter of fact, this is the first time I have been in the house."

"You were specially engaged to come down here," the Inspector said.

"I was. There is no need to disguise it. Mr. Lascelles engaged me and paid me my fee. I was to come here, but nobody was to know that I was Zana. My idea was to bring a make-up with me, and change into it in my car at the last moment. I drove through the gates of the park about midnight, and, near the house my car was stopped and my driver was sent back another way. That I was told was necessary in order to have the traffic properly regulated. I took this for granted, and placed myself in the hands of the man who said he was sent to guide me. We seemed to be going away from the house, and I mentioned the fact. The reply I got was a violent blow on the head which stunned me. When I came to my senses I was on my back in a dry ditch, my make-up was gone, and I was bound hand and foot by ropes. As there was a gag in my mouth I could not call for help. Of course I realised that some mischief was afoot, but what it was I could not imagine. My one idea was to get out of those confounded ropes. I had just managed to do so when I was pounced on by half a dozen of these gentlemen, and dragged here before I had an opportunity of offering a word of explanation. For the moment I was too sick and upset to resist, but I am feeling better now, and I want to know what it all means."

The guests looked from one to the other a little disappointed. The dramatic possibilities of the situation had changed. They felt that they were no longer confronted with a cool and daring theft, but a justifiably angry man. The vehemence of Zana's statement seemed to emphasise its truth. Still, the puzzle and the mystery of the situation remained.

"The man seems to me to be speaking the truth, your Grace," Gillispie said. "If he is, then we shall have to look a good deal further. Evidently it was a very clever and carefully prepared job. What I should very much like to know is where the thieves got the information that Zana was coming here. I suppose you could recognise your assailant, Mr. Zana?"

"I am afraid not," Zana responded. "You see it was very dark, and not thinking of any such business as this, I did not take much notice of the man. I was anxious to get to my performance, and I took him, naturally, for one of the household servants. No. I'm afraid I can't help you much there."

The Inspector wasted no time in further questioning. All he wanted now was a lantern and a chance to find some clue in the grounds. But the search party had already done much to obliterate any hurried trace the thief might have left. The Inspector therefore was not sanguine. He would commit himself to no theory, he had nothing to suggest beyond a cautiously hazarded guess that the robbery might be the work of the same gang that had obtained possession of Van der Knoot's precious miniatures. Intimating that he could always find Zana if he wanted him for further particulars the officer went off.

"He will find nothing," Madame Desterre declared. "It is hopeless. Moreover, it is time I was getting back home. I have my motor here—can I take you with me, Dr. Gilray?"

"That is very good of you," Gilray said gratefully, glad enough to have his home getting problem solved so conveniently. The man with the taxi-cab could doubtless look to himself. "I am quite ready."

It had been a night of surprises, and Gilray was quite prepared for more of them. He gave no sign therefore when he recognised Ninon Desterre's motor car as the one he had followed from the Park Gardens. He would not say anything, he would not give the game away—yet. There would be plenty of time when Madame Desterre began to show her hand.

"A very mysterious affair," he said as the car rolled along, and the lights of London began to twinkle in the distance. "Very cleverly planned, too. Those people are evidently educated, they use the latest methods. The chloroforming of the Princess—"

"You really think that they used an anaesthetic of some kind, doctor?"

"I am absolutely certain of it. I see scores of my patients under the influence of one every week. The yellowish-white colour of the face, the slight contraction of the pupils of the eyes. That shows the first stage of chloroform poisoning. In the last the pupils are dilated, but then, of course, the patient is comatose. The drug was administered by somebody quite up to his work."

Ninon yawned, as if the conversation had no further interest for her. She would go out of her way if he liked, and put him down by his own door. But Gilray preferred to walk. He was not tired, and he wanted to think. He was still thinking as he let himself into the house and switched on the lights in his study.

"Now what does it all mean?" he asked himself. "What is it for? And where do all those other people come in? And what became—by Jove! it never occurred to me before. Where on earth did Vorley vanish to, and what became of him?"

CHAPTER XV

HARLEY ASKS A FAVOUR

Following the disappearance of Van der Knoot's miniatures, the loss of Princess Helena's diamonds created something like a sensation of dismay. It had, of course, been impossible to keep the matter private, there are far too many society people dabbling in journalism to make such a thing practicable. The first edition of the evening papers had the news displayed with a score or so of 'scare heads.' There was not one of the journals but had its special account by 'one who was present.' A great many of them had also reached the theory stage.

According to one writer this was the work of a daring and audacious gang of international thieves. The diamonds had vanished in the capacious maw that had swallowed the miniatures. The police 'already had a clue.' According to another authority, this latest outrage was a political move on the part of certain foreign revolutionists to obtain possession of what they rightly or wrongly regarded as crown jewels that had disappeared when their country became a republic.

Gilray read these accounts with a tolerating smile. He knew perfectly well that the police had no clue, and that Gillispie was as much in the dark as anybody else. Could Madame Desterre have thrown any light on the mystery? he wondered. Had she anything to do with the disappearance of the glittering stones? But then the Princess would hardly be a party to the disappearance of her own gems. Still, there was that mystery of the 'Blue Anchor' to be accounted for. The Princess was in that. Whatever secrets Ninon Desterre had, the Princess certainly shared them. Some day, when he could spare the time, Gilray made up his mind to investigate the 'Blue Anchor' business. Here was emphatically a case where knowledge was power. Desperately situated as he was, the truth might mean something very substantial in the way of money.

And heaven only knew he wanted money badly enough. No sooner was he out of one difficulty that he was up to his neck in another. Directly one hydra head was cut off two more seemed to grow in the same place. He must find some way to see Enid Harley again, the good impression must not be allowed to fade away. It was something gained that he had formed a compact with Enid. True, Geoffrey Herepath was in the way, but Gilray knew how to get rid of him. It almost looked as if the fates were playing into his hands. Yes, he must in some way gain the freedom of the house at Poplar.

He worked on till late in the afternoon, taking his cases almost mechanically. It was past four before he had finished and was free to do as he pleased. He was glad that he had no engagement for this evening, so that he could retire early after the fatigue and excitement of the previous night. He was snatching a hasty cup of tea when his solicitor was announced.

"Take a cup too, Barker," he said. "Is there anything fresh?"

The dapper man of law helped himself to tea and toast.

"Nothing good," he said. "Why didn't you come and see me as promised? Or, at any rate, you could have telephoned me. Smith's people are very nasty. They say that there is no reliance to be placed on your promises. And, upon my word, you have tried their patience. They decline to withdraw that bankruptcy petition unless they have a thousand by Saturday. If you don't want to find yourself gazetted you must find it."

"But, my dear fellow, it's out of the question," Gilray said irritably. "I couldn't do it. There is absolutely nothing that I can put my hands on. Every stick and stone in this house is mortgaged, even the lease has been assigned to raise money. You'll have to find some way, Barker. Bankruptcy would be ruin to me in more ways than one. Nobody would come to me afterwards. And Smith's is not the only trouble."

"I know it," said Barker gravely. "You have a pressing need for 5000 pounds. Give me that and I can get you six months' breathing time. By then, with economy, you should have made enough professionally to clear yourself. But I can do nothing more for the moment. There is not a Jew in London who would touch your papers. Can't you do a little in the way of borrowing? You have many rich lady patients who would probably help you. And I've had letters from some of your constituents in the North. I understand that strange rumours are flying about."

To all of this Gilray listened moodily. He was feeling dreadfully helpless and impatient. There was real danger here, and he must face the fact. An idea took root in his brain; there was just the chance of the suggestion succeeding.

"I'll think it over," he said. "There is somebody who might...Yes, I'll go and see her and to-morrow morning I'll let you know how I get on."

Half an hour later a taxi dropped him at Park Gardens. He was fortunate in finding Ninon Desterre at home, and equally fortunate to learn that she was alone. She received him in her own sanctum, pink and gold room reserved for her intimates. She looked fresh and charming as ever, there was no suggestion on her smooth cheek or in her clear eyes that she and sleep had been strangers for a night or more.

"Do you know I was half expecting you," she said as she pushed over the silver cigarette box. "You have come to make terms with me. You have come to tell me that no longer are you going to interfere with my plans for the happiness of a certain lady."

"I am to do you a favour, eh?" Gilray said with a wry smile. "Well, perhaps! But in this cold and selfish world very few of us do good kind things for nothing. It was nice of you to give me an opening, so I'll come to the point without delay. Have you ever done any gambling?"

"My dear man, my whole life is a gamble," Ninon said coolly. "How true it is that one half the world does not know how the other half lives! Have you anything promising? Anything that one could make a fortune out of without risk?"

"I've not found it yet," Gilray said. "On the contrary, I have been most shockingly unlucky lately. I have been compelled to give everything as security to certain people. Of course, I am still making a good income. But I am in urgent need of a considerable sum of ready money. I want to borrow 5000 pounds."

"You don't say so," Ninon remarked demurely. "It is a remarkable coincidence, but I know exactly a score of people who are in precisely the same predicament. My clear, clever optimist, do you suggest me as your Chancellor of the Exchequer?"

"I thought that perhaps you could find the money, Madame Desterre."

"Oh, you did! I am greatly obliged by the compliment. It is so flattering! And now, behold, I will proceed to be as candid as yourself. I have no money. I never had half that sum in my life. Like the birds, I live on the grubs and the odds and ends that Providence finds day by day. Farther than that I give no details. But I might raise the money for you at a price."

"I am prepared to pay pretty handsomely," Gilray whispered. "May I hear the terms?"

"Oh, we are a long way yet from the question of terms. I may fail altogether. If you really are in earnest you must make me a promise."

"I will do my best, Madame. Tell me what that promise is."

Ninon's manner changed suddenly. The smile left her face, she looked hard and serious.

"Put that silly marriage dream out of your mind," she said. "Think no more of a certain girl who shall be nameless. Believe me, I am acting as your friend in giving you this advice. It can only end in trouble and disaster. Now think over what I said and come to me again in a day or two. If you pledge your word and are still in the same mind—Ah, my dear Lady Blessister, how are you? I have not seen you for ages."

She was the old Ninon again in the presence of a suddenly appearing visitor. She seemed to have forgotten everything but the frivolity of the moment. Gilray slipped away a moment later, and walked home with no other company than his moody thoughts. He told himself he was not going to be tricked in this way—he would not turn back where Enid Harley was concerned.

He ate his solitary dinner, making up his mind that he would not go out that night, but would retire early. He had meant to tell his man to take the receiver off the telephone so that be should not be disturbed. Confound it, there was the wretched thing trilling away now! In an angry mood, Gilray crossed the hall, and put the receiver to his ear.

"Yes, I am Dr. Gilray," he said. "You can speak freely. Nobody can hear."

"I am Daniel Harley," a hoarse voice responded. "You came here a night or two ago in your professional capacity. It so happens that I have need of your services again...What? Oh, yes, to-night. You will be well paid. Eh? Oh, there will be no trouble about that. My daughter will meet you at Shadwell Station, and conduct you here on foot. Somebody shall see you part of the way home. Can you come now?"

Gilray demurred for an instant. It was the proper professional thing to do. But not for a second did he really hesitate. Here in his grasp was the opportunity for which he had been so strenuously longing. Ah! he would show Ninon Desterre now what it was to play with him. He would carry his scheme to success, and laugh at the finish in the face of the clever Frenchwoman.

"It is rather late," he said, "but I fancy I can manage it. Give me just a moment to refer to my book...Are you there? Yes. I'll come, Mr. Harley. I find that I can get to Shadwell Station in about half an hour. For the present, good-night."

Here at last was Shadwell Station, and here also was Enid, patiently waiting. Her lovely face flushed as she caught sight of Gilray. Just for a moment he held her hand in his. There was no mistaking the admiration in his eyes.

"This is quite an unexpected pleasure," he murmured. "Is it very far from here to your house?"

Keeping step with his fair guide Gilray excited himself to please. He was sufficiently clever to keep off personal topics. Scrupulously he made no allusion to the compact between them. He saw presently as they walked along that Enid had relaxed her guard, that she was disposed to be grateful for his attentions. She was smiling now, and a pink flush was on her cheeks. Gilray chuckled to himself. He was making headway all right, and he would know how to remove the big obstacle from his path when the time was ripe for it.

Anyway, for him the time passed all too quickly. It appeared only a matter of minutes before the dark old house was reached, and Gilray found himself once more face to face with Daniel Harley. He did not care now whether the secretive old man with the hooked nose and the piercing eyes was rich or not. It seemed to him that he was fiercely anxious to get Enid, even if she came to him without a penny.

"Sit down," the old man said. "Sit where I can see your face. Enid, my child, you may leave us. If I want you I will ring the bell. Now then, doctor, we are alone, and there is very little chance of our being disturbed. You are in need of a large sum of money?"

Gilray stammered before the sudden attack in his question. The words had been shot at him as if they had formed part of some deadly accusation.

"Why not?" he stammered. "There are very few people who do not want money. I certainly am not one of the few."

The old man gesticulated impatiently. He leant forward, his eyes gleaming like a cat's. He laid a yellow claw with a quivering grip in it on Gilray's arm.

"Shall I show you how to earn it?" he croaked. "Shall I show you how to make the money you want so badly?"

CHAPTER XVI

A SPORTING CHANCE

Gilray thought hard as he looked at Daniel Harley. So these people were thieves, after all. Nobody but a criminal with some shady proposition would have approached a man in this way. In ordinary circumstances, as a man of reputation, Gilray would have risen to his feet and left the house without another word. There was no occasion to tell him that Daniel Harley was going to make some dishonourable proposal. The very attitude of the miser was eloquent of that, the furtive glance, the hoarse whisper, all were so many signs that something underhand was intended.

Gilray hesitated. He knew perfectly well that he was not to be permitted to obtain this money he needed by legitimate means. People do not scatter sums of five thousand pounds as one scatters crumbs for the birds. Neither was such a sum as this to be gained by the performance of any ordinary undertaking.

Harley's suggestion would be a criminal one, without a doubt. There was danger ahead. But then, argued Gilray to himself, would the danger be any greater than the peril he stood in at that moment? So far as he was personally concerned, bankruptcy was only a shade better than gaol. He would have to trust to his own cleverness for a way out of the trouble. And he was going to be paid 5000 pounds. Much satisfaction lay in that.

Also, he remembered, Harley knew all about him, Harley knew how terribly he was pressed for money, or he would not have made the suggestion he did. Harley was waiting now for him to speak, watching him with eyes that never wavered.

"You seem to take a flattering interest in my welfare," Gilray said at last. "You assume that I am in urgent need of 5000 pounds. Did you invite me down here to tell me so?"

"Nothing of the kind," Harley said, angrily. "Do you expect to gain anything by fencing with me? Would you have come here had you not expected to benefit by your visit? I tell you there are those of us in London who know everybody's business. Or can know it if there is need. Let us suppose that a man came here to me for a loan, I mean to arrange for a loan from the gentleman who employs me."

"I understand," Gilray sneered. "I also have had costly experiences at the hands of the money-lenders. I know all the Shibboleths. I never yet met a man who advanced money himself—there was always somebody behind him. You are not exactly dealing with a fool, Mr. Harley. What do you want? Speak plainly, and let us have no humbug."

Harley turned to his desk with a snarl. Furtively unlocking a drawer he produced a pocket-book, and extracted a packet of Bank of England notes. They crackled unsteadily in his yellow, tremulous fingers.

"There," he said. "Take them and count them for yourself. You will find that there are fifty notes for a hundred each. Good paper of the Governor and Company of the Bank of England, every bit of it. No suggestion of forgery there, what? No, not yet. Hand them back to me for the moment. Their destiny lies in your hands. Regard me as the principal in this matter if you like. Now, are you ready to deal with me?"

"Perhaps. It all depends upon what you require me to do."

"Not so very much, after all. Take one of those cigarettes. You will find them good, even to your fastidious taste. A cup of coffee? Here it is, all ready, made by myself from berries specially imported. A liqueur? What do you say to brandy of 1820? All you have to do is to ask, and there it is. In the days when I wore the Queen's uniform, and the Household Brigade were—I'll go and get that brandy."

The old man checked his speech as if fearful that he was saying too much. He shuffled out, leaving the door open behind him.

"Make yourself at home for ten minutes," he called out. "I have to open one of my bins at the back of the cellar, and that takes time."

Gilray nodded absently. There were many things to admire in that strange, dirty old room, with its faded curtains and shabby carpet. There were pictures of price on the walls, and for the moment the worried surgeon forgot his forebodings and troubles in examining them. As he stood near the door studying an old master he was conscious of voices close by. Surely it was Enid Harley who was speaking. Instinctively he looked across the dim hall to a room on the far side, where a lamp was burning. The door was open, and he saw plainly into the lighted chamber.

He started, and something like an oath escaped him as his eyes fell upon two people there. As he had surmised, one of them was Enid Harley. The other figure, equally familiar, was Geoffrey Herepath. The latter was leaning on the mantelpiece, his eyes shaded by his hand. His attitude was one of utter dejection.

"You have been very foolish, Geoffrey," Enid said, tenderly. Her accent was low and caressing; there was no mistaking the affection in her eyes.

Gilray saw one of her slender arms moved forward and placed gently on Herepath's shoulder. Well, he would find a way to stop all this before long. He had Geoffrey Herepath's future in the hollow of his hand. He could drive a wedge between these two which would part them for ever.

As a gentleman he should have turned his back upon them, should have declined to listen any longer. But some strange fascination kept his attention fixed. The demon of jealousy was driving him on. He was doing a thing now that a year ago he would have scorned.

Herepath turned from the fireplace and caught the girl in his arms. Gilray could see her hands seeking his shoulders, her lips responding to his. He watched with something like murder rising in his heart. Oh, anything to stop this; he would do anything!

"I couldn't help, it," Herepath was saying. "I had to go on. I went to Dr. Gilray, and he examined my eyes. He told me to give up all kinds of desk work, and that I was not to look at a plan for some time. But what can I do? I have more than one rival treading close upon my heels. That scoundrelly assistant of mine nearly betrayed me. And there was one little flaw in my invention that kept me awake at night. I was tossing about on my bed when the solution came to me like an inspiration. I forgot all about my eyes. I forgot everything but the fact that I had found what I had long sought. I have been working at those drawings ever since. Yes, up to an hour or so ago. And now the thing is perfect."

"And you have perhaps done yourself irreparable damage, Geoffrey."

"Possibly. For the time being I was mad. I was not responsible for my actions. As soon as I had drawn the last line my sight failed me. Everything was black as night. I was in the most intense darkness. It did not last for half an hour, and yet to me it was an eternity. That is why I came to you directly that horrible mist cleared away. I had to have somebody's loving sympathy. I dreaded my own company. If I could only have had another week I should have been safe. My plans would have been beyond the reach of my rivals. I should be duly protected by the law. Only one little week, but what a difference it would have made! A year from now and I could have taken you away from here. But it is no use to talk of this, now that I fear the mischief is done. I shall go to Gilray again the day after tomorrow and get my verdict."

The despair of Herepath's last words was eloquent. They betrayed that deep down in his mind he had a strong conviction as to his future prospects. Gilray's jealous glare was slow and cruel as he stood there in the shadow watching the scene in the room opposite.

"Oh, don't talk like that," Enid cried. "Fate could not be so cruel. Surely you have not hopelessly injured your sight. At the very worst it can only mean a few months of enforced idleness. They say that Dr. Gilray is one of the cleverest oculists in England, that there is nobody quite like him. He will surely put you right, Geoffrey."

Herepath stooped to kiss the quivering red lips.

"I'm afraid I am talking like a coward," he said. "But just now my nerves are badly shaken, and I have slept but poorly lately. If only I could find somebody I could trust! My dear girl, if I hear the worst I shall never come near you again."

"Geoffrey! As if that could make any difference. How cruel of you to think so. I should come to you, I should refuse to stay. Nobody could keep you from me."

Her voice trailed away in a whisper as Harley's shuffling feet were heard in the passage. Then the door of the room opposite was pushed to, and Gilray heard and saw no more. Well, he had heard enough. He knew all about the game now, and it seemed to him that the best cards were his. There was a thin smile of triumph on his lips as Harley came into the room hugging a bottle covered with a thick cake of dust and cobwebs.

"There!" he croaked. "Give me the corkscrew. What do you think of that for brandy? Note the aroma of it, the exquisite bouquet. See how it trickles into the glass like drops of oil. Drink it and confess that you have never before tasted anything like it. Cigarette good?"

"I never smoked a better," Gilray said. "They are of a brand made only for epicures and multi-millionaires. And the coffee is nectar for the gods. Let me compliment you on the excellence of your taste, Mr. Harley. Your youth must have been a well-trained one."

Harley gave vent to a low chuckle. His wrinkled features were twisted in a smile.

"Never mind my youth," he said. "Yes, I have heard the chimes at midnight. And now let us get to business. I am not likely to detain you long."

"I am all attention, Mr. Harley. What is it that you want?"

"Let me put my suggestion in the way of a story," Harley said. "I got it from a very clever tale I read the other day. It was all about an ambitious barrister, who, like you, was a member of Parliament. Like you he was up to his ears in debt, and to carry the similitude further, he also represented a Puritan constituency. He got into the hands of a clever capitalist, who was fighting an action over some mines. If the capitalist won, it meant millions to him. If he lost, he would be ruined. And this barrister, who was fighting the case for the other side, knew where the capitalist's weak spot lay. He had only to ask certain questions, and the capitalist was—well—done for. If, on the other hand, he omitted to ask those questions, the capitalist was an easy winner. It was in appearance, all a matter of judgment. If the barrister failed to ask these particular questions it would be merely assumed that he had taken a wrong line of policy. But, and this is the crucial point, the barrister knew that if he did ask those questions, the capitalist could ruin him body and soul. The price of silence was ten thousand pounds."

"And what did he do?" Gilray asked. "Did he sell his brief!"

"What does it matter whether he sold it or not?" Harley said impatiently. "What does it matter how the story ended? It is the possibility of such a position between two men that I want to drive home. Suppose now that I want to prove that on a certain day it was physically impossible for me to have written a certain letter. Suppose I put you in the witness-box to prove that physical inability on my part. I call you as an expert medical witness. You swear that on the day in question, at the hour in question, I was in your consulting-room...That is all. There were fifty hundred pound notes in that bundle you looked at, I think?"

Gilray started. His mind worked quickly, he was beginning to understand. Here was a service of no great risk, for which the price would be an uncommonly good one. But why should it not be a bigger price still?

"It is not the money so much that I need," he said solemnly. "Mr. Harley, you have a daughter."

Harley's eyes blazed, the devil of murder danced in them, his fists clenched.

"Go on!" he said hoarsely. "Go on, doctor. I have a daughter. Don't be afraid to speak."

CHAPTER XVII

A GREAT INVENTION

It was indeed hard for Geoffrey Herepath to realise the full measure of his misfortune. But a little time before he had seen his way clear to the goal of his ambition. He had all the sanguine outlook of the inventor, but he had never been a mere dreamer of dreams, had never wasted his time and intelligence on Utopian speculation. His was a strongly practical nature, and it was always the working value of the machine that appealed to him.

Machinery! New and ingenious devices for the saving of labour, contrivances that turned waste material into articles of commerce! In these things he saw the way to fortune, to the employment of thousands of hands, to power in the country, to an honoured name amongst men. All these prizes of life Herepath would, he felt, be able to lay at Enid Harley's feet!

So, at least it had seemed to him but a little time before. A week or two longer and he would be able to show the world how to make new rubber from old. He was going to take the worn-out article and restore all its uses and elasticity. This he could do with the aid of his wonderful machine. He wanted but a little time to enable him to convince the commercial world that his project was good, a little time in which to remedy one or two minor mechanical defects, which he alone could detect.

He was certain these defects would disappear if a slight change could be made in the mechanism, and in his mind's eye he had seen exactly what to do. It meant a few hours of close unceasing application to the drawing board, and then his machine would be perfect.

But now a cloud had arisen that dimmed all his hopes. It was impossible for him to do the needful work in the present condition of his eyes, almost beyond his power to make out the letters of a newspaper. He had never needed his sight as he needed it at this moment. There was not a soul in the world able to perform his task for him, no one to whom he could explain the factors that would bring success. To attempt to do so might be to give his secret away. Suppose Gilray's final verdict was the one that in his heart he feared it would be. Suppose he was told that he was never to touch a drawing board again! That he was going blind!

Then indeed all his hopes would be dashed for ever. His cherished invention would never be perfected by himself; he would have to get what he could for the idea. There were a few small things, his patent time-lock, for instance, which might bring him in enough to live on, but the big thing would have to go, and with it all that he had striven for.

"It is only a rest that you need," his sister said soothingly. "Surely Dr. Gilray would have told you earlier had the case been so serious. Don't fret, Geoffrey."

"My dear Blanche, I am doing my best to control myself," Geoffrey said. "But do you, can you, really understand how much for me depends upon the next few days?"

Blanche Herepath hoped that she did. She was a dreamer of dreams in her way, but then her dreams were artistic ones. She was doing fairly well with some of the magazines as a black-and-white artist, yet she hated London as bitterly as one of her sweet and gentle nature could hate anything. She had seen her mother pine and die there for want of means to get away into the country she so loved and missed. And now there was Geoffrey to be looked after. Somebody had to oversee domestic affairs in the little house in West Kensington, and who could better do it than Geoffrey's sister? He would marry some of these days, of course, and then she would be free to take that old world cottage at Walton Heath that she had for many a long day so coveted. She had her own little romance, too, but she did not intrude it, for it had ever been Blanche's way to keep herself in the background.

"I am sure everything will come all right," she said. "What does Enid say? And why has she not been to see me for such a long time?"

"Her father keeps her close at home. And such a home. It is as much for Enid's sake as anything else that I am so anxious regarding the future. I want to get her away from that dreadful house. Some strange mystery hangs about it, and it is no place, I am convinced, for a young innocent girl like Enid. What is wrong there I have not asked her. Nor do I think she herself knows. I was called in professionally to do certain work, which I should probably have declined had I not met Enid there. As it is, I feel very uneasy in my mind over it. What do they want all those elaborate electric alarms and devices in that shabby old house? It is not as if old Daniel Harley were a rich man. He continually complains of his poverty, yet he has spent great sums on these electric contrivances, and his strange visitors at times. If I would keep a wife in any anything like comfort, I should ask Enid to marry me to-morrow. That is, of course, if there is nothing really very much the matter with my eyes.

"You have probably overstrained them," Blanche suggested. "Why don't you put your work on one side altogether for a week or two? Why not go into the country and rest? Even the strongest of us needs a change sometimes."

Geoffrey shook his head impatiently. Women never understood these things.

"It is utterly impossible," he said. "I have a most important appointment this very morning with a capitalist who is coming to the shop in Long Acre to see my rubbish converter. He is to see some worn-out rubbish of his own made over again into veritable new rubber. I shall not tell him that I am unable just now to work continuously, because I've got it all set in my head, and if I could only see properly, could surmount all the difficulties in a few days. I do but need to alter the machinery slightly. And once that is done, I am the master of millions. Do you understand—millions!"

Blanche sighed quietly. These ambitions of her brother had been the source of all the mischief. He had been warned against continuing this night work, from which he would not stay away. And now he was paying the penalty of his rashness.

"I must be off at once," Herepath exclaimed as he reached for his coat. "I had no idea that it was so late. Oh, no, you need not come with me. I can get about the streets all right. I can see well enough for that. It is only when I come to read or work that everything goes black before me. Ta-ta! Perhaps by this time to-morrow I shall be more cheerful. Though I must confess I dread seeing Gilray."

Herepath put his troubles out of his mind as he turned into Long Acre, and entered the old carriage works where he conducted his experiments. He had a few trained mechanics on the premises, but no personal assistant. He did not believe in letting anybody share his secrets. He had had more than one possible fortune wrested from him by tricky associates, and did not intend that it should happen again. He was the keen inventor now with a critical eye for the machine, the child of his brain, that stood in the centre of the floor.

It was small and compact, and, to the casual eye, might have seemed a little cheap, with nothing out-of-the-way about it. But inside that brass case Herepath had worked miracles. He had summoned hitherto unknown powers of electricity to his aid, and the response had been marvellous. There was apparently no heat nor smell nor friction about the mechanism, nothing but a steady whirr of wheels, a feeding of the brazen monster with waste-heap scraps of old perished india-rubber, and the belching out at the other end of dark grey cubes identical in every way with the raw, resilient high-priced rubber of commerce.

Herepath watched the converting process with grim satisfaction. It could be done successfully upon a small scale, but what he needed, and what the trade needed, was a means of doing it in large quantities at a price to successfully compete with the fresh article. Give Herepath the full use of his eyes and a drawing board, and he was sure he could alter things to cut the cost of conversion, and make his machine a gigantic commercial success within a week. As he was fixed he was a like a man armed with a powerful weapon, and at the same time deprived of the use of his hands.

He was still watching the smooth working of the process when a stranger came into the workshop and accosted him. The newcomer, a short and dapper man, looked at Herepath with a shrewd pair of eyes, whose keenness was partly hidden by the glasses he was wearing.

"I'm a little late," the newcomer said, "and I cannot give you more than half an hour. I have been speaking to one or two of my capitalist friends about the machine, and think that I have succeeded in interesting them. I have no money of my own for the process—I make it a rule never to touch any patent."

"I have heard the argument before, Mr. Brigden," Herepath said drily. "More money lost in patents than in mines; and all the other stock phrases are old familiar frauds. As a matter of fact, the prosperity of Britain has been built up on patents. You have only to go to Yorkshire and Lancashire to see that. Oh, I admit that patents are kittle cattle to deal with. Mine, however, is quite out of the ordinary, and would be hard to infringe. Shall we put your stuff through?"

The other nodded. He was no mean judge in matters concerning rubber. At a sign from Herepath one of the workmen came forward with a great bale of stuff, which bore in the corner the impression of half a dozen seals in red wax.

"Better see that the seals are intact before you open the sack," Herepath suggested. "Perhaps you would like to feed the stuff into the hopper yourself, Mr. Brigden."

Brigden signified that he would be quite content to watch one of the hands do this. At the same time, it might be just as well perhaps to have a look at the inside of the machine in case anything had been placed there. Capitalists were shy and suspicious people, and Brigden would be better pleased if he could convince them that everything had been shown to him, and that the demonstration was entirely open and above board.

"I was about to make the same suggestion myself," Herepath said. "See here."

He raised the brass flaps from the sides of the machine, and disclosed its strange interior. There were queer rods and fans, and something, resembling a glass disc, which things Herepath was well aware could convey nothing of the real secret to the looker-on. With a wave of his hand Brigden intimated that he was perfectly satisfied.

A moment later and the machinery began to move. Then the contents of the huge sack disappeared in the hopper, and in a few seconds the grey cubes commenced to fall from the shoot at the further end of the machine. In a few minutes the whole operation was complete, and Brigden was standing in wonder carefully examining the result of the experiment.

"Absolutely marvellous," he said. "This seems to be the real stuff. And done apparently without chemicals of any kind. I'll take some of the product with me, and put it through some practical tests. If it comes out all right, as I feel convinced it will, you shall at once hear from me again. We ought to have a company with a capital of at least a million, and mills all over the world. Meanwhile, of course, you will not mention this business to anybody else."

"You may rely upon that," Herepath said. "I shall be glad of a few days to myself, for there are one or two little improvements I want to make, especially in the feed."

Brigden bustled out and went his way. But, though he had overstayed his time, he no longer seemed to be in any violent hurry. He walked slowly and thoughtfully along till he came to his office in Cheapside, and entered his private room. There he threw himself down in his chair, and seemed utterly lost to the busy city life around him.

"The old ruffian was right," he muttered. "Right, as he always is. Now I wonder what his little game is this time. Shall I tell him the truth, or try to work without him?"

His musings were interrupted by the entrance of a clerk. "Mr. Daniel Harley has rung up, sir," he said. "He wants you to go over to him without delay. He will be waiting for you."

"Very well," said Brigden quietly, dismissing the man with a nod. But as he picked up his hat and went out to obey Harley's summons, he clenched his teeth and swore softly to himself.

CHAPTER XVIII

"THE SENTENCE OF THE COURT"

We left Daniel Harley and Dr. Gilray engaged in a brisk battle of wits in a miser's study in that strange old house by the riverside.

After Gilray's pointed allusion to the fact that Harley had a daughter, and his thinly-veiled hint that she might be part of the price he should require for any risky business he was asked to undertake, the two men faced each other for some time in silence.

It was as though each was trying to read the other's thoughts. But both were wearing their usual inscrutable business masks, and neither found any advantage accrue from that silent scrutiny.

"Go on," Harley croaked at last. "Go on, young man. You are here with some project in your mind."

"I came because you sent for me, sir. I must ask you to remember that."

"True, true," Harley muttered. "Still, all the same, you were not sorry for the opportunity, eh? You are young, also ambitious, and—poor as a rat. If you could get on your legs again, you might go very far indeed. Is that the reason you want to marry my child?"

Gilray made no reply for a moment, He was wondering what line to pursue with the cunning old man. Perhaps it would be best to be absolutely candid.

"At first it was," he said coolly enough, "I came here quite by accident to begin with, and I concluded that you were a man of considerable means."

"You are making it your business to find out," Harley sneered.

"No, I am not making it my business to find out, sir. If I did, I very much doubt if I should be successful. I am prepared to take the risk of mistake. After I met your daughter, it seemed to me that my chance had come. Now that I have seen more of Miss Harley I am prepared to make her my wife, even if you could convince me that you do not possess a shilling to your name."

"The young man is in love," Harley cried. "Generously in love. So you have not so much caution as I imagined. And suppose I have nothing? Suppose my daughter must marry a man who can keep her? Are you that man? You who might be a bankrupt at any moment. Still, you seemed to be in earnest."

"I am," Gilray said grimly. "Give me my opportunity, and I'll ask you for no money."

All this time the dark, glittering eyes of the old man had been regarding Gilray searchingly. There was a sinister light in them as the conversation proceeded. Gilray had a rather uneasy feeling that Harley was playing with him, that in some way he was at the miser's mercy.

"All roads lead to Rome," the old man quoted. "But there are a goodly number, and it is possible to travel them in many different ways. I know that my daughter is beautiful and fascinating. I also know that she is good and pure. Others are aware of the fact, too. I have tried to keep my child to myself, but that has proved a task beyond my power. To revert to metaphor again, does it not occur to you that you are not the only pebble on the beach?"

The name of Geoffrey Herepath was on Gilray's lips, but he stayed its utterance just in time.

"In other words; I have a rival," he suggested.

"Precisely. You have a rival, and a dangerous one. At least he thinks so. And I am rather afraid that my poor little girl is very fond of him. But he has me to deal with."

Harley broke off, and shook a yellow hand at some imaginary foe. His eyes were gleaming again, his brows were knitted in a frown.

"I must try to keep my temper," he muttered. "I am too given to these sudden outbreaks." Then he continued: "When I found out what was going on I could have killed the man. He was recommended me by a friend. They told me he was a mechanical genius. To give him his due, so he is. I paid him well for the work he did, and dismissed him. I wanted nobody prying about here. He came again and again, and I was fortunate enough to see—well—never mind that."

"You mean that Mr.—I mean the man did not come to you openly?"

"Just so," the old man snarled. "Oh, I know the lover's formula in such cases. 'I am poor, darling, and your wealthy father would spurn my suit.' 'I am young and clever, and I shall be rich some of these early days.' 'Let us keep our secret till that day comes, and then I can claim the right to marry you before all the world.' My dear Doctor Gilray, it is the kind of thing that no young girl can resist. At first I was going to say what I had noticed. I was going to command my daughter to think no more of this man. That is, of course, the way fathers do it on the stage."

The old man paused, and a sinister smile hovered about the corners of his mouth. Then he went on:

"Now that stage-father method is exactly the one to bring about the very opposite to the result you require. Nobody can be answerable for the vagaries of the persecuted heroine. So I just watch and say nothing. I just go on in ignorance. But I bide my time. Doctor Gilray, I bide my time. I'll ruin that fellow yet."

"Suppose I could ruin him for you and save you the trouble?" Gilray suggested with eagerness in his tone.

The cigarette that Harley was smoking dropped from his fingers, and lay unheeded on the table. The old man seemed to be utterly taken aback. It was as though it had suddenly occurred to him that he was up against an intellect as keen as his own, that he was dealing with a fellow mind utterly selfish and unscrupulous.

"Do you happen to know the name of the man?" he asked.

"I do," Gilray replied. "No matter where the information came from, but I have it. Should I be far wrong in suggesting that you have some other motive for injuring Geoffrey Herepath apart from his presumption in making love to your daughter? One has these little intuitions, you know."

The old man picked up his cigarette again. He writhed and wriggled in his chair, shaking from head to foot with a noiseless mirth not pleasant to see. Gilray would have given a good deal to know what was the mainspring of it all.

Harley suddenly grew grave.

"You are correct," he said. "You are a remarkable young man, and I am sorry that we have not met before. You recognise the fact that you have a powerful rival in Geoffrey Herepath. So much the better. All is fair in love and war, you know. You have some idea in your head that you can get rid of your rival?"

"I can sweep him from my path, as I could sweep away a fly," Gilray exclaimed. "I gather that you would be glad to see me do so. But you have other motives beyond a mere desire to give a presumptuous young man a severe lesson. What is the motive?"

"If I am convinced that your boast is correct," Harley said, "I might confide it to you."

"Then be assured that I can make my boast good. I can do it by lunch-time to-morrow. But at a price. I have nothing to convince me as yet that I am not merely a tool in your hands, and that when I have served your purpose I shall be cast aside like an old glove. You see your way to benefit materially by the suppression of Herepath. A man like you would take no real risks for anything but money."

"You are vastly polite to me in my own house," Harley growled.

"Because it is just as well to be candid. The first thing I want is your daughter. I am taking the risk of her coming to me with empty hands. On the other hand, I can help you in your scheme against Herepath. In this matter our interests are identical. But that is no reason why I should do all the work and you get all the plunder. This invention of Herepath's—"

Harley started. A cry escaped him. It was a bow drawn at a venture, but the arrow had gone home. Like a flash Gilray saw the way clear before him.

"It is a game that two can play at," he said. "Did you flatter yourself that you were the only man that had heard of Herepath's great invention?"

It was bluff of the purest kind, but Harley cunningly swallowed it. His manner assured Gilray that there really was a great invention somewhere, that it did not exist merely in the inventor's imagination, and that the old miser knew all about it, and was, moreover, planning at this moment to get hold to it. Once Herepath was out of the way, the thing was done. But this was not so easy as it looked. The one man who could do it successfully—and safely—was he, Gilray, and if he was to take a hand in this conspiracy, he was going to get his price.

"I can do it," he whispered. "I can render Herepath as good as dead. The thing can be finished before the hands of the clock go round again. The one question is: How much?"

Harley appeared to be chewing something rapidly. Here was a problem that required careful consideration. Before he could reply, the door of the sitting-room burst open and a little man came hurriedly in.

"It's good!" he cried; "It's perfect! There's a million in it. Herepath is a genius. He—"

The speaker paused, seeing for the first time that Harley was not alone. He stammered some apology.

"Glad to see you, Brigden," Harley said. "I have been expecting you all day. You can speak quite freely before Doctor Gilray, who is by way of being my partner in this business. So you have seen Herepath's invention, and are quite satisfied that it is all he claims for it? Now tell us everything!"

Brigden proceeded to explain. He was wildly enthusiastic. If this invention were placed in the hands of one or two keen men of business there would be literally millions in it. And Herepath had pledged his word to approach nobody else. Brigden was still discoursing eloquently after he had smoked two cigarettes. If anything was to be done, then it should be done without the slightest delay. Harley held up a hand for silence.

"That will do," he said. "I do not require anybody to teach me my business. Come back here at the same time to-morrow night, Brigden, and I will give you my instructions. Meanwhile I have something to say to Doctor Gilray that is for his private ear alone. You understand?"

Brigden accepted the hint and departed meekly enough. No sooner had the door closed on him than Harley turned to his companion with a fierce energy all his own.

"You heard all that?" he asked. "Now can you do what you promised? If you can come back to me with proofs of your success there is a cheque for you for 10,000 pounds. And far more to follow. Now, don't tell me your scheme but go and carry it out. And now I'll see you part of the way home."

The morning after his momentous interview with Harley, Gilray was feeling decidedly easier in his mind. He had slept well for the first time for many nights, and he was quite ready for Herepath when the inventor arrived according to his appointment. Gilray was going to earn his 10,000 pounds and the big money to follow. With that in his possession he would be able to look the whole world in the face again. He would soon now be absolutely rid once for all of a dangerous rival, would have his path clear to the heart of Enid Harley.

And the whole thing, he told himself, was so ridiculously easy—so easy and so safe. Even if the conspiracy failed and became known, nobody could possibly connect him with it. Fortune was on his side at last!

Thinking these things, he turned briskly to Herepath. "Let us get on," he said. "Will you remove your clothing as before? Oh, yes, I shall be able to give you a definite opinion to-day. Don't speak any more now."

At the end of half an hour Herepath struggled into his clothes again. He was desperately anxious to hear the verdict; he could feel his heart hammering against his ribs. So much depended on that one word.

"Speak out," he said hoarsely, "and let me hear the best—or worst. What is it?"

Gilray spoke clearly and distinctly. There was a proper suggestion of regret in his tone.

"You must give up your work for a year," he said. "I will give you a prescription for some glasses which you must wear always. You must do nothing and read nothing—not use your eyes at all, in fact! Moreover, you must have a complete change. You must go for a long voyage at once."

Herepath gasped as he listened. A wild feeling of anger gripped him.

"But this is ruin," he cried, "absolute ruin! I shall have nothing left by that time. Can't you patch me up in some way for a week or two? I must finish my work."

"I'm very sorry," Gilray said, "but it is impossible. If you choose to go on in defiance of my opinion—"

"Well, go on, man. If I choose to go on?"

Gilray shrugged his shoulders. There was a compassionate tone in his voice.

"You will bitterly regret it," he said. "I tell you, I am bound to tell you, that unless you follow my directions to the letter, there can be only one result. You will be stone blind in three months."

CHAPTER XIX

AFTER THE VERDICT

Herepath staggered back before the force of the cruel blow. In his heart of hearts he had never dreamt of anything quite so bad as this. He thought that perhaps he might have to wear glasses, would have to be careful, that his reading would be restricted, but nothing more than that. He had hoped to get those precious drawings finished a bit at a time. If he carried out the commands of his doctor he would be compelled to spend every penny he possessed. On his return to England he would have to begin the world all over again.

Hitherto he had felt so strong and self-reliant. Now he had a curious feeling of weakness and utter dependency. He would have to rely on strangers in future, he would have to trust his fortunes to those whom he could not even see.

Slowly and gradually the blood crept back to his cheeks again, the roaring in his ears died away.

"I shall have to keep a dog," he said bitterly. "A dog at the end of a string."

"It won't be quite as bad as that," Gilray replied. "You will be able to see your way about when you get accustomed to the glasses that I shall provide for you. But you will have to follow my directions implicitly. At the end of a year or so you will probably be quite well again, and may go back to your great work. You will be able after a time to read and write in moderation, but I should advise you not to do any mechanical drawing again. Really, Mr. Herepath, it might be a great deal worse."

"Oh, it might," Geoffrey said in the same bitter strain. "I might have lost my sight entirely. I might be reduced to begging my living in the streets. Well, I'll try to bear up against it. It is fortunate perhaps that I have a little money by me. What about these glasses?"

Gilray proceeded to write some instructions on a sheet of notepaper.

"This is all you need," he explained. "Take this to Gothard's in the Strand. I am giving you more or less a stock prescription, so that you will find yourself suited whilst you wait. Now, there is no occasion for you to come to me again. All I ask you to do is to implicitly follow my directions."

Herepath stumbled out of the house, trying hard to get a grip on himself. So far as he could gather, his eyes seemed better. Either he was suffering from some delirium, or he was making objects out more sharply than he had done for some time past. A kind of reaction, probably. Certainly he was not quite the same. He found his way to the Strand and obtained his spectacles. His rate of progress was much slower then. But all the same, that irritating smarting of the eyes had gone.

Well, there was only one thing to be done, and that was to make the best of the catastrophe. If only he had finished that last set of drawings. Now, if he was to make anything of the invention, he would have to place himself in the hands of other people and trust them implicitly. He would have to make the matter plain to Brigden, and somehow he did not like Brigden. He would have to make clear to some mechanical draughtsman exactly what he wanted done, and thus give his precious secret away.

He knew quite well the danger of trusting inventive ideas to outsiders. A year or two before over another matter he had convinced the head of a great manufacturing trust that he could save him thousands a year by a certain ingenious contrivance. The great man was a pillar of his church and party. He could have had a peerage for the asking. But, great man as he was, he had not hesitated to take the idea to his own engineers, and to put them to work upon it. So he made his extra thousands a year, and blandly told Herepath that there was nothing in the conception. It had been a bitter lesson to Geoffrey. And he was none the less bitter because he had found other inventors who had suffered in the same way. Perhaps the best thing he could do would be to destroy his model and recent commercial figures and hide his drawings until he came back.

He went on to Brigden's office, and told him everything. Brigden was superficially sympathetic, as usual. It would be a great nuisance, of course; but it could not be helped. There was just a suggestion in his manner that he regarded the trouble as an exaggerated one. Herepath controlled himself with an effort. "It is only a postponement," he said. "The invention has not been talked about. Only you and that mysterious client of yours are in the secret. The machine will not suffer by the delay."

"That's all very well," was Brigden's reply. "But my client is a hard nut to crack. Don't forget that you have mortgaged a certain proportion of your prospective profits to him, and that he has advanced you over a thousand pounds. Suppose that he refuses to believe what you say, and suppose he insists upon your going on?"

"But, my dear sir, with my eyes in this perilous state, it is impossible."

"What strange ideas of business you inventors have," Brigden responded. "You owe my client this money. From what you tell me, it is possible that you may lose your sight altogether, and what then? My client drops his money. The only honourable thing to do is to pass over the machine to him as it stands, and let him put it into expert hands. I have no doubt he will pay you your share of the profits. Dash it all, man, you have had his money. And no fellow, however rich, likes to lose a thousand pounds. Suppose he cuts up rough."

"It is no fault of mine that my eyes have betrayed me."

"No, but it might easily be your misfortune," Brigden said with an unmistakable sneer. "My man brings an action against you and recovers his money, or gets a judgment, which comes to the same thing. You have no effects, and he makes you a bankrupt. If he does that, your machine no longer belongs to you, but to your creditors. It is the property of the official receiver. He will sell the machine for scrap iron, patent rights and all. And everything goes to the man who buys it."

Herepath bit his lips savagely. The trap was plain now. Nobody would believe that his patent was any good. It was no use telling people that there were millions in it. And the purchaser, beyond a doubt, would be the mysterious client who had advanced the thousand pounds.

"I quite understand," he said, speaking as calmly as possible. It was useless to fly into a rage. By so doing he would play straight into Brigden's hands. "Yes, I see now there are two sides to the question. I am afraid I was only looking at it from my own standpoint. I will see what can be done. This has been a knockdown blow for me, and I am not myself yet. I'll call on you again in a day or two."

Brigden rubbed his hands cheerfully. His foxy little eyes twinkled behind his gold rimmed glasses. It seemed to him that he had successfully put Herepath in his place. And he had not expected him to take it quite so calmly. It had been one of the easiest victories in his twisted career.

"I'm glad you understand," he said. "My dear fellow, you are absolutely safe with us. But business is business, as you know. Drop in and see me on Friday at 4 o'clock."

He hold out his hand in token of friendship, and Herepath forced himself to take it. Whatever happened, he must keep his temper now. It would never do for this little rascal to find out that he had seen the trap and the bait inside it. Well, he would know how to act—if he did not benefit by his invention he would see that nobody else did.

There was one thing more to be done before he returned to his flat to begin his preparations for the voyage. He would have just enough to take him on that sea trip and bring him back again. It was fortunate, too, that Blanche was capable of getting her own living. Harold Gay, the figure in his sister's quiet romance, would look after her in the meantime. Now that Gay had obtained that stewardship to the eccentric Lord Southlands and the control of his estates, he would be asking Blanche to share his home. But she would never consent if she knew how really bad her brother's eyes were. For her sake he must make light of his misfortune. He would have to be cheerful, and declare that the sea voyage would put him all right again. Perhaps his trip would expedite matters between Gay and Blanche. He would do his best to help them.

But there was one to whom the bitter truth must be told, and that without delay. In honour bound he must absolve Enid Harley from her promise to marry him. She must be freed if only for the time being. If he came back absolutely cured, and she was still without ties, then it would be a different matter. But she must give him back that little ring that she wore as yet about her neck. He would go to Poplar this very night and see her. He would give her the signal. She would let him into the house, and he would make a full confession of the trouble.

It was not a difficult matter to see Enid. He followed her along the dimly-lighted passage to the oak-panelled room, where so many interviews had taken place. At the sight of his face she grew pale and frightened.

"Geoffrey," she whispered. "Geoffrey, tell me what has happened."

He took her in his arms and kissed her passionately. Then gently but firmly he put her aside.

"That is for the last time," he said. "My dear girl, you must have courage and listen to what I say. I have been to see Gilray again. And he gave me what is practically my sentence of ruin. I am not to use my eyes for anything but finding my way about. I am not even to read a poster on a hoarding. And I am to go away for a long voyage. If I do not follow these directions I shall be stone blind in three months."

"And if you do follow them, dear? Will you get quite well again?"

"I understand so," Herepath said quietly. "But don't you see what it means, darling? I am practically ruined. By the time I get back to England I shall have nothing left. I cannot perfect my great invention. I must hand it over to a man who lent me a thousand pounds. If I don't do that, I shall be made a bankrupt, and my machine will go to my creditors. Brigden as good as told me so."

"Brigden," Enid cried. "He is acting for your creditors? I wonder—"

She paused in some slight confusion. Herepath could not see how the blood flowed into her face.

"Do you know the name of your creditor?" she asked. "But of course you do."

"Of course, I don't, darling. From the very first he has remained anonymous. It was his wish that his name should not be mentioned. It does not matter so far as I am now concerned. I shall know soon enough."

Enid was silent for a time. She looked greatly disturbed and troubled.

"Oh, if you only know how sorry I am for you," she said prettily. "But I am going to hope for the best, and this trouble shall make no difference to me. There will never, never be anyone but you, Geoff, dearest, and I shall not take back my freedom. If I did it would be quite meaningless. What does Blanche say?"

"Blanche does not know. I am making light of the whole thing to her. If I did tell her, she would make up her mind to sacrifice her life to me, and throw Harold Gay over. And Gay has just got the stewardship of the Southlands estates, that belongs to that eccentric old nobleman that nobody ever sees."

"What name did you say?" Enid questioned. "Southlands. What an amazing—but never mind that. Some day perhaps, but go on, dear. It is a good thing for Blanche. And now that Harold has got that post, you are anxious for them to marry before they find out how serious your trouble is. That is very noble of you, dear."

"Is it?" Herepath said dreamily. "It would be very selfish of me to do anything else. But I did not come to talk of Blanche, but of you."

It was an hour later when Herepath left the house. As the door closed behind him one of the panels in the wall slid away, and Daniel Harley crept out. His dry, wrinkled old face was wreathed in smiles, his wicked dark eyes twinkled with pleasure.

"I can stop that little romance when I like," he chuckled. "Meanwhile let these two young fools play the game for me. Now, how did Gilray manage it? What risks did he take? Has he had the nerve to destroy the eyesight of our brilliant young inventor?"

He chuckled again as he hobbled along to his own room and closed the door.

"That's it," he said, "Gilray has done it. Done it for the sake of 10,000 pounds. Well, he's earned the money, he's earned his reward all right. And, by Jove, he shall have it too, the dog, he shall have it."

CHAPTER XX

SMASH!

Herepath determined that Blanche should not know—at least, not yet—of his terrible misfortune. There was no need to spoil her life with his troubles. It would be good at any rate to know that she was provided for. Harold Gay was a fine fellow, who had had more than his share of misfortunes, most of which had been made for him by other people. Doubtless he would be over from Camford in a day or two, and then all the news could be discussed.

But Gay was over already. Herepath found him there when he got home. He seemed to fill the little sitting-room in the flat, a long lean, bronzed man, hard as nails, and clear of eye as a child. Not a handsome man, perhaps, but good to look upon, and a face that invited confidence at the first glance.

"Well, here you are, old man," he cried with a handgrip that made Geoffrey wince. "I was wondering how long you would be. I hear that Blanche has told you all about my luck. As a matter of fact, I have been expecting the appointment for some time, but I did not like to mention it in case of disappointment. As soon as I knew for certain I came over at once. I'm about the happiest man at this moment in London."

"You certainly look it." Herepath smiled. "But why this violent hurry?"

"Hurry, my dear chap? Haven't Blanche and I been waiting for something like this for three years? And that dear little girl so good and patient all this time. I get a thousand a year and a house. The most delightful old house, black and white timbered, and going back to the time of Charles II. There is all that old furniture of mine in store ready to go in it. Everything will just drop into place as if made for it. You never saw such a lovely old garden; Blanche will love the whole thing."

Blanche sighed gently. Her face was flushed with delight, but there was still a tinge of regret in her eyes.

"It sounds heavenly," she said. "It is the kind of place one dreams of, the sort of home I often promised myself when I was building castles in the air. But I have been telling Harold all about you, Geoff."

"Lord, what a selfish beast I am!" Gay said contritely. "Is it a very bad job, old chap?"

Herepath lied manfully enough. He knew exactly what Gay wanted. He was anxious to get his house furnished and marry Blanche without a moment's delay. And the thing must be done.

"No, it isn't," he said. "As a matter of fact I have been giving myself a great deal of unnecessary anxiety. I suppose it is only natural when a man's eyes are concerned. I'm to be careful and do nothing in the way of reading or writing for some little time to come, and I am to wear these glasses constantly. Also I am commanded to get a complete change by taking a little sea trip. I must do it, but till I came in just now I couldn't see my way. I didn't want to leave Blanche here all by herself."

"Capital!" Gay cried. "Fortune seems to be smiling on us all round just now. Now my dear girl you cannot possibly object to our programme any longer. Listen to me old chap. You can go off on your voyage with the assurance that Blanche is going to be looked after. She's going to marry me before you start."

"You are ridiculous, Harold!" said Blanche blushing.

"Not a bit of it. Never more sane and practical than at the present moment. I am not going to listen to a lot of nonsense about having no clothes. You can get them afterwards. I'll procure a special license tomorrow and we'll be married this week. Then we'll go straight back to Camford, and take rooms at the jolly old hotel there till the house is ready. I've practically arranged it all now. Geoff, help me to persuade this hard-hearted girl to consent."

That was no difficult matter. Herepath's declaration had removed Blanche's chief reason for objecting to an early marriage, and the way was clear. So she gave Harold permission to get the license without further ado.

"It's the only thing I was anxious to have settled," Herepath said as he stooped to kiss his sister. "I dreaded leaving Blanche in case anything happened to me! A sea voyage is no great undertaking, but one never can tell."

"Then that's all over," Gay cried. "You must come down with me and see the house. Can you spare us a few days, Geoff? It would be a nice change for you."

Herepath responded grimly that he could spare the time all right. He was likely to have plenty of it on his hands for some months to come. He would very much like to see the house.

"How did this good fortune come your way?" he asked.

"Oh, I had a friend at Court," Gay explained. "As a matter of fact, the Law Courts had the appointment. You see the estate is vested in trustees. It is over twenty years since Lord Southlands disappeared. He was over fifty then, and, had not long come into the title. The whole place was mortgaged up to the last penny. It was a toss up whether it had to be sold or not. It was at this critical time Southlands vanished."

"Do you mean that he has never been heard of since?"

"In a sense, yes. He disappeared, leaving everything to trustees under the Court of Chancery. He is still alive, for letters come from him from time to time, but he refuses to see anybody, and his hiding place is a secret. Every now and again he sends large sums of money to his trustees to pay off the mortgages. He has found over half a million one way and another. There is still a great burden on the property, but I am sure that if that man lives long enough he will pay it all off. Once he does so, I have an idea that he will return to the house of his fathers. Bit of a romance, isn't it?"

"Very much so," Herepath said. "Does nobody whatever see his lordship?"

"Nobody. From the day he disappeared till this present moment no friend has ever set eyes on him. Even his family solicitors, to whom he remits the money, have no idea where he is, and what he is like. Not that it matters one penny to me. Even if the old chap should come back and take a dislike to me, I need not worry; I am only responsible to the trustees. But I am not anticipating any such unlikely event."

Gay was not disposed to let the grass grow under his feet. He returned the following day flourishing the special license in the blushing, happy face of his pretty sweetheart, and declaring that the ceremony would take place on the Saturday.

"No fuss, no bother, not anything," he said. "We'll get married at twelve o'clock, and I'll treat the whole party of three to lunch at the Ritz afterwards."

"You'll have to harden your heart and pay for one more," said Blanche, smiling. "I really must ask Enid Harley. You haven't met her, Harold. She's the daughter of a queer old miser that Geoff works for. I am practically the only girl she knows, and she comes here more or less secretly. She is afraid that if her father finds out, he may forbid her to visit me, because, you see, Geoff is in love with her."

"I hope to marry her one of these days, please God," Herepath said simply. "You had better write to her and tell her all about it, Blanche."

"Oh, she's coming here to tea this afternoon," Blanche explained. "I'm going out with Harold, and, as we may be back rather late, I daresay you will forgive me, Geoff."

Herepath thought it might be possible. He was glad to hear that Enid was coming, glad to know that he would have a chance to explain everything to her before she met Blanche again. For Blanche must not know for some time to come what a tragedy hung over her brother's life.

"I'll try and make up for your absence," he said. "Go and enjoy yourselves. I should like to come with you, but the glare of the lights is not good for my eyes!"

Enid came in timidly, glad to find Herepath awaiting her. He made no effort to take her in his arms, and sternly refused to notice the quivering lips held up to his.

"Are you not going to kiss me, dear?" she whispered.

"As if I am not longing to," Herepath cried. "You know I am. And yet it is better not."

"Then I am going to kiss you, darling," Enid said. "Oh, my dear, my dear, do you suppose that I could let you leave me like this? I will not be free, Geoff."

He bent and kissed her, then he held her close in his arms.

"It is so good to have you near me," he said. "And now, before the others come back, let us be serious. You got Blanche's letter. You know she is to be married on Saturday?"

"Oh, yes. And I do hope she will be happy."

"She must be happy," Herepath declared. "It shall be our task to make her so. And so that there shall be no cloud for the present I have deliberately lied to her."

"You mean that you have told her nothing of Dr. Gilray's verdict?"

"Not one word, dear. It was my intention to partly tell her the truth, but when I got home Harold was there bursting with his good news. It was good to see the dear little girl's face. Had I told her even part of the truth then she would have declined to marry Harold. She would have insisted on sacrificing herself to me. So I made light of everything. I pretended that I had greatly exaggerated the trouble, and that a few weeks would see me well. You must keep up the deception, Enid. I shall never tell her until I am compelled to do so."

"Ah, it is like you to think of others besides yourself. Geoff. You can rely on me. Not one word will I say to spoil Blanche's happiness. Where is she going to live?"

"At a place called Camford. There is an eccentric old nobleman called Southlands—"

Herepath paused as Enid started. It seemed to him that she had suddenly turned pale.

"What is the matter?" he asked. "Have you heard the name before?"

"A good many times," Enid said. "I—I know something of the family. But the secret is not altogether mine, and I am not permitted to speak more freely. But it is very, very strange, Geoff. So Mr. Gay is going to be the steward of Camford, and Blanche is electing to live in the house where I was—a house I know quite well. Some of these days I will tell you all about it."

Herepath restrained his curiosity. He could see that Enid was uneasy and disturbed.

"I was going to speak of you and your invention," she went on. "What are you going to do about it?"

"My dear girl, what can I do?" Herepath asked hopelessly. "Let it go sooner or later. I am in the power of some mysterious individual, to whom I owe a thousand pounds. If he does as Brigden suggests, he will take proceedings and make me a bankrupt. I am in honour bound."

"You are in honour bound to nothing," Enid cried. "You are the victim of a conspiracy. I dare not tell how I know this, but I do know it as surely as if I were one of the conspirators. You are justified in meeting these men in any way you please. What if you defied them, if you took a hammer and smacked your machine. Could they put it together again? Could any legal firm compel you to make good the mischief you had done?'

"Well, no, I suppose not," Herepath admitted. "If I took a certain glass disc away not all the engineering experts in England could make that machine earn a penny."

"Then do it," Enid cried vehemently. "Do it and defy the consequences. Oh, I know what I am talking about. And if it becomes necessary—but, hush, here come the others, and I must go home."

The warning had come in time. Enid had been seen part of the way home by Herepath, and now he was returning slowly and thoughtfully back, pondering on what the girl had said. It was all very mysterious and disturbing, and the more he dwelt on the matter the less he liked the look if it.

Suppose he did as Enid suggested. Suppose he quietly took away that magic crystal disc that looked so trivial and meant so much! Then he could go on his voyage, and leave Brigden to do as he liked. Why should he not remove the disc now? He had the key of the workshop in his pocket, for there had been many nights when he had laboured there alone.

Almost unconsciously he turned his steps in the direction of Long Acre. The well-oiled lock gave easily, and he stepped quietly inside, fumbling for the switch of the electric light. Then he drew his fingers quickly away, as there came to his ears the sound of voices—voices in the direction of the machine. Somebody was flashing a naked bulb on the end of a long flex, somebody was explaining.

"That's it," the voice said. "Now look here, this is what I mean. You take this feed—" The light flashed on the faces of the two men, and Herepath moved noiselessly into the shadow. He knew who one man was, but he was not by any means sure of the other. Then he got his chance. He bit back the cry that was on his lips.

The other man was Daniel Harley!

CHAPTER XXI

THE GLASS DISC

Herepath held himself in hand with difficulty. His first impulse was to fall upon these rascals and kill them. He had the strength and courage for the fray, and he was a desperate man. It seemed to him that he was ruined beyond all hope of redemption, that nothing in the world mattered so far as he was concerned. Well, at any rate, he would prevent these people prospering out of his misfortunes. He would quickly prove to them that their greed had bred disaster.

So Daniel Hurley was Brigden's mysterious client. Herepath was not in the least surprised to make the discovery. Enid had more or less prepared him for it. He recalled her strange agitation at the mention of Brigden's name. This was the conspiracy she hinted at, and he could see her reasons now for not being plainer with him. It was one more turn in the maze of mystery in which Enid's life was involved, and she had not been more explicit because she was afraid of her father's part in it.

He could not hear what those men were saying, They were muttering to themselves in whispers; they seemed to be dissatisfied about something. Herepath smiled grimly. They should have much greater cause for dissatisfaction before he had finished with them. He came forward and addressed them by name.

"This is quite an unexpected pleasure, gentlemen," he said. "Good evening, Mr. Brigden. Mr. Harley, I am delighted to see you here. But just one question. How did you get here, and where did the key come from?"

Brigden shuffled uncomfortably. For once in his life he was at a loss for a reply. He could only stammer something utterly unintelligible. On the other hand, Harley seemed quite at his ease. There was a smile on his sinister face, a queer kind of chuckle in his throat, as he turned to Brigden.

"Why don't you speak out?" he asked. "You were the pioneer of the expedition. It was your suggestion that I should come here. You told me you had the run of the place, that you could get in at any moment. I understood that you were by way of being a partner with Mr. Herepath. Don't blame me in the matter."

All this was said with the utmost coolness and effrontery, and it was quite amusing to see the clever way in which the elder rascal shouldered the blame on to Brigden. The latter could only writhe and wriggle and put up with it. Evidently he was entirely under Harley's thumb, another pawn in the mysterious game.

"Then Mr. Brigden brought you here?" Herepath demanded.

"Of course he did. I am too old and feeble to take up burglary as a sport. Brigden interested me in your machine. He told me that there was money in it. I have heard that kind of story before. I always like to look into these things for myself when the inventor is not present. I asked for that opportunity, and Brigden said he could give it me at once. Would I come now? I was in the mood and I came. If you have anything to complain of, Mr. Herepath, you must blame Brigden."

"Stop a moment," said Herepath. "You are just a little too clever for me. Let us have a clear understanding. You came here to-night, you say, on the spur of the moment, at Brigden's request. You have only lately heard of my invention?"

"Only a few hours ago," Harley said. "If I am to put money into it—"

Herepath interrupted him abruptly. "You are a contemptible old liar," he said slowly and coldly. "You have known all about this invention of mine for months. You have put money into it. At the present moment I am your debtor to the extent of a thousand pounds. You are the mysterious client with whom Brigden has been threatening me. Stop. If you interrupt me I shall forget that you are an old man, and do you a mischief. If I can stay here to prove my invention, then I may get a share of the profits. If I have to go away leaving things as they are, then you will take action against me, and everything I possess will fall into your hands. Well, I congratulate you, Mr. Harley. So far your dirty scheme has been eminently successful. I am compelled to go away, and I have not the slightest idea when I shall be back. I have practically lost my sight, and it may never return. You had better see about getting your money back."

"You are taking a great deal for granted," Harley said coolly. "You have no right to assume that I am in this business at all. Brigden did not tell you so."

Herepath jumped forward angrily. He gripped Harley's arm with a force and energy that caused the old miser to whimper and cower before the inventor's righteous rage.

"Don't palter with me, or by heaven I'll kill you," Herepath cried. "Are you my creditor? Tell me, or I will tear the truth out of you. Speak, you hoary rascal."

"You are strong, very strong," Harley whimpered angrily. "But you will find that the law is stronger. If you must have it, then I am your creditor."

Herepath relaxed his grip on the old man's arm. His rage had fallen from him as a tempest suddenly lulls. But there was a glitter in his eye, and a hardness about his mouth, that looked ominous. He was beginning to see his way.

"I am glad that we have got somewhere near the truth at last," he said. "I am not what you call a 'business man,' but, thanks to Mr. Brigden, I am beginning to glimpse the facts. So the law is going to give you everything, Mr. Harley. It is a good thing to understand the vagaries of the law. You will be able to shrug your shoulders and say that you have lost a thousand pounds, and that your only return was so much metal. And later on, you will call in some clever pirate in the way of an engineer, who will breathe life into that old metal of yours, and the fortune is made. But there is just one little thing that you have forgotten. Out of the way."

He pushed Harley roughly on one side, and laid a hand on the electric light switch. The long workshop was flooded with the yellow glare; the rays gleamed on the polished sides of the machine. Herepath threw back the bonnet, and disclosed the delicate mechanism inside. Then, at a part where two revolving rods made contact, he removed very carefully a gleaming glass disc.

"Now here in my hand I hold the heart of my invention," he said. "There is only one disc in the world fashioned like this one. Also it is tempered and overlaid in a peculiar way. I made it myself, I ground it with infinite care, and also I practically lost my sight in the fashioning of it. Without this tiny fragment of glass, made in this peculiar form, the machine is useless. You can call a conference of all the engineers in the world, and not one of them can discover the secret of my machine if the disc is not there. They can fashion a million discs, but not one will serve the purpose. Now you may have a claim on the machine, and you can take it now if you like. You can have all the drawings, and the office, and the workmen so long as I retain this little disc. Now what are you prepared to give me for it, Mr. Harley?"

"It is part and parcel of the invention," Harley growled.

"No, it is not. It is a separate installation. But that has nothing to do with the question. Is this little disc worth ten thousand pounds to you?"

"No, not ten pence," Harley went on. "What are you driving at?"

With a grim smile on his face Herepath held the disc up to the light. Then it slipped through his fingers, or seemed to do so, and smashed into fragments on the concrete floor. Harley looked at Herepath in a sour, puzzled way.

"What does this theatrical display mean?" he asked. "What you have done once you can do again, I suppose? I am not to be bluffed, young man. It will be a bad day for you when you put your wits against mine."

"It might have been an accident. It might have been an intention of Providence, Daniel Harley. At any rate, I defy you or any man to prove that it wasn't an accident. I tell you that the heart of my machine lies there smashed in a thousand pieces on the floor. All the King's horses and all the King's men couldn't put Humpty Dumpty together again. If this had happened a month or two ago I should simply have smiled and ground another disc. Now it is impossible for me to do so, for I am practically blind. If I use my eyes again for any but the most ordinary purposes of sight, then I shall never see again. You are more than ever dependent upon me if you wish to make anything of my invention, and I in turn am utterly dependent on the future. On that point I have had the best evidence that Harley-street has to offer. I have been to Dr. Gilray, and he pronounced the sentence of the Court. He gave it me in cold, plain language that there was no mistaking. If the voyage I am to undertake serves its purpose, then all will be well. If not, then my invention is no more than an empty body without a heart, and your thousand pounds lies there at your feet. Old man, you have made a mistake this time. You are beaten."

The queer grin faded from Harley's face, his lips quivered with rage. He danced over the floor like an infuriated ape behind the bars of a cage. He was utterly beside himself, for Herepath had touched him at last.

"The fool!" he choked, "the idiot! This is the way in which...to think that a man should so far forget himself as to...What was I saying? Lord! how I wish I had Gilray here at this moment! I'd grind his face in that broken glass, I'd force the splinters into his eyes, the thrice accursed idiot! To gain that money—curse, curse—"

Harley grow utterly incoherent in his rage, gibbering and mouthing like an epileptic on the verge of a seizure. It was impossible to follow what he was saying. To Herepath himself the whole thing was meaningless. It was to him merely an outbreak of senile rage against a perfectly innocent person. But all this was to recur to him, with illuminating force, before long.

He watched Harley now gradually growing weaker under the strain. The old man dropped on to a pile of refuse and gasped for breath. His cunning eyes turned from one to the other of his companions inquiringly. He was wondering what he had said, how far he had betrayed himself. But he could see no signs of suspicion in Herepath's contemptuous eyes. The fact reassured him.

"I get like that sometimes," he said in a tone that Herepath regarded as apologetic. "There are so many fools in the world. So Gilray told you all that, did he? I happen to know Dr. Gilray—he has done work for me. And I think, I rather think, he is under an obligation or two. I'll ask him about your case."

"You are quite welcome to do so," Herepath said coldly. "Meanwhile, it is getting late, and if you gentlemen have quite finished with my workshop, I should like to lock up. Though it seems apparently to be of little use."

Without another word Harley stepped towards the door. He vanished, into the night, followed by Brigden, who muttered some kind of apology. Herepath snapped off the lights, and the last thing he saw as the illumination died away was the glitter of a thousand pinpoints of flame from the powdered fragments of the disc upon the floor.

CHAPTER XXII

A CHECK

Daniel Harley with Brigden by his side shuffled along the road muttering angrily to himself, eager to find anybody upon whom to put the blame for this unexpected reverse. He had been beaten by an honest man in a perfectly legitimate way and this fact angered the old rogue more than the loss of his money. He looked forward to a fortune from the great invention and had made up his avaricious mind that Geoffrey Herepath should benefit nothing by it, and here in a moment the whole thing had slipped through his fingers. Oh, somebody should pay dearly for this wretched fiasco.

"It's rather awkward," Brigden ventured at last somewhat nervously. "Who would have guessed that Herepath would show fight like that?"

"You should have guessed it," Harley grunted wrathfully. "Nobody but an idiot would have put his head into a trap like that. If I hadn't been deluded into going to Long Acre everything would have gone right."

"But you wanted to go to Long Acre," replied Brigden with some spirit. "You desired to have a private look at the machine. And when I suggested that I had a key that fitted the door and that we should be safe if we went after dark, you jumped at the notion. Didn't I tell you there was a risk that Herepath might put in an appearance?"

"Yes, but you said it was very remote," Harley growled. "It was a million to one against his turning up you said. Bah, and when he did come, why didn't you appear more friendly? Why didn't you try and humbug him? What on earth do you think I pay you all the money for, you miserable, worthless muddler?"

"I earn every penny of the money you pay me with tears of blood," Brigden retorted hoarsely. "Is there never to be an end to your bullying and growling? Now, don't you drive me too far. There are other ways of getting money besides being always at the beck and call of a dirty old ruffian like you. You were eager enough to come to Long Acre to-night, quite ready to take all the risks. And because you have been found out you want to blame me for it. Herepath has got the best of you and it serves you right. I'm not particular to a shade, but I'm fly enough to know when the crooked lay is a losing one. If I'd been in your place, I should have played the straight game with Herepath. You could have made a million or two by doing so, but you wanted it all. Now, like the greedy dog crossing the stream with the bone in his mouth, you've dropped the bit you had to get nothing." Then lowering his tone he added. "But there, when you are in one of those vile rages there is no doing anything with you."

Harley made no response. There was, he admitted to himself, a good deal of common sense in Brigden's plain speaking. By a change of policy it might yet be possible to get on terms with Herepath. Harley's murderous passion was now ill directed against Gilray. An hour or two before he was prepared to regard Gilray in the light of his best friend—now he cursed him as his bitterest enemy. But a little time back he had chuckled that the unscrupulous doctor had earned every penny of the money promised him—now he would take care he should never see the colour of it. He would teach Gilray a lesson before he went to bed.

"Perhaps you are right," he muttered turning to Brigden. "I must have time to think. I want to be alone to give this business my undivided attention. Call me the first taxi that passes. And be where I can get you on the telephone to-morrow morning."

Brigden was glad enough to let it go at that. He too wanted to think. He had not forgotten Harley's strange references to Gilray, and he was anxious to puzzle out where it was the doctor came into the plot, and in what capacity.

He would have been fully enlightened had he been present an hour or so later in Harley's study with the old man and Gilray.

Gilray had come down to the dockside house none too willingly. He had been literally dragged away from a pleasant dinner party in response to an imperative telephone call from Harley, who had told Gilray's butler that he must speak to the doctor at any cost. Harley would take no refusal. He didn't care whether Gilray was enjoying himself or not. There were far more important matters than dinner parties. He refused one single word of explanation, contenting himself with a hint to the effect that if Gilray did not choose to come, then so much the worse for him.

Gilray thought of the promised 10,000 pounds and decided to obey the command, for indeed it was little less than that. It was an easy matter to plead an urgent professional call. All the same, he was feeling not a little sore and angry when he arrived at the mysterious old house beyond Shadwell. He tossed his hat and coat on a table in the study and sulkily demanded to know what all the hurry was about.

Harley showed his teeth in an evil grin. He was feeling murderously inclined toward the man, whom he held to be the source of his recent discomfiture, through which he had lost the vast fortune he was counting on.

"Don't you take that tone with me," he snarled in answer to Gilray's query. "I could smash you to-morrow if I liked. I could pull you up by the roots and throw you into the nearest ditch as if you were a weed. When I want you, you've got to come like a dog and lick my hand. A nice mess you have made of things. And yet you expect me to find you all that money."

"On certain terms you promised to find it," Gilray retorted. "There is no occasion for us to go beating about the bush. I was to get Herepath out of your way. I was to render him a child in your hands, and I have done it."

"Yes, but how? I didn't tell you to destroy the poor fellow's sight. Good heavens, if I liked to speak I could get you twenty years' penal servitude."

Gilray opened his lips, but no sound came. He struggled hard to keep his feelings under control. There were certain things that he could not disclose to this villainous old rascal. The time was not yet.

"So you think I did my work all too effectively," he said quietly. "We will defer any immediate discussion as to that, if you don't mind. What I want to know is, what has happened to cause you to bring me down here in this hasty fashion?"

"I'm going to tell you. One of my men and myself paid a secret visit to Herepath's workshop to-night. He came and caught us there. It was an occasion that made it impossible to give a satisfactory explanation for our visit. Of course, Herepath knew well enough why we were there. He told us that he was doing no work for the present, that he had been to you, and that you told him he would go blind if he tried to do any work. Then he took out a part of a certain machine in which I was deeply interested and had put money, and destroyed it before our eyes. After that he sarcastically assured us that the thing could not be replaced, and that without it his invention was worth nothing. It was pretty clever, when you come to think of it."

"But there are such things as actions at law. You can proceed against him."

"If we could prove that the thing was not an accident, yes. But Herepath was very careful not to defy us that way. As things stand at present, everything depends upon his eyesight. If he gets no better, I am the poorer by at least a million. If I wait till he gets well—if ever he does get well—then I stand a chance of having something out of the million I expected, and he gets a vast fortune for himself. But he won't get well, curse it! Your work has been too thorough for that. You have gone too far."

"I deny it," Gilray said coldly. "Prove your words. How? In a Court of Law? Are you going to confess that you tried to bribe me to make sure that Herepath should stay in his present unhappy physical condition so that you could steal his invention? Your greed blinds your judgment, sir. You are not your astute self to-night."

Harley gasped in speechless anger. He had pulled the strings of his puppets only to find that they refused to work. Evidently there was nothing for the moment to be gained by threatening Gilray.

"Now, listen," he hissed. "That man must be made to see. My whole future depends upon it. You must find some excuse to see his eyes. You must give him fresh hope. You must work to restore his eyesight as you have never before worked to give vision to any patient. Those two pupils of his represent a million of money to me. Unless it is too late. If it is, then look out for yourself."

"That will do," Gilray said grimly. "We shall get on better without threats. May I take it that you no longer assume as certain that I have deliberately tampered with Herepath's eyes."

"If you like to put it that way. Though, to be sure, 10,000 pounds is a tempting lot of money."

Gilray did not appear to be listening. For the moment he was occupied with his own bitter thoughts. A few hours before he had believed that the money he so needed was in his grasp, that he could silence his pressing creditors and clear the way for future fortune. He had flattered himself that he had for ever got rid of a powerful and dangerous rival, and that it was only a question of time before he made Enid Harley his wife and gained possession of David Harley's wealth.

And here everything was suddenly dashed to the ground. Herepath's failure of sight, which had promised to open up comfort and fortune to Gilray, had suddenly become an overpowering misfortune that threatened to haul him back into the old slough of poverty and disgrace. If he failed to make

Herepath's eyes once more those of a normal man he would never touch one farthing of that desperately needed 10,000 pounds. Nor would his calamities end there. He would make of Harley a deadly and malignant enemy, who would pursue him day by day and hour by hour, till finally he was landed in the gutter.

What prudence and foresight could have anticipated a fiasco like this? To defy Harley meant ruin, to restore the sight of Herepath's eyes meant that Gilray's hopes of Enid Harley would be shattered. He must have time to think, time to see in which direction lay the greatest personal advantage.

"Very well," he said at length. "I'll do all I can. But you are a hard man to please, Mr. Harley. One day you want one difficult and dangerous thing done, and the next you want it reversed. Still, don't forget that modern surgery can work wonders. I'll see Herepath as soon as possible—but it won't be before Saturday evening, as to-morrow I go to Yorkshire to operate on Lady Cunningdale and cannot be back until the end of the week."

Harley nodded sulkily. There was nothing for it now but to wait. And he had given Gilray his lesson, he had brought him obediently to heel. But Gilray was not thinking of how best to secure the interests of his employer as he walked home, nor did he consider Harley as he journeyed north, or during the time he was away from London. He was still in the same mind on his return, still undecided as to his course when he reached Herepath's flat in West Kensington late on Saturday evening. Even as he stood outside the flat with his finger on the bell, he was still puzzled and anxious how to proceed.

A neat, pretty-looking woman came to the door and asked Gilray his business.

"But Mr. Herepath is not here," she said. "Only myself, my husband, and my maid. My husband is an engineer, who will be in London for a year or so on business, and Mr. Herepath has let us the flat for that time. We—we only came to-day."

"You mean that Mr. Herepath has gone into lodgings?" Gilray asked.

"I really don't know," the lady said. "I have never seen him. All the business was done in the greatest hurry between my husband and Mr. Herepath."

"But I suppose he left an address in case of letters and all that sort of thing?"

"No. He is ill and needs rest. He wished, he said, that nobody should know his whereabouts for some long time to come."

CHAPTER XXIII

A GLIMPSE OF THE GEMS

The thing was done, the boats were burnt, the Rubicon was crossed. There had been a conspiracy to deprive Herepath of the fruits of his toil, and if he was to get nothing he would see to it that the plotters were in no better case. He no longer doubted the existence of the conspiracy. It had been amply proved when he found Daniel Harley in his workshop.

In bitterness of spirit and the heat of the moment he had defied the father of the girl whom he had hoped to make his wife. Evidently the man was a criminal; indeed, his mysterious life in the strange riverside house pointed to that. Some day the police would lay hands on him, and a great scandal would result. What was to become of Enid then? Herepath groaned as he thought of it. In ordinary circumstances it would not have much mattered. His love for Enid was a pure and brilliant flame, and no family disgrace could have dimmed it. Besides, Enid knew little or nothing of what was going on under that mysterious roof. No shadow of crime had touched her. On this score Herepath had never entertained a single doubt.

And yet there were one or two disquieting little things. He remembered how, the first time he mentioned Brigden's name to her, she seemed confused and uneasy, as if half afraid to say anything. Again, there was a strange agitation when he had mentioned Gay's name in connection with Camford.

Well, after all, these things did not point to any guilty knowledge. And what did it matter in any case? Enid was lost to him for ever. He could not hope to marry her now. He did not believe for a moment that his normal sight would ever come back to him. He would never be able to devote himself to his old work. The glass disc was destroyed; there was nobody else who could make another. For all practical purposes the greatest invention of modern times was as if it had never existed.

But of these things that so oppressed his thoughts he said nothing. He showed no feeling of despondency before Blanche and her happy lover. He determined that they should guess nothing of his real emotions. But when he had seen them bright and smiling on the way to their new home he felt the weight of bitterness that oppressed him lie heavier on his soul than ever. Enid, who had come to see them off, laid a timid hand on his arm.

"You have been very brave and generous," she whispered.

There were tears in her eyes as she spoke. She could see Blanche's handkerchief still fluttering from the window as the train drew out of the great station. And her sorrow was greater than that of the man by her side.

"Because Blanche has been very brave and generous to me," he said. "It has been very hard work, Enid. But I could not dim her happiness at this hour. If she had guessed the truth about my eyes she would never have married Harold."

"But your recovery is only a matter of time, dear," Enid pleaded. "You always said that there was a glowing prospect before you—before us."

Ah, if she only knew. If he only dared to tell her. He smiled sadly.

"There is no 'us' at all," he said. "Oh, I am going to give the cure every chance. But I have very little hopes of it. And I shall require all the money I can scrape together. I have already let the flat furnished to an American engineer friend of mine, and I have secured a bed-sitting room, where my goods have already been taken. I suppose a week or so from now will see me in the Bay of Biscay."

"But you will come and see me before you go, darling?"

"I will see you before I go, sweetheart, but not at your house. There are many reasons why I should not come there again. But a letter will find you, of course. Where are you going now?"

"I am going to lunch with Ninon Desterre," Enid explained. "Now that Blanche has gone she is the only woman friend I have in the world."

"Are you quite sure that she is your friend, Enid?"

The girl looked up startled at the question.

"Oh, surely," she said. "How could I possibly doubt it? She has been so very kind. I know she is a bit of a mystery, and I cannot understand what a strange tie it is that binds her to my father. So far as I know, they never meet, and yet in some way I am certain that they are closely connected in business. I carry all kinds of parcels backwards and forwards. And, Geoffrey, I am going to tell you a secret. I must tell somebody."

"My dear girl, anything you tell me will be perfectly safe."

"Oh, I know that. Well, you remember all that sensation over the disappearance of those Cosway miniatures of Mrs. Van der Knoot's? They were stolen from the house in Parklane, and nothing has been heard of them since. The other night, when you and I met in Park Gardens, Mrs. Van der Knoot was there, and, as you know, the subject of her loss was discussed."

"I thought she took it very coolly, indeed," Herepath said.

"Yes, very coolly. I wonder what she would have said had she known that those miniatures were in my possession all the time. Her stolen miniatures."

"Enid, you are joking. Do you mean to say that you were actually a party—"

Enid stopped him with a gesture.

"You make it difficult for me to go on, Geoffrey," she said. "I discovered the truth quite by accident. I never see the daily papers, and I did not guess about the miniatures till I heard the story of the robbery discussed in Ninon Desterre's drawing-room. And there is somebody else who knows—I am speaking of Dr. Gilray."

"I shall wake up presently," Herepath murmured. "How could he possibly know?"

"Because he saw the miniatures in our house. He came down very late one night, and very secretly, to attend a man who was staying with us, who had had an accident to his eyes. These miniatures were lying on my father's table in the study when the doctor went in there. He knows, and because he knows, without so much as one word on either side, he has forced me into a kind of compact with him. I am sure that he regards me as being in his power. He has not made love to me, but a girl understands some things by instinct. I know that he means to ask me to be his wife. I also know that he regards me as helpless to resist him. And, oh, Geoffrey, you are going away, and I have nobody in the world to protect me."

The words were quietly spoken, but they cut Geoffrey Herepath to the quick. Up to now he had regarded his action as single-minded and unselfish. Now he could see that there was another side to it. It disturbed and filled him with hot anger to find that Gilray was acting like a scoundrel. But he repressed any sign of heat.

"I am very sorry, dear," he said humbly. "You see, I did not suspect anything of this. Did you put any questions to Madame Desterre? Did she offer any explanation?"

"Oh, yes. That is the most puzzling part of the whole thing. I demanded an explanation, for I was exceedingly angry. I said that I was being made use of as an intermediary in a very queer and possibly criminal business. And Madame Desterre laughed. She did not deny that I was the quite innocent possessor for the time being of the Van der Knoot miniatures. She told me not to worry in regard to the pictures, not to imagine that there was anything wrong or criminal in my father's possession of them. Funniest of all, she offered to make Mrs. Van der Knoot tell me so herself if I wanted to be further satisfied. Geoffrey, what does it all mean?"

Herepath shook his head hopelessly. He felt altogether out of his depth. But strange as the story was, there were more pressing things to occupy his attention. He had been thinking far too much about himself. He had brooded over his misfortune to the exclusion of the rights of others. What he had just heard rendered it impossible for him to go away and leave the girl he loved alone and unprotected. Suppose she found herself dragged into the black business that evidently occupied her father. Suppose that sooner or later she was forced into the dock? The idea was intolerable. After all, it could not very much matter whether he went on a sea voyage or not. The sparing of his eyesight was the main thing. Then a sudden suspicion flashed into his mind. Perhaps Gilray had detected him as a rival, and had taken this course to get him out of the way. Suppose, therefore, he only pretended to take this voyage, and really remained secretly in London to protect Enid and watch events?

The idea appealed to him. Yes, he would remain in England. He would save all the expenses of that trip abroad, and have a little money to spare to help him unravel this tangle. But of this change of plans he would say nothing to anybody yet, not even to Enid.

"It is all very strange and mysterious," he told her. "More bewildering than any detective story. At any rate, I will so arrange that you shall be safe, whatever happens. I may be deceived, and Madame Desterre may be nothing more than a smart adventuress, but I like Madame Desterre. Shall I come with you, Enid?"

"I think you had better not," Enid replied. "Let us walk as far as Park Gardens; it is a lovely morning, and the walk will do me good. And you won't go away without letting me know, and you will give me your address, dear? Something tells me that I shall need you, that events are going to happen. And there is nobody but you."

Naturally Herepath gave her the desired assurance. No doubt existed in his mind now as to the course he meant to take. He would not turn his back on England and leave this beautiful, innocent sweetheart of his to the tender mercy of two such ruffians as Harley and Gilray. It was not for him to tell Enid that he had made a lasting and bitter enemy of her father. The poor child had quite enough on her mind as it was. He stopped presently, and handed Enid a card and pencil.

"Here, take down my address," he said. "I am afraid I cannot see to write it. It is there that you will always hear of me in case of need. If I were you I should say nothing about our two selves to anybody, not even to Madame Desterre, friendly as she appears to be."

They parted presently near Regent's Park, and Enid went her way much easier in her mind. She could have told Herepath a good deal more had she not lacked the courage to do so, and now she chided herself for her reticence. Still, there were certain secrets that were not altogether her own, while in many matters concerning the riverside house she was as utterly in the dark as the merest stranger.

Herepath went on to his new lodgings very quietly and thoughtfully. He had plenty to occupy his mind. He was more disturbed by Enid's confession than he cared to admit. Was it possible that this innocent child was unknowingly acting as a tool to a gang of international thieves? Were Daniel Harley's associates also at the bottom of the disappearance of Princess Helena's jewels? Yet Madame Desterre had not acted towards Enid as if the latter had caught her conniving at a crime. Also Herepath had a very vivid recollection of Van der Knoot's demeanour when speaking of her loss. She was not merely diffident, but had even resented any allusion to it.

Those matters occupied Herepath's mind till long after tea, and he had got all his possessions unpacked in the snug bed-sitting room. He was just filling a pipe when his landlady gave a knock and came in with a telegram in her hand.

"Please read it to me," Herepath said. "As I explained to you, my eyes are very bad."

"That's all right, sir," the woman answered. "It says: 'Dine me eight to-night, green room, Royal Empire Hotel, alone, and very urgent. No need reply'—that's all, sir."

Herepath dismissed the woman with a nod. He would not go. Why should he? Yet just before 8 he was waiting for Madame Desterre in the vestibule of the Royal Empire.

CHAPTER XXIV

VOLUNTEER OR PRESSED MAN?

A stream of men and women in evening dress was pouring into the great pink and gold dining-room. It was the place to dine at in London just then, the last word in luxury—until some new capitalist should come along with something still more sinfully extravagant.

Herepath's lips curled scornfully as he saw the flashing jewels, the expensive dresses, and the fleet of gleaming cars that came purring gently up to the pavement. What those people wasted in a year would keep a hundred families in comfort and happiness. There was not one of them who would have lent him a sovereign to protect him from starvation, and yet he had something hidden in the back of his mind that would have meant a fortune to half of them.

Yet perhaps the show of gaiety was not all as easy and devoid of care as it appeared. For instance, he did not look like poverty himself with his Bond-street cut dress clothes, his immaculate linen and polished shoes. There was just the suggestion of a cynical smile on his lips, and he would easily pass as part and parcel of that giddy throng, living on the money of others, and having no thought for anything but pleasure and the pursuits of the morrow. Who was to know that he was out of touch with fortune, and at the end of his resources?

A gentle hand was laid upon his arm, a gay voice rang in his ear.

"How good of you to come. I am afraid I am dreadfully late, Mr. Herepath."

He turned round to find Madame Desterre by his side. Her long white opera cloak was thrown open, exposing some amazing salmon pink confection underneath. Her clear, beautiful eyes looked into Herepath's with frank pleasure and innocence.

Herepath felt just a little ashamed of himself. Surely it was the last thing in absurdity to connect this woman with a crime! Herepath followed her docilely, and was permitted to remove her cloak and find the table she had engaged. Half a dozen waiters were proudly eager to see what they could do to meet her wishes. The occupants of other tables looked round and whispered one to another. Evidently Ninon Desterre was a familiar figure to the people through whose midst she passed as gaily and serenely as some dainty butterfly, unconscious of the admiration she was creating. There were well dressed men, men whose names were household words, who looked enviously at the fellow-creature who was to have the honour of dining tete-a-tete with Madame Desterre.

Herepath was feeling slightly intoxicated by this atmosphere. He would have been more than human otherwise. Why should he not enjoy himself just for this evening, at any rate?

"You must not altogether despise we insects," Ninon said. "We are not all working bees."

"I don't know that I do despise you," Herepath replied. "Had I been born to the environment, I dare say that I should be one with you. But the possession of a fortune must be very enervating. Do you never get tired of it?"

"Never," Ninon said, showing her teeth in a dazzling smile. "You see, I am naturally contented. Give me a nice house and pretty clothes and plenty of money and I'm never bored. Did you ever see anything more exquisite than these flowers?"

She bent over the table, and snapped off a trailing spray of pink orchids, heedless of the fact that it would mean another sovereign to the bill. She arranged the blooms in her corsage, and smiled as she noted their striking effect.

"I can't resist them," she said. "I left the dinner entirely to that adorable Jules, the chef here, and I am sure he will do his best for me. But you shall choose the wines. Like most women, I am no judge of wines. And I want you to please yourself entirely."

Herepath gave himself over to the spirit of the evening. He chose the wines and liqueur recklessly, and without the slightest heed of the cost. It would probably be many a long day before he was in a world like this again. Probably he would be called upon to earn his dinner presently, but for the time being he had not to consider that. He ate with zest and the appetite of one who lives hard and cleanly. By the time the coffee and the cigarettes had arrived it seemed to him that this world was a very good place to live in after all. He passed the cigarettes across the table.

"I am forced to say no," Ninon murmured. "There is nothing I enjoy more after a good dinner, and it has been a good dinner, has it not? But it is one of my rules never to smoke in a public dining-room. Mr. Herepath—Enid came to see me to-day."

The attack was as sudden as it was unexpected. Herepath could only stammer in reply. Ninon Desterre sat with her chin propped on her hands, looking her guest fully in the face.

"Do you trust me well enough to confide in me?" she asked.

"Well, really," Herepath stammered, "I hardly understand you. Certainly we are very good friends."

"And always shall be. Now Enid is an innocent, transparent little soul. It is not a difficult matter to get anything out of her. And she told me quite a lot at lunch time. Mr. Herepath, whatever happens, as you value Enid's happiness and your own, don't go away."

"I have already made up my mind to stay," the bewildered Herepath said.

"Come, that is good hearing at any rate. You have a rival in Dr. Gilray. Now don't run away with the idea that Enid told me so. And please do not regard me as an altogether frivolous little butterfly, whose one idea is to flit from flower to flower sipping honey all day. The honey I get is collected in quite a different fashion. I see a great deal more than people give me credit for. And I see where your danger lies. To save you from that danger I asked you to meet me here and dine tonight. I am perhaps a fool to interfere in the business of other people, but I am very fond of Enid, and I have a great regard for you. If you will only do as I tell you there will be no further danger from Gilray."

"I don't quite understand how much you know," Herepath said guardedly.

"Oh, you are quite right to be cautious. Gilray wants to marry Enid Harley for two reasons. In the first place, he has fallen madly in love with her, and in the second he imagines that Daniel Harley is a man of considerable means. That is quite correct. But where Gilray makes the mistake is in thinking that Harley is under his thumb. Daniel Harley is under the thumb of no man—he is too astute for that. He has been too astute for you."

"I am not quite so sure of that, Madame Desterre."

"Oh, yes he has. He would have robbed you of your patent; he and that little fox of a Brigden together. You have checkmated them. But what is going to happen when you get well again? That is a question that you cannot answer; but it is possible I can. I think I know exactly what will happen; but I am not going to discuss that point till I am sure of my ground. Now, what do you make out of that stolen miniature business?"

"Did Enid tell you everything that we had been discussing this morning?"

"Pretty well," Ninon said coolly. "My dear, good man, I extracted the information. There are more ways than one whereby the butterfly draws the honey. And I really am your friend. Now let us be quite serious for a moment. I cannot tell you the secret of those miniatures. But I swear to you that there is nothing criminal in the business. Oh, you are not going to live to see the father of the girl you love languishing in a dungeon over that affair. The same remark applies also to the disappearance of the jewels of my friend, the Princess Helena. In a way Daniel Harley is a public benefactor. It will be all made quite plain one of these days."

"That is certainly very hard to believe," Herepath said. "Yet when I look into your face I cannot doubt what you tell me."

"That is one of the prettiest compliments I have ever had paid me. But I must be serious. You have already promised not to go away. Now, what I want you to do is this—leave London and hide yourself in some quiet place, so that Gilray will imagine that you have departed on that suggested voyage. But your hiding-place must be where I can reach you with a telegram at any moment. Your whole happiness rests on this—your happiness and the disclosure of a conspiracy that will bring three men to your feet begging you to make your own terms."

"Will it bring back the use of my eyes?" Herepath asked bitterly.

"Before Heaven, I think it will," Ninon whispered. "The Princess told me—but, hush!"

She paused. At a near table somebody who had just arrived was speaking of Princess Helena in loud and excited tones. It was quite easy to hear what the newcomer said.

"Had it as a fact," he vociferated. "The police have tracked the thief, and they expect to arrest him at any moment with Princess Helena's diamonds in his possession. One of those journalist chaps who knew everything told me. He says that the thief is dining here to-night, and that we may look for something lively at any moment. What?"

Herepath glanced at his companion. It was very curious to hear all this at the moment Ninon had spoken of the Princess. She sat there tense and rigid, her face pale and set, her eyes narrowed to pinpoints of flame, The only restlessness about her was in her hands, which moved quickly over each other as if she were making signs. As this restless movement ceased a man rose from close by, and went quickly towards the door. As he passed he carelessly pitched an evening paper on to the table next that occupied by Ninon and Herepath. Near the door somebody accosted the late diner, and he vanished noisily.

"They tell me it is a certainty," Ninon said aloud. Herepath stared at her in amazement. He had not the least idea what she was talking about. "An absolute certainty."

"I am quite at a loss to follow you," Herepath said.

"I'm not in the least interested in horses as a rule," Ninon went on. "I regard them as stupid creatures that do silly things at inconvenient moments, such as running away and all that kind of thing. But I am going to back Polestar for a lot of money, because I had what you call the tip from a friend of mine who is, as they say, in the know."

"You mean to back Polestar for the Gold Cup?" Herepath asked.

"Precisely. For a lot of money. In the jargon of the ring, I can get a good price. I should think quite ten to one. Do you know what the horse stands at now?"

"I haven't the remotest notion," said Herepath; indeed, just at that moment he had not the remotest notion of anything. "If you are really interested—"

"Oh, I am. There is a paper that some kind man has left on the next table. Please get it for me and we will see what the betting is. And carry that paper just as it is folded."

The last words came in a whisper, and they covered a stern command. Herepath gripped the fact that there was more meant than met the ordinary ear. Very carefully he took the paper from the next table, and brought it over to the one where Ninon was seated. She seemed to carelessly flick over the first page, but the second one she was more careful with. As she raised a corner of it she disclosed to Herepath's astonished eyes the cover of a shabby leather case.

"Don't look at it," she whispered. "Go on talking about racing or anything else, but talk, talk. And whilst you are chatting try to make out what I am saying to you. That's what I mean...Yes, I dare say you are disgusted and not a little weary, and so am I. The situation was saved just in the nick of time. Otherwise I should have had all my pains for nothing. Now I dare say you have guessed what is in the case—"

"You don't mean to say that they are Princess Helena's diamonds—"

"Hush, hush. That is precisely what they are. And now I am going to ask you a favour, a great favour, that you will never regret, believe me. Slip that case carefully from the folds of the newspaper and put it in your pocket. And when you have done that go on talking to me just as if nothing had happened."

With a feeling that he was being hypnotised, Herepath obeyed.

CHAPTER XXV

THE DANGER ZONE

Almost before the thing was done Herepath regretted it. He would have regarded such an act as incredible folly on the part of anybody else. If he were caught with those stones in his possession there could only be one end to the adventure. Assuredly he would be arrested as either the thief or an accomplice.

Had he been lured here for the very purpose of being duped? Had he been deliberately marked down for a catspaw? These questions raced through his mind rapidly. After all was said and done, he knew very little of Ninon Desterre. She was beautiful and fascinating, and apparently rich. She was a prime favourite in the most exclusive circles, but Herepath had never heard anything of her family or of her relations.

She seemed to read these troubled reflections as they flashed upon Herepath. But she was not in the least discomposed. On the contrary, she looked like somebody sitting in the stalls of a theatre witnessing a comedy. The dazzling smile was still on her face, her eyes danced with something very like mischief.

"You are very kind," she said. "And the way you are trusting me is a pretty and sincere compliment. There is nothing to be afraid of."

"Perhaps not," Herepath retorted; "but I am not feeling very happy all the same. This is the first time I have ever been the receiver of stolen goods. You seem to have successfully transformed a fool into a knave, Madame Desterre."

"And presently I shall be able to prove that you are neither," Ninon said coolly. "Mr. Herepath, I give you my word, my solemn word, that I never anticipated anything like this when I asked you to meet me here. Moreover, I pledge you my honour that nothing is really wrong. A carefully laid scheme has gone astray; that is the worst that can be said. In helping me now you are helping yourself and one you love to an extent you do not dream of. Come with me, please."

Herepath shrugged his shoulders helplessly as he rose. After all, what did it matter, what did anything matter now? His life was practically wrecked, he would never have the free use of his eyes again, and what was left of his great invention would soon be in other hands. And this woman possessed, at any rate, the reputation of being loyal to her friends. Let the adventure proceed—he was ready.

In the vestibule a little knot of people had gathered round the man who had so cunningly passed over the diamonds to his confederate. There was no fuss or bother—no signs that the management had been consulted. The thief stood there quite calmly and coolly, a smile on his lips as he listened to the questions of the police officer fronting him. His face lighted up as he saw Ninon Desterre approaching.

"Well, here is a lady who will say a good word for me," he exclaimed. "Madame Desterre."

"Victor Player, Count Victor Player," Ninon cried. "'So you are back from Amsterdam. I had not expected you to return so soon."

"You know this gentleman, madam?" the officer asked.

"A great deal better than I know you, Inspector Gillispie," Ninon replied. "You have not yet discovered anything in regard to the disappearance of the Princess Helena's jewels?"

"I rather fancy that I have, madam," Gillispie said drily. "You were present, I remember, at the Duke's entertainment the night the diamonds were stolen. I have been following up a clue ever since, and that clue brings me here to-night. I am about to arrest this gentleman on a charge of being concerned in the robbery. He is just back from Amsterdam, where he has been attempting to dispose of one of the largest of the missing diamonds. I shrewdly suspect that he has the stone upon him at the present time."

Herepath listened to this with intense uneasiness. It seemed to him as if he had suddenly become the leading actor in some hideous nightmare drama. It was almost impossible to realise that he had the missing gems in the pocket of his overcoat. And here were the police in reach of his hand in total ignorance of what had happened.

He made a more or less successful attempt to appear absolutely indifferent. He stood a little aloof, as if declining to be dragged into an unsavoury business, as if he were merely waiting to escort his companion to her car.

"It is perhaps unfortunate that I have a valuable diamond in my possession," the man called Count Victor Player said quite coolly. "It was very good of the police to follow me about all Amsterdam so that I should not be robbed. Probably they tracked me home, so that they could take me red-handed with the balance of the gems in my possession. But it is a difficult matter to identify a loose stone, my good Mr. Policeman."

"Very possibly; sir," Gillispie said with some asperity. "And it is only fair to tell you, sir, that you are making dangerous admissions that will be used in evidence against you. You admit that you are in possession of a diamond that you have secretly attempted to dispose of."

The Count carefully selected a cigarette from his case and lighted it.

"By no means," he said. "True, I had and still have—a valuable diamond to dispose of. I tried to sell it here, but your London brigands would give me no kind of a price. It is a very little trip to take across the water to Amsterdam. Now, look you, my dear Mr. Policeman, you are making a great mistake. I am by no means a man of wealth, and I have to augment my income by business methods. It is one of my fortunate gifts that I am a good judge of gems. My friends know that, and frequently they come to me with valuables to dispose of. I find them good markets, and they pay me what you call a commission. It is not all gold that glitters, hein? My lady has had a bad time at bridge, or my lord has a big betting account to settle on Monday. Well, well, that being the case, some of the family stones must cease to be of the family, er?"

"If you will give me the name and address of the owner of the stone the matter can soon be settled, sir," said Gillispie.

"'My dear Mr. Policeman, I could do what you wish with the greatest possible ease. I could take you to the real owner of the stone at present in my possession, most excellent policeman, and prove to you that this is his property. But no; I do not choose to do so. Suspicion falls upon me because I frequently go over to Holland, and I am known to transact secret sales of stones. But to tell whose stone this is would be a breach of confidence. The owner of the property would be rightly angry. He does not want anybody to know that he is pressed for money."

The Count gesticulated picturesquely with his cigarette as he spoke. He made little staccato movements which Ninon Desterre appeared to be following with close attention though she still smiled as if the whole thing were some joke arranged for her benefit. Yet all the time she fidgeted at her throat, and Herepath could see that in his turn the Count was watching Ninon's every movement. Undoubtedly under the very eyes of the police they were signalling to each other with a sort of code not unlike army flag signalling.

"Very well, you can explain to the magistrate," Gillispie said shortly. "If what you say is true, of course you will be completely exonerated. But I have to do my duty, and you will have to come with me, sir."

"And then I must of course betray my client," the Count cried. "My dear Mr. Policeman, you are making matters worse. Instead of helping me to avoid scandal, and are deliberately forcing me to make it. My client is a lady. Think of her feelings when all this becomes public property. And also, Mr. Policeman, think of your feelings when you are, as you will be, reprimanded for your stupid blunder."

"I take it that you only need proof of what the Count says?" Ninon suddenly asked.

"That would certainly justify me, Madame, in not making an immediate arrest," Gillispie admitted, palpably shaken by the Count's allusion to the reprimand that awaited him if it was shown that he had blundered. "Otherwise, of course, I must arrest him now."

"Well, I don't fancy there will be any 'otherwise,' Inspector," said Ninon drily. "I happen to know that the stone in question is, as the Count says, 'the property of a lady.' Now let me describe it. The stone is what you call a blue diamond, hexagon in shape, and weighing exactly 75 carats. It is in a little blue box, on which is the monogram N.D. in silver. If the Count will, as things have gone so far, produce the stone, you will find that my description is correct." Without any further waiting the Count took a tiny blue box from a pocket inside his vest, and handed it over to Gillispie. The latter examined the case and its contents grimly before he passed it over to one of his subordinates.

"What do you say, Motley?" he asked. "You are a judge of these things."

"It's a blue stone all right, sir," the other man muttered. "And I should say that the weight is 75 carats as near as no matter. Also the monogram is on the box."

Gillispie looked uneasy. He was not pleased with the aspect of affairs.

"May I ask, Madame," he queried gruffly, "how you came to know all this? Am I to take it that you have done some business with this gentleman?"

"On one occasion only," Ninon retorted, smilingly, "namely, the present one. You see the diamond happens to be mine."

She spoke quite calmly and easily. Gillispie's face fell as he caught a smothered chuckle from one of his subordinates. He twiddled the little box in his fingers, plainly at a loss to know what to do next.

"The Count was introduced to me by a lady friend," Ninon explained. "You see, Inspector, I have a very large income, but unfortunately I have no notion of the value of money, and I spend my dividends sometimes a wee bit faster than they come in. And I am the unluckiest woman at bridge that ever touched a card. When I go into the city to try and get some of my money back again I lose once more. So I need three thousand pounds. The Count came to me, and I gave him my stone to sell. He will not part with it under a certain price, and there is an end of it. You can please yourself, Mr. Gillespie, as to what you do now in the matter."

There was just the suggestion of a threat behind Ninon's dazzling smile. The whole thing had been so coolly and beautifully engineered that Gillespie was staggered. It was impossible to doubt the evidence of ownership that Ninon had laid before him. To go any further was to court censure from his chiefs, and possibly something worse.

"I am greatly obliged to you, Madame," he said, "I am afraid there has been some mistake here. I acted on information supplied by the Dutch police. Of course, if any question should arise later I know where to find you, and through you the Count, to whom I apologise."

The Count was graciously pleased to take the matter amiably. He would have handed the tiny jewel case to Ninon, but at a sign from her he returned it to his pocket.

"What a thing it is to enjoy the confidence of a lady so beautiful and distinguished," he said as he bowed and turned away. "It is with deep regret that I have dragged Madame into this. And she has acted in a manner that has made me her slave for ever. Good night, Mr. Policeman, and should you ever want my services Madame Desterre will tell you where to find me."

He took off his hat with a flourish and vanished smilingly into the night. Gillespie was all apologies. It seemed as if he could not say enough.

"There is no occasion for another word," Ninon told him. "Your zeal is wonderful. Well it is said that the English police force is the most intelligent in the world. Good night."

She watched the inspector till the swing doors of the vestibule closed behind him. Then she turned to Herepath with a challenge in her eye.

"Come," she said, "admit that you are puzzled, that you want to know all about it."

CHAPTER XXVI

THE FAMILY PICTURES

"The admittance would be just as well, perhaps," Herepath said a trifle coldly.

"My dear boy, you have just been watching a little comedy of the most brilliant type. It is rather unfortunate that you are not in the mood to appreciate it. Now, by my cleverness, backed up by the natural astuteness of the Count, I have averted a great scandal—and incidentally saved that excellent Gillispie from a severe wigging. That diamond is not mine—"

"I could see that from the first," Herepath replied. "You arranged the whole thing by signal under the very eyes of the police. It staggered me that they didn't see it."

"L'audace, l'audace et toujours l'audace," Ninon quote mockingly. "My word, your eyes are not so hopeless if you could follow all that. But that is another side of the question which we will discuss in due season. In the meantime, please do not run away with the idea that because the blue diamond is not mine therefore it belongs to the Princess. It does not belong to the Princess. She would be the first to tell you so."

"And what would she say if she could see into my pocket at the present moment?"

"'Oh, she has a fine sense of humour," said Ninon laughing. "She might be a little dismayed, but she would certainly not be angry—except perhaps with me."

"Still, the sooner I get the things out of my possession—"

"Dear friend, you are not going to get them out of your possession just yet. You will leave London as soon as possible, and take the gems with you. Stay away in hiding until your presence is needed here again, and until then put the stones in some safe place."

"But, my dear Madame Desterre, you are asking me to become an accomplice in a felony," Herepath protested. "You are asking me to risk everlasting disgrace, let alone a long term of imprisonment. Everybody in England knows that these diamonds were stolen from the Princess Helena by an audacious trick."

"Nonsense! Pray do not argue. The Princess would not attempt to interfere—unless she did so on your behalf. I am your friend—one of the best friends, if you only knew it, you have in the world. I want to make the path smooth for you and Enid Harley, and I am the only person who can do so. I can even give you back your sight. I can restore your precious invention. And it is because I am eager to do these things that I am apparently placing you in so dangerous a position. But no campaign was ever won without risks and danger, and the particular campaign I am engaged upon is far from being an exception to the rule. Now, do you want the things I can give you, or do you not? Are you going to be cautious, are you going to play the careful coward! Think of it! On the one side a big struggle to live; poverty, blindness, endless anxiety. On the other side, restored sight, Enid, fortune, fame, a name that any man might envy! It is for you to make your choice."

Ninon was smiling no longer, her face was pale and set: she spoke with passionate energy. There was an earnestness in her appeal that carried Herepath away.

"Very well," he said; "I cannot but believe you. You are either my best friend or the most consummate actress in the world. What shall I do?"

The flashing smile was back again, the beautiful eyes were luminous.

"Ah, that is the way to speak!" she cried. "Only do as I tell you. Get away from London and hide those precious stones as soon as possible. Go down to Camford, and stay at the same hotel with your sister and her husband. You see, I know all about it. I have had to arrange the movements of a score of people on your behalf—and Enid's. Only have patience and trust me. And, now, see me into my car."

Ninon declined to discuss affairs any further. She was once again the gay and inconsequent woman of society. Herepath turned away from the car and made his way home to his lodgings. He was desperately anxious to get rid of the burden of those stolen gems. He wondered what would happen were he suddenly to become involved in some street accident and his pockets were searched. It was a relief to find himself in that humble bed-sitting-room again.

He felt that he had no option but to let things take their course, to trust Ninon Desterre. After all, he could not well be worse off than he was at that moment. He would lie low for a day or two, and then go down to Camford. He was certain of a welcome there.

In this latter respect he was certainly not disappointed. He was met at the quaint village hotel, where Blanche and Gay were quartered for the moment, with open arms. They arranged that he must share their sitting-room, and take his meals with them. He could make himself useful in helping to get into the new house.

"A perfect gem of a place," Blanche cried. "So beautifully old and restful. If you like pictures and works of art Camford can supply all your needs. It is a veritable museum of treasures."

"I thought it was let on a long lease," Herepath said.

"It was," Gay explained. "But the tenancy expired some weeks ago, and the family have gone abroad for a time. Now the glorious old house is in the hands of two ancient servitors as caretakers. Would you like to see the place?"

Herepath expressed himself anxious to do so. He very much wanted to go over this house in which Enid was evidently so interested. She had told him that her association with it was not her secret, but he did not doubt that she knew all about Camford.

It proved to be a magnificent grey pile of buildings, that dated back to the time of the Stuarts, and was lined throughout with old carved oak panelling. The mansion, as Blanche had said, was a veritable museum of works of art and furniture, but its chief glory was its pictures.

"They are marvellous," Herepath exclaimed when his inspection was finished. "Still, if the house belonged to me I should be contented with fewer of them. There are so many that they hide and detract from the beauty of much of that wonderful carved oak. If Lord Southlands is so anxious to clear the estate, why doesn't he sell some of the canvasses?"

"He can't," Gay said. "They are heirlooms. They go with the property. So far as we know, Southlands has no family; indeed, I never heard that he was married. In any case, I am sure the next-of-kin would object to such a sale."

Herepath stopped to admire a small gem in the gallery, one of the finest specimens of a Corot he had ever seen. There were six pictures in a panel, with no frames beyond the old carved oak into which they had been embedded.

"Well, I dare say the sale would be a wrench," he said. "Just cast your eyes over this, Harold. Did you ever see anything more exquisite? Really, I shall have to come here again and again. It is a positive pleasure to wander about this fine old place."

"Come whenever you like," Gay said. "I have told the old man and his wife that you are free of the place. I'm glad you're interested. It gives you something to think about, and makes you forget your troubles. We are only waiting to hear that you are not going on that proposed sea trip of yours, and we shall be happy."

"Upon my word, I had forgotten all about it," Herepath confessed. "For the present, at any rate, I'm not going. I dare say a month or two here will do me just as much good, and not cost a quarter of the money. It may be only my fancy, but it seems to me that my eyes are getting better."

Gay was unfeignedly glad to hear it. He, of course, knew nothing of the trouble that was holding Herepath up, nothing of the history of those stolen jewels, and the hiding place that had been chosen for them. There was plenty here to occupy Herepath's attention. He had the run of Camford with its lovely park, and he made himself busy, too, in helping Gay and Blanche to get into their new home. He could not read or write, but fortunately the weather was fine, and he gradually fell into a habit of taking long walks after dinner.

He had commenced them at first out of a natural desire not to intrude too much upon the evening leisure of Blanche and her husband. Besides, the exercise was good for his health, and he slept all the better for it. He seldom met anybody in the park, and as a rule had the wide leafy solitude all to himself. The calmness of the place suited his mood. It mattered little what time he returned, but it was generally midnight before he crossed the long avenue in front of the house on his way to the little hotel.

After one of his rambles he was coming back that way about the witching hour when he paused for a moment with his face turned in the direction of the house. He fancied he could see something like a dim light in one of the windows. Whilst he was wondering whether or not his bad sight had played him false, the light vanished, and then he distinctly saw it reappear in another window.

"That's odd," he said to himself. "Somebody is wandering about the picture gallery with a candle. It can hardly be the old caretaker or his wife at this hour. Besides, their quarters are on the far side of the house—"

Herepath moved towards the building till he stood on the wide flagged terrace. He could see then that he was not mistaken, that somebody was really in the picture gallery with a candle. He was half inclined to knock up the aged caretakers to see if they knew who it was moving about the old place. On second thoughts, however, he abandoned the idea. Burglars do not wander about a house with a naked light, however large and solitary it may be. There was, too, nothing they could carry off at Camford except furniture and pictures. Pictures were not of much use to the average burglar, and the furniture was too bulky. He would speak about the matter in the morning, and no doubt Gay would make inquiries.

"I'm getting too full of fancies," he told himself. "I begin to scent mysteries everywhere. Probably a cat has got shut up in one of the rooms and the old man is looking for it. I'd better go to bed and sleep this fidgetiness off."

Herepath mentioned what he had seen to Gay at breakfast-time next morning. It was not a matter of any moment, and Gay made light of it. But he looked a little less easy at lunch time, and drew Herepath on one side quietly.

"I didn't ask and didn't question the old couple," he explained, "about that moving light you saw, but I got some information. I'm quite sure that neither of them was out of their room from ten last night till daybreak. There's something strange about the matter after all, Geoff, and I'll look into it."

"Very well, and I'll have a hunt round the picture gallery for myself," said Herepath.

For an hour or two in the afternoon Herepath busied himself in the gallery. He looked grave and puzzled as he came out and made his way to Gay's office at the back of the house.

"Just come, this way," he said. "I suppose you can spare me ten minutes. I've made a discovery that calls for your earnest attention. Come as for as the gallery...Now look here. Just cast your eye over that panel of pictures I admired so much the other day. You will, of course, remember that wonderful Corot. What has become of it?"

Gay looked eagerly at the panel in question. His face was a study as he turned to Herepath.

"Why, they have all gone," he cried. "Those are not the same pictures at all. Those are the kind of treacle-coloured things that one sees in the windows of cheap dealers in copied old miniatures. And how neatly and artistically the edges of the panelling have been fitted to them."

"Yes. The thief, whoever, he is, understands his work, and must know the house well. Shall we call in the police or bide our time for the rascal's return. If he thinks no suspicion has been aroused he is sure to come again."

CHAPTER XXVII

HARD PRESSED

We must now return to Dr. Gilray, whom we left outside Herepath's former lodgings, where he had been to seek the inventor, only to be told that he had gone away, leaving no address.

Gilray turned away from Herepath's flat with a foreboding of coming trouble. He would have found it difficult to account for this, but there it was. And Daniel Harley would not let this matter drop on the mere assurance that Herepath was not to be found. Harley was a hard man to deal with. He did not appear to know his own mind for two days together. Take this very matter of Herepath's, for instance. At first Harley had appeared to be more than satisfied when he thought Herepath had been rendered helpless by his failure of sight. He had been free with his praise, and had not hesitated to say that Gilray, in convincing Herepath that his case was hopeless, had earned his money twice over.

Then almost before he had made a mental division of this money, which was he believed, so soon to be at his disposal, the whole ground was cut from under his feet, and the blackness of despair filled him once more.

Harley had suspected him of a crime, the crime of rendering Herepath blind, and for that crime he was at first prepared to pay the unscrupulous surgeon handsomely.

It mattered little to Gilray whether the crime had been actually committed or not, so long as the money came to him. Now everything was wrong, he was to get nothing unless he found some way of undoing all his work, and of giving back to Herepath his normal sight. Even then Harley might make some excuse for not fulfilling his contract. If he did, Gilray was in no position to enforce it. And if he took back everything, and put the inventor once more in a position to work, then he raised up a powerful rival again. What a nuisance this money was, why couldn't people do without it? And all the while angry creditors were clamouring on his doorstep.

By hook or crook he would have to find Herepath, and do Harley's bidding, but meanwhile it was necessary to get some cash on account. His solicitor, Barker, was at him again. Unless he fulfilled his promise to produce 5000 pounds, sure and early bankruptcy stared him in the face.

"My dear fellow, it's no use blaming me," the solicitor said. "You made me a certain promise for to-day, and you tell me now that you have failed to raise the money. If I am to save you I must have a cheque by post time."

Gilray groaned in despair. He was utterly at the end of his resources. His one and only chance was to get the money from Harley. He determined that he would go and do so, that he would drag it out of the old man, if necessary. Why should he be played fast and loose with in this way?

"I'll get it," he said desperately. "I'll get it this very afternoon, and come back here before your office closes. I'll be back here with that five thousand pounds."

Barker shrugged his shoulders. He had heard all this before.

"Very good," he said. "I shall be here till six. And please understand that I have done everything I possibly can for you. Now, once for all, remember that the bankruptcy petition will be filed to-morrow unless you keep your promise. If you are not ready with the money you will be adjudicated a bankrupt, and the Official Receiver will take possession of everything. You know what this means to you?"

In his mind Gilray took an imaginary Harley by the throat.

"I do," he said hoarsely. "It means absolute, hopeless ruin. But I will get that money. I will get it, even if I have to commit murder to do so."

It was nearly 3 o'clock before Gilray dismissed his taxi and made his way across the open space that led to the mysterious old house beyond Shadwell. In the garish light of day it looked not a bit less forbidding than it did at night. Gilray thought of the occasion on which he had first seen it. He wondered where was the mysterious basement door by which he had so nervously entered. This time at any rate he would gain admission by the orthodox way. He rang the bell, but nobody came. He rang again and again before he heard footsteps in the hall. Then the door seemed to open by itself in some mysterious way, and Gilray found himself in darkness. The door closed behind him, and he heard the latch click. His heart was beating just a little faster. The darkness and the silence of the place oppressed him. He had placed himself now entirely in Harley's power. The man might murder him and throw his body in the river, and nobody would be any the wiser. Nobody knew that he had come there. There would be no clue if he was never seen again.

Then he comforted himself with the thought that Harley could not do without him. To his mind it was quite clear that he was absolutely essential to the wicked old man's plans. Yes, he would put up a bluff, meet Harley with a bold face, and carry the matter of like a man. He might as well be dead as bankrupt; indeed, the former condition would be preferable.

"Anybody in?" he shouted. "Where are you, Mr. Harley?"

A door in the distance opened, and a ray of light streamed out. The gay voice that answered the call was certainly not Harley's.

"It is the good Dr. Gilray," the voice said. "Pray come this way. I shall be most delighted to see you and thank you for all your kindness to me. This way, doctor."

Gilray walked on, feeling not in the least surprised. Nothing in that amazing house could surprise him. At any rate the voice sounded friendly. He entered a room into which he had never been before, a long plain room with discoloured walls and dirty ceiling, yet filled with the most beautiful and artistic old furniture. A good-looking young man, with a reckless face and a pair of amused blue eyes, was bent over a table engaged on some task of carpentry.

"Enter, my good doctor," he cried. "Behold me, Victor Player, at work. Such a phenomenon has not been witnessed since the days when I was at school. Now have you any knowledge of the way in which to construct a picture frame?"

Gilray shook his head impatiently. He had not come here for this foolery, excellent as it might be. He had, too, a feeling that the fellow was laughing at him. And there was something oddly familiar about his face.

"That is a great pity," Player went on gravely. "I want to restore a broken portion of this lovely old Florentine frame. It got broken in the—er—hurry of moving. Is it possible, my dear doctor, that you fail to recognise your grateful Victor Player?"

"I seem to have seen you before," Gilray said stiffly. "But you have the advantage of me."

"But yet it is not so long ago, doctor. You came here one night to attend a patient. He had something the matter with his eyes. Goodness knows what it was, but you came here. I was your patient, my dear doctor. Behold me!"

"I remember you now," Gilray said. "No thanks are necessary. It was merely a professional matter, and incidentally I was well paid for it. But I came here to-day to see Mr. Harley. I have business with him of the greatest importance. I hope he is at home."

"Oh, he is at home all right," replied Player with a shrug. "But you've come at a most unfortunate time. The old man is in a devil of a temper. He has even lost his temper with me, which, when you come to think of it, is a most amazing thing. Take my advice and come some other time."

"I must ask you to tell Mr. Harley that I am here," Gilray insisted.

Player shrugged his shoulders again, but expostulated no further. With a genial smile he left the room, and Gilray could hear him softly whistling to himself as he walked along the passages. There should be no more of this nonsense, Gilray determined. If Harley did not see him in the course of a few minutes he would know the reason why.

But a good quarter of an hour elapsed, and there was no sign of Harley. Gilray wandered restlessly about the room examining its various art treasures. In an idle kind of way he wondered what his late patient had been doing. On the table lay an exquisite Florentine frame in four pieces, and by it a small painting, which Gilray's critical eye at once appraised as a gem. This was some recent purchase of Harley's, he decided, something that had come to him in the way of business. But why should such business be done in this hole-and-corner way in this mysterious house? Why was not Harley keeping one of those fine art establishments in Bond-street?

Gilray was pondering this problem, when the door opened and Harley came in. There was a frown on his face and unmistakable anger in his eyes.

"What do you mean by coming down here like this?" he demanded.

"I came to see you on urgent business," Gilray replied. "And I warn you, Mr. Harley—"

The old man stepped across the room with an agility remarkable for one of his years and snapped his long yellow fingers under Gilray's nose.

"Hoity, toity!" he cried. "The young bantam fancies himself, or he would not be defying the wily old cock in this fashion. You warn me! Oh, oh, that is good, very good! Why, I could smash you in an hour if I chose. I could break you up in little bits. Or, on the contrary, I could save you from disaster. I have only to hold up my hand and that petition in bankruptcy to-morrow would never be filed."

He skipped and danced in front of the disconcerted Gilray, his features convulsed with rage, and yet with a sardonic smile in his eyes. Exhausted at length by his exertions, he dropped panting on a chair.

"Oh, oh!" he coughed "I forgot that I was not so young as I was. But when you come into my own house and begin to threaten me I am myself again."

"I beg your pardon," Gilray said hoarsely. The man's knowledge of his private affairs filled him with wondering trepidation. "I came to see you, and you—well, you are not polite."

"I never am polite. Politeness is an art I have no use for. Go on."

"Well, I went to see Mr. Herepath, as you suggested. You gave me certain instructions—"

"No. I gave you no instructions. You are a free agent in the matter."

"You are very cautious," Gilray said bitterly. "But this is no time for diplomacy. Mr. Harley, I am a desperate man. I stand face to face with ruin."

"Well, most of us do at times," Harley said coolly. "A good many men are bankrupts if they only knew it. I was pretty close to it myself once. You want me to help you?"

"I want you to keep to your bargain. If I did certain things I was to get 10,000 pounds. I did what I bargained to do, and you pronounced yourself satisfied."

Harley sat there listening, with his head on one side like some evil old parrot.

"Here, what's that, what's that?" he shrieked. "I made a bargain with you! Never!"

"Oh, yes, you did. I am going to speak quite plainly. Geoffrey Herepath stood in your way. He has invented a wonderful machine that you made up your mind should be yours. You had already advanced a thousand pounds through your creature Brigden, and you thought that the money would not be repaid, and that you could step in and take everything. But Herepath was just a little too smart for you.

He had pushed his invention to the commercial stage before you were ready. And then his eyes went wrong."

"Where did you get all your knowledge from?" Harley sneered. "And what has it got to do with me? Suppose that I admit that what you say is true? What then? It was a mere business transaction, sharp practice, if you like, but the kind of thing that is done every day in the City. You can go and proclaim your story from the housetops, if you like. Nobody would listen to you. We do not make profits out of bankrupt doctors, my friend. You cannot suggest fraud."

"That is exactly what I do suggest," Gilray said defiantly. "Fraud on your part and on mine. If I become bankrupt then you go to gaol as sure as there is a heaven above us."

CHAPTER XXVIII

ENID SPEAKS OUT

Harley sent his head parrot-like again. He and Gilray were coming to grips now.

"Go on!" he croaked. "Don't mince your words. So I am party to fraud, am I?"

"Yes, and I am another. Herepath has beaten you. He did not turn out to be the average inventor, who does nothing but dream of untold gold so long as he has a sovereign in his pocket. He pushed his machine on. He satisfied Brigden that he had only to go to the trade to get all the money he needed. In that case you would only have had a share of the profits for your thousand pounds. That share was a huge fortune in itself, and would have more than satisfied an average man. But you are not an average man. You cast about in your avaricious mind for some scheme whereby you could get everything."

"I am not admitting a word of this, Dr. Gilray. But go on, my eloquent accuser, go on."

"Pooh! what does it matter whether you admit your villainy or not? Keep your denials for the dock, where you will find yourself before long. I say you looked round deliberately for some way to rob Herepath of the fruits of his brain. And fortune favoured you. Herepath had given his eyes too much to do, and he came to me to cure him. And by good fortune I happened to be more or less in your power. Do you follow me?"

"I am listening, my fellow criminal. It will be my turn to speak presently. Go on."

"Herepath came to me. I told him certain facts. Practically I deprived him of the full use of his eyes. I stopped him from doing the crowning work that was to render his machine perfect. And by so doing I threw the invention practically into your hands. And I did it at your request."

"A pretty confession, truly," Harley sneered. "At my request you say you deprived Herepath of the full use of his eyes! So that he would be powerless, and that I could steal his machine! And this you are prepared to repeat?"

"Anywhere!" Gilray cried. "Everywhere! To anybody! As I said before, I am a desperate man. If you repudiate your bargain with me and I go down, by the Maker who made us, you go down, too. And now, are you going to let me have the money you promised me?"

Harley's mood suddenly appeared to change. He sat with his chin in his hand thoughtfully.

"Circumstances alter cases," he said. "You have been frank with me, so I will be equally frank with you. I am obliged to you for your confession that you deliberately deprived Geoffrey Herepath of the full use of his eyes for the sake of ten thousand pounds. I will pass for a moment your statement that you did this at my request. What I want you to understand is that I never part with money unless I get full value for it."

"That is the truest thing you ever said," Gilray retorted bitterly.

"Well, it's a fact, anyway. Now, suppose that Herepath gets the better of both of us, after all. Suppose that he has destroyed a certain small part of his machine, so that its secret should not fall into my hands? Suppose that he has discovered that Brigden and myself are working together."

"Oh, a truce to all this fooling!" Gilray cried. "Herepath has found you out and I know it. He was beside himself with despair. There was just the chance that he would get better in the course of months, but that would be too late. By that time everything would be in your hands. So he deliberately destroyed the essential portion of his machine."

"Since you know it, I'll admit he did all that," Harley said grudgingly. "He caught Brigden and myself in his workshop at night. And he spoke pretty plainly. He said that the odds were against him ever seeing properly again, and, as he did not trust us, he took from his machine a glass disc and smashed it. There you are. That's just how we stand to-day."

"Then you have lost everything, including your thousand pounds?"

"Confound it, yes," Harley burst out. "You were too premature; you destroyed, or practically destroyed, the fellow's eyesight, and now the whole nicely-arranged scheme has come to nothing."

"I did what I did at your suggestion, remember. And, moreover, you said that I had earned my money twice over. Now, instead of paying me, you fly into a passion and declare that I have ruined everything. I'm not the man to stand that sort of thing, Harley, and the sooner you realise that the better."

"You will stand everything I ask you to stand," Harley said coolly. "If you could restore that fellow's sight I could make terms with him. I could go on the old lines and take half that he makes. It would come to millions in time. I've over-reached myself this time, and I don't mind confessing it. You can't do what I suggest?"

"And if I could do it, what then?" Gilray queried.

His voice sank to a whisper, he thrust his head forward till he could see the yellow specks in Harley's glittering eyes. His whole body tingled with excitement.

"Do you mean to say that you can?" Harley said eagerly.

"I don't say so. I only asked you a question. You don't have the chance to play fast and loose with me again. What do I get if I can undo this mischief, can bring back Herepath to his normal self?"

"Well, you got your ten thousand pounds to begin with."

"Ah, that's better," Gilray cried. "To begin with. You'll have to trust me—a thing that with you will go sorely against the grain, but you will have to do it. Meanwhile, I'll take this. It is a beautiful picture, and I can easily raise a thousand or two on it."

He picked up the little gem of paint and colour from the table, and proceeded to pack it carefully. With something like a cry of horror Harley came forward.

"Do you want to ruin me altogether?" he cried. "Do you want to ruin yourself at the same time? You little dream of the mischief that would be caused if it got abroad that that picture was in my possession: Put it down, man, put it down! To offer it for sale would be ruin. No good could possibly come of a mad action such as that would be. Can you do what you boast you can?"

"I am not boasting. And I have promised nothing. I said you would have to trust me. Do so and I will try my best. Give me five thousand pounds now, and the rest when I can prove to you that success has been achieved. If I fail, you can easily take your revenge, for five thousand pounds will not go far towards clearing off my debts. Give me a cheque for what I ask you now, and the balance later on."

"Um! It sounds so far reasonable. And will you be satisfied with, that ten thousand?"

"No, I shall not," Gilray said boldly. "Remember what I asked before. I don't want any more money; at least I shall not require any more until you have done with it. You have a child for whose sake I would do anything. With her by my side I could go far. Is this to be part of our bargain?"

Once more the ruddy sparks flashed in Harley's eyes, once more his yellow fingers crooked with a suggestion that they were strangling somebody, He laughed in a horrible silent way, unpleasant to see.

"My daughter shall please herself," he said. "You are free to ask her to marry you if you like. But I shall put no pressure on her, understand. If she refuses you, then there is an end to the matter, and it is not to be mentioned again."

Gilray expressed himself perfectly willing to fall in with this arrangement. It would be strange indeed, if, with the hold he thought he had on her, he did not win this girl. In the meantime he would be able to save his position, would stave off the exposure and disgrace that hung over him like a cloud. He would show Barker that he could keep his word. The money would be paid before 6 o'clock.

But the situation was not without its danger. To earn the whole of his reward he would be compelled to place his rival on a pedestal again, a strong man with a gigantic fortune before him. And Enid Harley loved this rival from the bottom of her heart.

Well, he must chance it. There could be no drawing back now. There was just one loophole, perhaps, but Gilray would not count too much on that. The one great thing now was to get hold of that money.

He nodded in the direction of Harley's desk.

"There has been enough and more than enough of talk," he said. "Give me my pound of flesh and let me go. To-morrow will be too late."

Harley shuffled slowly, almost painfully, across the room. He was going to part with some of his beloved money, he was going to lose some of the yellow gold that was his very heart's blood. And he was not getting anything tangible for it. He was exchanging hard cash for a more promise. Gilray watched him with a cynical smile. He rejoiced in the struggle with the demon of avarice, tearing the miser's soul. Harley dug his pen viciously into the paper of the cheque, dried it, and with a sigh handed it over to his confederate.

"There," he said, "take it and hide it from my sight. This is a very painful business for me, very painful indeed. Good-day. Come again as soon as you have any news."

There was no occasion to wait for anything more, and Gilray let himself out of the house, feeling that he had not wasted his time. He would walk as far as the Tower, where he could take a taxi to Barker's office. As he turned into the first street he heard his name softly called, and looking round, saw Enid Harley behind him.

"This is quite an unexpected pleasure," he said.

"Is it?" the girl said coldly. "I followed you from the house, Dr. Gilray. I have just had time to pack some of my things and send them by a messenger to the station. It may perhaps interest you to hear that I am leaving home to-day, and that I have not the slightest intention of returning. I should be glad if you would lose no time in telling my father this, for you are mainly to blame for my action."

"I to blame?" Gilray cried. "My dear Miss Harley, how can that be possible?"

"I listened," Enid calmly explained. "I was in the next room doing some of my painting. There is only a thin partition between the rooms, and I heard everything that was said. There was not one word of your vile conspiracy that failed to reach my ears. For a long time I have been meditating this step, but to-day I knew I must remain under that roof no longer. I will say nothing now of the wicked, abominable crime my father and you have committed against Mr. Herepath. And remember this, Dr. Gilray, even if you fail to restore to him the precious thing you have taken away, it will alter nothing between us. I love Geoffrey Herepath, and shall love him till I die. No, I will not listen to a word from you. Go back to my father, and tell him what I have said. If he wants to know where I have gone, tell him to Camford. He will understand quite well what that means."

She turned and disappeared down a side street before Gilray was sufficiently recovered from his surprise to follow her. All his plans seemed to have failed, the house of dreams had collapsed. But the girl must be stopped in her flight, she must be brought home at any cost. He ran panting back to the house and thundered on the door. He could hear Harley's shuffling feet as he came along the passage, he heard the angry voice asking what was wrong now.

"Your daughter," Gilray gasped. "She heard everything. She was in the next room. I met her in the street just now. She has gone, never to return. She told me to tell you so. And I was to say particularly that she had gone to Camford."

Harley grabbed Gilray by the coat collar and dragged him into the house.

"A thousand curses," he foamed. "Let me get a timetable, quick. She must be stopped at any cost, ay, at the cost of half my fortune, if necessary."

CHAPTER XXIX

A GRAVE SUSPICION

At the end of a week Gay and Herepath were no nearer to a solution of the mystery of the missing pictures. It was annoying and disturbing, and none the less so because they had said nothing to the police. True, Gay had communicated the loss to the solicitors to the estate, and asked for instructions, but had received no satisfactory reply. The matter, he was informed, had been reported to the trustees, who were "taking steps." Meanwhile, would Mr. Gay be so kind as to keep the matter a secret till he heard from them again.

"Very far from satisfactory," Gay commented. "Still I've done my duty in the matter. Perhaps those chaps know something, and are keeping it to themselves."

"Perhaps it has happened before," Herepath suggested. "Perhaps I have stumbled upon some family scandal. Well, we have done all we can, Harold. But I've still got the idea that the thief will turn up again. It will amuse me to look out for him."

For the moment there was no more to be said or done. Besides, they were all very busy getting Gay's house in order. By the end of the week the last curtain was in its place, the last rug upon the floor. Blanche surveyed it all with tears of pride in her eyes.

"I was never so happy in my life," she whispered. "I'm selfishly happy. If only Geoff were all right I should have nothing to wish for."

Herepath turned away so that Blanche should not see his face. He did not want to spoil the exquisite pleasure of that moment. He would go out and see if there was anything he could do in the garden. It needed nobody to tell him that Gay and Blanche wanted to be alone. A feeling of depression was upon him. A long walk was what he required to get rid of it. Those walks always gave him an excuse for retiring early. He could always plead after dinner that he was tired out.

He struck off across the country in for him a new direction altogether. He walked on mile after mile till he was tired and thirsty, and in need of tea. Presently by the roadside he found a quaint old inn that appealed to him invitingly. He could just make out the sign of 'The Green Man' swinging on a post in front of the house.

The door stood hospitably open, and he turned in. Here was the passage, and the bar with the old black tap-room beyond, and beyond that again the snuggery. Herepath rapped on the counter, but nobody came. But for its furniture one might have imagined the place deserted. He rapped again, and shouted at the top of his lungs.

A gay voice in the distance answered him in light and easy tones. It was not exactly the way for a landlord to address a customer, and Herepath was conscious of a certain irritation. He called again sharply.

"Why don't you come down?" he demanded. "Is everybody asleep here?"

Out of the brown shadow a slender figure of a man emerged. He was dressed in a suit of perfectly fitting flannels. Herepath's sense of smell told him that the cigarette he was smoking was an Egyptian of the most expensive blend.

"Now this is quite an unexpected pleasure," the man said. "I anticipated finding some thirsty carman in search of beer. Instead, I behold my friend, Mr. Herepath."

"Player," Herepath gasped. "Count Victor Player! What—what are you doing here?"

"Victor Player, at your service," the Count said coolly. "The victim of a ridiculous mistake on the part of a stupid constabulary. The delicate plant that might to-day be languishing in gaol but for the intelligence of the beautiful and talented Ninon Desterre. My dear sir, do you know that you are in great demand. Do you know that Mr. Daniel Harley would give much of his money to stand face to face with you as I do?"

Herepath shrugged his shoulders impatiently. He had small reason to trust this man, whom he had come to regard as little better than a clever thief. At any rate, there was no getting away from the fact that the Count had had a hand in the stealing of Princess Helena's diamonds. That those stones were now in Herepath's possession made very little difference. He would not part with them lightly.

"Come into the private bar and sit down," Player suggested hospitably. "I have an aged retainer here who will get us some tea presently."

"You seem to be quite at home here," Herepath suggested.

"Oh, I am," the Count smiled. "You see the house belongs to me. I bought it some time ago from a young swell, what you call a Johnnie, on condition that I kept the house open till the license could be transferred to another inn now being built on the far side of the village. Otherwise the license would have gone altogether. For the moment it is my whim to pass as a village landlord; that is when I have any spare time. The villagers who assemble here at night to absorb beer regard me as an amiable French lunatic. Between ourselves, they are a little afraid of me. When I make this place into a private residence and settle down they will know me better. Meanwhile, there are amusing comedies to be acted here. Ah, yes. I am not sure that we are a long way from a comedy now. And, by the way, what happened to those diamonds the other night?"

Player spoke quite coolly. There was not the least sign of shame or confession about him.

"You mean the diamonds stolen from the Princess Helena of Pau?" Herepath asked coldly.

"The same. But your description is not strictly accurate. Don't forget just now that I spoke of comedies. Well, those jewels form part of a comedy. You have read all about them, of course. You are aware that they formed part of the crown jewels of the Principality, and that the rebels strove to get them back. My friend, that is all nonsense, what you call flap-doodle. There never has been any rebellion in the State of Pau. It is a fiction, a nicely got up newspaper sensation. The Prince of Pau resigned, gave up his job, as you say, because he had no money to carry it on. The jewels truly belonged to Princess Helena. At one time they were her mother's, bought with her own money after a successful flutter upon the Stock Exchange. You see, she had opportunities, as a Princess, of inside information. Very useful, eh? The whole, what you call yarn, was the invention of a clever journalist, and it has never been contradicted, because, well, because, it was not worth anybody's while to do so. For certain purposes, too, the story has been useful."

"Pardon me for a moment," Herepath interrupted. "All this may be fact, but we can't get away from the knowledge that the Princess has been robbed."

The Count's eyes twinkled as he applied a match to a fresh cigarette.

"So it would seem," he said coolly. "You know that they were in my possession, and therefore you think you have evidence that I am a thief. But do clear your mind of all that nonsense about political alarums and excursions. The time will come when you will see more clearly, when you will positively enjoy the situation. Meanwhile, I shall be grateful if you will withhold your judgment as to my moral character, and believe that I am your good friend and well-wisher. I am, indeed, Herepath."

There was something sincere and convincing the way the Count spoke. Herepath had proved him, as he thought, to be a cool and audacious thief. Yet in spite of all this, he felt attracted by the man. He looked him frankly in the face, and there was no suggestion of the furtive-eyed criminal of fiction about him. He went on without giving Herepath a chance of reply.

"Madame Desterre is your good friend too. Oh, we know what is going on, I assure you. They say it is not possible to serve God and Mammon, but I'm not so sure even of that. You must not condemn the servant because the master is a blackguard. I presume that you are staying somewhere in this neighbourhood, Mr. Herepath."

"I am staying with relatives," Count.

"Quite right. Be guarded. Don't tell me too much. After all, knowing what you do about me, why should you tell me anything? And the less I know the less other people can get out of me. Keep where you are, and don't go near old Harley for the moment. If he finds you now, as he hopes to do, well then—"

The Count shrugged his shoulders with an eloquent gesture.

It was all very puzzling and bewildering but at the same time it was evident that this volatile Frenchman meant well.

"I am absolutely helpless," Herepath said bitterly. "I am deprived of my sight and practically of the means of obtaining my living. I am one of Fate's footballs."

"Ah, my friend, but some day you will be in the possession of a fortune. Some day you will get to work again and perfect that rubber invention of yours, yes? Meanwhile you laugh in Harley's face. You tell him that the game is his if only he can make another of those pretty glass marbles of yours. That was a strong card, my friend, a very strong card indeed. Then just at the critical moment you disappear, and Harley does not know where to find you. And I give you my word he wants to find you very badly indeed. And so does the clever Gilray."

"Gilray! What do you know about him?"

Player winked solemnly. He was as near gravity now as he ever got.

"A great deal, a very great deal," he said. "Sir, I am not quite so brainless as you imagine, and that sometimes it suits me to appear. Now listen, I set myself a task, and that task is nearly finished. Once it is ended, Daniel Harley and your humble servant part company for all time. Then I come and settle down here, and become a respectable member of society. Ah, yes. I am shortly to lead to the altar, as you say, the most lovely and accomplished of her sex. No, I don't mean Madame Desterre, who has views of her own on the subject. The lady waits for me in Paris. Now come up to my rooms, and I'll get some tea for you. The old woman who helps me here is very old and feeble, and I save her all the trouble I can."

Herepath followed wonderingly. He was just a little annoyed with himself at falling so easily under the fascination of this free and easy stranger. But he could not resist. He found himself presently in a beautiful old room, in the centre of which was a table on which a cloth had been spread and laid out. There was golden butter and honey and homemade bread. A silver teapot of exquisite design stood on a tray, and this Player took in his hand.

"I shall have to go downstairs and get some hot water," he said. "If I leave it to my poor old woman we shall wait all the night. Excuse me for a moment. Are you any judge of old oak? If so, there is plenty of it here to interest you."

Herepath wandered round the room admiring the blue china, the wonderful old punch bowls, and the half-dozen carved chests that stood ranged in front of the mullioned windows. He forgot everything else in the enthusiasm of the moment.

They were wonderful chests carved by a master-hand, and adorned on the lids and sides by incidents from the Canterbury Tales. A more perfect collection it would have been hard to find. Herepath wondered if there were carvings inside the lids, for more than one of the chests had bracket arms that suggested a double lid, so that at will the chests could be converted into window seats. He raised one of the tops almost reverently.

But there was no double lid here, nothing but an empty chest, save for a picture or two lying on the bottom. Herepath took one of them in his hand carelessly, then threw it back with a clatter into the chest again.

He had found the panel pictures recently stolen from Camford!

CHAPTER XXX

THE FACE BEHIND THE GLASS

It was fortunate perhaps for Herepath that he was alone just at that moment. He had quite recovered from his surprise by the time that Player returned with the tea. Herepath decided that he would say nothing of his discovery to anybody; at least nobody should know except Harold Gay. At any rate, he knew who the thief was now, and nothing would be gained by betraying his suddenly gained knowledge to Player.

He would get away as soon as possible and return home. He had plenty of food for thought as he walked along. It was nearly 7 o'clock by the time he reached the quaint and charming old house near the lodge gates of Camford. Apparently Gay had finished work for the day, for he was in the garden smoking a peaceful pipe. Blanche was nowhere to be seen, for which Herepath was grateful.

"Been for a long tramp?" Gay asked. "You might have been miles by your boots. And what's the matter with you, old chap? You look mysteriously wise."

"Well, I've discovered who stole those missing pictures," Herepath said. "What's more, I know where they are, for I have actually had them in my hand."

"The deuce you have," Gay cried. "Did you bring them back again?"

"No, I didn't. I did not betray myself at all. The man who has the pictures has not the remotest idea that I have seen them. He does not even guess that I am aware of their existence. He could not possibly connect me with Camford. I believe I am correct in believing that he has no idea of my present hiding-place."

"But my dear fellow, why do you speak of this delightful old house as a hiding-place?"

"Well, more or less it is, as all in good time I shall prove to you. Now, since you have been in these parts, have you ever heard of a public-house called 'The Green Man?'"

"Of course, I have. It's quite a landmark in the country. I heard a rumour the other day to the effect that the old hostel had been sold to a Frenchman, and that the licence was being transferred to a new building. Why?"

"Because I have had tea with the Frenchman—a man called Count Victor Player. I have met him before, but that is quite another story, and one that I cannot go into at present. I dropped into the house to have tea in the ordinary way, and Player told me very much what you have been saying. He left me in his own sitting-room whilst he went to make tea, and invited me to admire his old oak chests. Lifting the lid of one of them I came bang upon the missing pictures."

"My dear chap, are you quite sure you are not mistaken?"

"Mistaken! I'm prepared to stake my reputation on what I say."

"Well, upon my word, Geoff, this is amazing," Gay cried. "Did you by any chance say anything?"

"No, I didn't," Herepath said curtly. "I held my tongue. It seemed to me to be far more prudent just now to say nothing. We know where the pictures are, we know the name and identity of the thief, and we can put the police on his track at any time. Besides, I am inclined to think the fellow may have an explanation as to the pictures being where they are."

"Explanation?" Gay queried. "When you know how those pictures went?"

"Well, there may be an explanation. The strange part of the whole thing is that Player does not give one any impression of his being an ordinary thief. In the ordinary course of things I should call him rather a nice chap. I should like to go up to the house after dinner, and have another look at the panels the pictures were stolen from. I suppose I could get in without disturbing those ancient caretakers?"

"With the key in my possession, certainly," Gay said. "What's in your mind?"

"Nothing very particular. Only a theory I wish to test. Besides, it gives me something to do. Isn't that Blanche calling? She sounds quite excited I hope she hasn't broken any of those old bowls she is so fond of. Well, Blanche?"

Blanche came hurriedly down the rose-bordered path, her eyes shining like stars.

"Oh, the most wonderful thing!" she cried. "I was never more surprised and delighted in my life. Who do you think is there, Geoff? Who do you think has just come? She walked over from the station, and her luggage is followed in a cart. She was going to stay at the old Inn, but when she found that we were properly settled she came on here and asked if we would pardon her intrusion and put her up for a time."

"If I had a mother-in-law," Gay said, with a twinkle, "I should at once jump at the name of the invader."

"Oh, do be serious, dear. Can't you guess? Well, Geoff, perhaps you can."

Herepath was conscious that his heart was beating a little faster. It was bewildering and incredible, but Blanche's shining eyes let him into the secret.

"Blanche!" he cried. "Is it really true? Is Enid here?"

"Oh, yes, yes. And she knows that you are staying with us. I thought perhaps that she might not care to...you understand. But she seems to be glad. And she says that she is never going back to that dreadful old house in London again. She wants to remain with us a little time till she can look round and get something to do. She seems to think that she will be able to get a living doing gold brocade embroidery. She looks dreadfully ill, poor thing. I am quite sure something terrible has happened, that she has something on her mind."

Herepath went slowly up the path in the direction of the house. He would find Enid in the drawing-room, Blanche observed. And Gay was suddenly anxious to get information as to Blanche's views on the subject of a new flower border.

"Best leave them alone for a little while," he murmured. "Looks as if there was something wrong, dear. If so, she will confide in Geoff, and we shall hear all about it in good time. I should like to see those two people as happy as we are."

Enid rose as Geoffrey entered the long low drawing-room. He could see the tears in her eyes, could see the supplication on her face, and the yearning for love and sympathy in the droop of her lips. He had not meant to take her in his arms and kiss her, and he hardly realised that he had done so till her head lay on his shoulder like that of a tired child.

"Oh, I am so glad, so glad!" she murmured. "People may say that I am here after you, but I shall not mind. I couldn't stay when you had gone, Geoff. I couldn't really. You don't know what my life was like after you had gone."

He could feel the sobs shaking her from head to foot. He held her to him and soothed her as best he could. Then she grew calmer, and a beautiful smile lit up her warm face.

"Now tell me all about it, darling," he said tenderly.

"Oh, I couldn't, Geoff. At least not yet. It's all too terrible. And besides I'm not sure. You know how it is when you wake up from a hideous nightmare. At present everything is clear and vivid but afterwards it all goes dull again. And I should not like to condemn anybody on the evidence I heard until I was certain, positive. If what I heard was true, then how can I tell you my dearest boy? Oh, I couldn't. At least not just yet. Please do not press me till I feel a little stronger."

It was a puzzling situation, but, as Herepath plainly saw, no time for questions. There would be plenty of time for them later, and Enid was safe here. It was good to feel that she was far away from the blighting influence of that dreadful house in the region of Shadwell.

"Did you have any quarrel with your father?" he asked.

"No, Geoff," Enid replied. "I left him. Just left him. I made up my mind what to do on the spur of the moment. I am not without money. I am fairly well supplied with that. My first idea was to come down here at once, but I found something else to do which kept me in London for some days. Do you know that for the moment I had quite forgotten Blanche was here."

"Really! Then you didn't come here with the intention of seeking shelter from her?"

"No, Geoff. I had really forgotten all about Blanche. It may seem incredible, but it is true. But then I had so many dreadful things to worry me. It was not until I was halfway there that the idea of Blanche and her lovely house occurred to me. I was going to the inn."

"But why come here at all, darling?" Herepath asked. "It seems a strange coincidence."

"Oh, it was no coincidence. I sent a message to my father, saying that I was coming here."

Herepath suddenly recollected. It was not so long since Enid had told him that she knew Camford well, that this very house was familiar to her. She was looking just a little red and anxious as he gazed into her eyes.

"This is another of your secrets," he said smilingly. "Do you remember telling me that you were quite familiar with this house, that you knew Camford well? Yes, I can see that you do, Enid. You must have had some powerful reason for coming here. Are you going to tell me what it is?"

She lifted her clear eyes to him and shook her head.

"I cannot at present dear," she whispered. "That is not my secret. Some day you will know. Before long everybody will know. But now it would be a gross breach of trust for me to tell even you. You must be content with the knowledge that I feel quite safe here—it is the one place where I am safe, and where I can defy everybody."

"But if your father follows you down here, dearest?"

"My father will not follow me down here. Of that you may be certain. So long as I am in Camford I am as safe as I should be in Buckingham Palace. More than this you must not ask me to say. And now about yourself, dear? How are your eyes? Are you feeling better? Oh, if you only knew how I had longed to be near you?"

Herepath bent down and kissed the trembling red lips tenderly.

"I think I understand," he murmured. "I never felt better in my life. And, strange as it may seem, my eyes are not troubling me at all. At odd moments when I forget and take off these glasses I can see wonderfully well. It's very strange."

Enid's face grew pale, she trembled in Herepath's arms. It was as if she had had some bad news.

"That is very strange indeed," she whispered. "Oh, if only...but I'll not think of that. Let us go and find the others—they will think that we are very selfish. Geoff, Geoff, I begin to see a way out of all our troubles—"

But more than that Enid would not say. She seemed quite tranquil and happy during the evening, and it was some time past ten before Herepath was free to leave the house, and make his way across the path in the direction of Camford. He had the key of the house in his pocket. He was going to put his theory to the test without disturbing the caretakers. He was thinking more of what Enid had said than anything else as he made his way across the grass. He paused at length by the side door, the key to which was in his pocket, for it seemed to him that he could hear sounds of footsteps inside.

"It looks like a light under the door," he murmured. "By Jove, it is a light. And somebody is creeping along the passage. If I look into this window—"

He raised his head and stared into the passage through a window devoid of curtains. The dim light grew stronger as it came nearer to the glass. Then a man passed dimly and shakily along like some quivering figure on the film of a cinematograph.

"Harley," Herepath muttered "Harley for a million. The plot thickens with a vengeance."

CHAPTER XXXI

ON THE VERGE

Herepath stood for some minutes outside that window of Camford House taking in the bent, crafty-looking figure of Daniel Harley, and making quite sure that he was not mistaken. His identification of the old miser did not surprise him: indeed, he had had so many surprises lately that they were losing their power to startle him. All the same, the puzzle of Harley's interest in Camford remained, and Herepath made up his mind that he would leave nothing undone to solve it.

He could see Harley looking here and there, as if in search of something. There was a scowl on the old man's face—his lips moved as if he were muttering something to himself. He appeared to have no fear of being discovered, but moved along as if he were on absolutely familiar ground. Then the light of the candle became more and more faint as the miser vanished in the distance.

Evidently something radically wrong was going on here, and possibly the old caretaker and his wife knew something about it. Still these people bore an excellent reputation, and it was just a little late in the day for them to take to crooked ways. Besides they slept on the far side of the house, and they were deaf and lame into the bargain. Any thief who knew the ropes would be comparatively safe, and there was nothing in the attitude of Daniel Harley to suggest that he had any fear of consequences.

Well, whatever he was after, Herepath was not going to lose sight of him. He had rambled all over the house many times now, and he knew it as well as, or better than, the people whose duty it was to look after the ancient mansion. Moreover, he had the key in his pocket, and an electric torch in case of accidents. He opened the door carefully and stepped into the corridor, intent on following the mysterious visitor. He could see a dim spot of light a long way ahead, and this he kept in view. Harley appeared to have some definite object before him now, for he continued his way until he came to a staircase leading to the gallery. It seemed to Herepath that he was getting warm.

Was it possible that Harley was in some way connected with the stealing of those pictures? At any rate the old man was after something in the gallery, and it was from the gallery that the pictures had been taken. It was not a pleasant thought and was certainly not made more attractive for Herepath by the remembrance that he was following Enid's father. It seemed rather strange that the old rascal should take these risks at his time of life when he had so many satellites about him who could do the work so much better.

Harley paused at length before a large picture in an oak frame, and placed his candle on a Chippendale pedestal beside it. Some thirty or forty feet away was a small chest draped with a piece of Gobelin tapestry, and behind this Herepath secreted himself so that he could see all that was going on without fear of discovery.

He knew that picture quite well—it was a Raeburn, and represented Cynthia, fifth Countess of Southlands, a noted beauty and flirt in her day; it was, moreover, a picture with a history. There was no finer specimen of a portrait in the gallery, and none more admired by visitors.

It seemed impossible that Harley had any sinister designs on this work of art. He was too old and feeble to carry it away, and no man in his senses would run the risk of cutting it out of the frame. Besides, it would have no commercial value, nobody would ever dare to become the purchaser of so well-known an art treasure. Just for a moment it occurred to Herepath that Harley was bent on doing the painting some mischief.

But if so, there was a good deal of method in his mischief, for he dragged forward an oak chair and proceeded to place it in front of the picture to form a step ladder. He took from his pocket a tape measure, with which he went carefully over the surface of the picture, making notes of certain measurements on a sheet of paper. Apparently these figures were not pleasing, for he paused and muttered to himself. A minute later he climbed down from the chair and replaced it, putting his notes in his pocket at the same time. Then very deliberately he pulled the iron handle of the bell on the wall close by with the air of one who knows exactly what he is doing.

Herepath could hear the harsh jingle of the bell in the distance. He knew perfectly well that it communicated with the old caretaker's bedroom, and the fact seemed equally well known to the intruder. Again and again the bell clanged harshly, and presently in the distance Herepath could see the figure of the caretaker limping down the gallery.

"Oh, lor', oh, lor', whatever is a-doin' of now?" he asked sharply. "Is the place afire, sir? What do 'ee mean a-frightenin' honest folk in their beds this-a-way?"

He was half angry and half frightened, and his palsied head jerked from side to side as if a string were pulling it. Then the candle he carried in his hand fell with a crash on the floor, and he gazed at Harley as if he had seen a ghost.

"I be mad," he shuddered, "clean gone off my head I be. I'll come to myself a-soon and find as it's all a dream. How many years is it, my—"

"Daniel Harley," the other rasped out. "If you dare to forget that name, I'll—I'll skin you alive, you sallow old image. What's my name, you rascal?"

"Daniel Harley, it be, Mr. Daniel Harley, of Lunnon," the caretaker said with the air o' a child repeating a lesson. "An' I humbly axes your pardon, sir. You see it be so many years sin' I seed 'ee last that I be apt to forget, I be."

"Well, don't forget in future. You can keep a secret, James."

"Nobody beant better, sir, wi' keepin' a secret than I be," the old man said with a touch of pride. "Aint kep' one for twenty years an' more an' nor another body the wiser as the saying is? What is it you might be pleased to be a-wantin'?"

"Nothing except answers to some of my questions. First of all, why has the portrait of the Countess been moved? And where has the tanseag frame gone?"

"It were done two or three years back," the caretaker explained. "The trustees they sent a gentleman down, from some place in Lunnon, Chrissie, I think 'twas they called it, and' he had most everythink altered, he did. Here for a month or more she were, an' the galry were turned about no end."

"Yes, yes," said Harley impatiently, "but what became of the old frame?"

"That be somewhere down in the cellars, sir, I do believe. The visitors as comes here to see the picter do say as how that there frame be a great improvement."

"Um! from their point of view perhaps it is. Between you and me, James, there was a lot of useless lumber here, and it's just as well that it was taken away. But that frame doesn't quite suit me, and I'm disappointed in it, James. Got any petrol in the house?"

"Lor' no, sir," the bewildered caretaker replied. "If so be as you wants to set it afire an' burn down the place I 'opes as 'ow you'll give me an' my old 'ooman a chance to get away fust."

"Burn down the place—who the dickens suggested such an idiotic idea? Did it never enter your thick head that petrol is a good thing to clean pictures with? I shall have to come again and bring some with me. I dare say I shall be here pretty often for some time to come. It's rather a nuisance that my visits must take place at night, but that is not distasteful to one of my modest and retiring nature. Now listen to me, James, and pay great attention to what I am saying."

As Harley spoke he crossed over to the old man's side, and whispered something in his ear. He was speaking vehemently. He was terribly in earnest, for his hand shook as he gripped James by the arm. It was quite impossible to hear a word that passed, to get any idea of Harley's commands, but that they were unpleasant and unusual the caretaker's blank face, and open mouth plainly indicated.

"But I couldn't do it, sir," he said "I really couldn't. It beant nat'ral. If so be as anythin' was to happen to you, sir, whatever would become o' me an' the old 'oman. I be an old man, I be, an' arter all these years o' sarvice to the family, I should take it mortal 'ard to see the end on't in prison."

"Then you mean to say that you refuse?"

The old man wrung his hands in an agony of distress.

"Now don't 'ee, don't 'ee force me to say them words," he implored. "Don't 'ee, sir. Us might be destroyed in our beds, us might. Lor', I do wish as 'ow I'd never been born, I do, an' that's Gospel."

"Was there ever such a doddering old image," Harley cried, forgetting his caution in the wild anger of the moment. "I tell you there's no danger whatever. I'll see to that. The whole thing will be over in ten minutes at the outside. And it will save a lot of talk afterwards. A few people will be sorry, there will he a paragraph or two in the papers, and then the incident will be forgotten. And you'll get fifty pounds."

"An' a fat lot o' good that 'ud be to me, sir," James retorted sturdily. "Me and the old 'oman ain't a-got a many years to live now between us, and we've done very tidy, so to speak, one way an' another. Since us 'ave held on 'ere, in the way o' puttin' a bit by, an us couldn't spend it all, leastways not by fair means, afore our time comes now, I tell 'ee, sir, as 'taint no money as'll tempt us."

"You are a wonderful man, James," Harley growled; "You're about the first man I have ever met who is not appealed to by money. As a matter of fact, money is not what I am thinking about. I am a comparatively poor man, James—"

"Ay, thanks to the father afore 'ee, you be, sir," James muttered.

"Well, never mind that. The fact remains. If I were alone in the world I would not mind, but you see I have a child to provide for. Can't forget that, James."

The old man smiled, and Herepath could see how his face softened.

"To be sure, sir, to be sure," he said. "I had bin near forgettin' Miss Enid. God bless her. I suppose us shall see her again some day, sir?"

It seemed to Herepath that there was cunning method in Harley's way of dealing with his rustic servitor. He had touched the right spot now, had touched the spring of affection that all his money could not move.

"Very soon, very soon now, James," he said. "In fact, Miss Enid is in this neighbourhood now. She came down here to stay with some friends, and that is also another reason for my coming here. We had a little difference of opinion, James, and I'm afraid she is rather annoyed with me. I should not be in the least surprised if she called to see you some of these days, James. Now, you will do this little thing for her sake, James?"

The old caretaker no longer protested. The look of yearning and affection was still on his face. It was all very bewildering and puzzling to the listener, who so far had gained nothing by his adventure. He would have given a great deal to know what those two had been talking about, and what it was that Harley was so keen on attaining.

"Very well, sir, if 'tis to help Miss Enid, I'll do it," said James grudgingly. "'Tis a mad thing and a wicked thing, I be sure, but for Miss Enid's sake it shall be done. But you'll have to be a-comin' 'ere a time or two to put me up to the way on't, sir, for I be certain sure I couldn't do it right off like so to speak. An' now, sir, if so be as it pleases you, I'll be going back to bed, sir—"

"Oh, go back as soon as you like," Harley grunted. "And mind you speak no word of this to anybody, not even to that old wife of yours. The less said the better. Good-night, James."

The old caretaker hobbled off without another word, and then in his turn Harley made his way along the gallery and down the stairs. He blew out his candle and vanished into the darkness, leaving Herepath doing his best to put together the pieces of this maddening puzzle.

CHAPTER XXXII

AN EYE FOR AN EYE

The sudden defection of his child had been a bitter blow to Harley. There were reasons for his rage and his seeming impotence in the matter far deeper than any that Gilray dreamt of. The miser had been taken by surprise.

Enid's rebellion was the last thing he would have expected. Hitherto the girl had been docile enough. Certainly she had protested and argued, and that was all, and Harley did not mind that. She had found the task of go-between, which had been thrust on her, a hateful one, and had speedily become suspicious that there was something very wrong about the business carried on so secretly, but so far she had never before dared to set that stern old father of hers at defiance.

When Gilray brought him the news of Enid's flight so dramatically Harley raged and turned for some time like a lunatic, and the doctor deemed it prudent not to interfere. But by and by the old man calmed down, and seemed prepared to face the situation.

"Your daughter will probably come back, sir," Gilray said.

"I tell you she won't," Harley snarled. "She's like her mother—very sweet and amiable up to a certain point and after that as obstinate as a mule. Up to now she has done everything I told her for the simple reason that she couldn't put as much as a little finger on anything actually wrong. But it's different now. She's got to know of the bargain between us, and she is in love with that fellow Herepath, curse him. She's got a certain amount of money of her own, so she is more or less independent of me, Gilray. It's up to you to put matters straight."

"And how can I put matters straight?" Gilray asked.

"Well, if you can't nobody can. I tell you that girl must be brought back. I can't have her hanging about Camford. It would upset the whole of my plans. Give me another three months, and the work of my life will be ended. I shall be able to turn my back on this filthy hole, and everybody can know everything that has occurred here, for all I care. But this is an infernally critical time, and I can't have everything disarranged because of a girlish whim. You can get that child back if you like, and after that—well, we'll see."

"You want me to set Herepath on his legs again?"

"Of course I do. Restore his sight to him, fetch him back to London. Once that is done, the great invention will become once more a practical proposition. If you do that Enid will come home if only to be near the man she loves."

Gilray caught his lips between his teeth savagely.

"You are very illogical," he said. "I am going to speak plainly, Mr. Harley; indeed as things are between us, the more plainly I speak the better. There was at one time, and not so very long ago either, an implied bargain, linking us together. You were to find me a large sum of money, and in return I was to deprive Herepath of the use of his eyes."

"But, confound it, I didn't say that you were to blind the fellow."

"You didn't say anything one way or the other. To be brutally frank, you did not care a row of pins whether Herepath was permanently deprived of his eyes or not. If you had had any choice in the matter at that time, you would have preferred the extreme course. I did what was necessary, and you were, or pretended to be, quite grateful. You told me that I had found a way out of all my money troubles, and I—well, I had at the same time disposed of a dangerous rival. When I came for my reward what happened?"

"I refused to give it you for the simple reason that circumstances had changed," Harley said with the greatest coolness. "Herepath had been too many for us. He was firmly convinced that his sight was going; he could see his chances slipping away. And when he caught Brigden and myself in his workshop that cursed night the whole plot was plain to him. If he could gain nothing then neither should I. That is why he destroyed the glass disc, and at the same moment deprived me of a prospective million. That million is utterly lost unless his sight is restored."

"Which is the task I have before me, eh?"

"Precisely. Give it him back again—if you can. You'll get nothing unless you do. I mean you'll get nothing beyond what you have already had, which is only enough to stave off your trouble for a month or two. Go down to Camford and see Enid. Tell her what you can do. Ask her where Herepath is to be found, because it's any odds she knows. Get him back to London, and keep him fiddlin' around for a week or two, and I am positive Enid will follow. But you'll have to eat humble pie. You will be told with unpleasant frankness that you are a criminal, probably you'll have to confess what you've done. Very, very nasty, of course, but, my dear sir, big money is not obtained so easily as you seem to imagine."

Gilray ground his teeth in impotent rage. There was no need for Harley to enter upon such an elaborate analysis of the situation. He could see all it meant quite plainly. He was to confess himself a coward and a blackguard and a criminal, he was to lower himself still further in Enid's eyes, and perhaps run the risk of a prosecution. If this last happened, he would take good care that Harley stood in the dock, too.

"You are a precious cool hand," he sneered. "I like the way in which you are piling everything on my shoulders. I am to confess my crime and leave Herepath to take his revenge. I am to let him know that he has been the victim of a vile conspiracy to deprive him at one fell stroke alike of his sight and the fruits of his genius. But it takes more than one to form a conspiracy, Mr. Harley. Remember that you were to be the principal beneficiary."

"Admitted," Harley said coolly. "If you go and proclaim the story on the housetops I dare say you could get me five years—we might even compare notes in gaol. But, you see, I am paying the piper, and it is for you to dance the tune. You are at your wits' end for money, and you come to me to make it for you. Now, Herepath could not very well prosecute you without prosecuting me, and he won't do that, for the simple reason that I am Enid's father. My dear sir, I have reasoned it all out."

"You are the most cold-hearted and calculating old scoundrel I have ever met," Gilray cried in a passion of rage. "I curse the day I ever met you."

Harley listened quite coolly. He seemed to accept the denunciation as a compliment.

"Not you," he said. "You've got 5000 pounds already and more to come. My good fellow, we are very well matched and very well met. And now, be off, and do as I tell you, without any further argument or waste of words. I'm getting tired of your company."

Gilray went back to Harley-street mad with rage and the sense of his importance. He could not see his way a yard before him, he could see no path to safety. If he defied that old rascal he was ruined. If he confessed to Enid he was disgraced for ever in her eyes, and could never hope to call her his wife. Perhaps that hope was already lost to him, for she had overheard the greater part of the conspiracy. He would have to go deliberately out of his way to put Herepath on his feet again. He would have to restore to the lovers the happiness they had lost. He might even be publicly disgraced and degraded.

And what was he going to get in return? He had had 5000 pounds of Daniel Harley's money, and there was as much again to come. This would help him out of some of his troubles, but a long and bitter struggle would still face him. It would be years before he was round the corner. Harley could order him about like a dog.

Moreover, he had yet to earn the remainder of his money. Part of the compact was that he should find some means of luring Enid back again to London. He was to go down to Camford and see her. He had not the least idea where she was to be found, but that made no difference. It was necessary that he should remain in London for the next few days to look after his work, but he generally had a free day on Saturday, and he determined to get away for the weekend.

He turned up Camford in the A.B.C., and found that accommodation could be obtained at the little hotel there. So he motored down, to look about him and make inquiries. It was not possible for Enid to be staying in the neighbourhood without somebody knowing it. The landlord of the hotel would doubtless be able to give all the information.

"Oh, yes, sir," he said. "There's a Miss Harley staying at Grange—that old house by the lodge gates at Camford House. She was going to stay here only she found out quite by accident that Mrs. Gay was a friend of hers."

"And who is Mrs. Gay?" Gilray asked.

"Oh, she's the wife of the new steward at Camford," the landlord went on. "They have only been married a few days, sir; only just settled in their house. Very nice lady, Mrs. Gay. They were here for a short time. Mrs. Gay was a Miss Herepath, sister to a wonderful inventor."

"Oh, really," Gilray exclaimed. "I—I happen to know him. Is he staying here, too?"

"Staying with his sister, yes, sir," the landlord explained. "Very nice gentleman but nearly blind. Sad case, sir, and him so young and clever and all."

Gilray turned aside without asking further questions. He had all the information he needed, and a good deal more. So Herepath and Enid were actually under the same roof. He thrilled with rage at the thought of it. It was as though the Fates everywhere conspired to make his task more difficult. He would have to explain to Enid, of course; but it was hardly possible to do so in the presence of Geoffrey Herepath. At last he decided to drop in casually and announce himself as Dr. Gilray, making the knowledge that one of his patients was in the neighbourhood the excuse for his visit.

But with all his coolness and audacity he felt miserably shaky and nervous as he walked up the drive leading to Gay's house. The beauty of the day and the brilliance of the sunshine did not appeal to him just then, he started and changed colour as he saw Enid seated on the lawn with a book in her hand.

"I—I came in the hope of seeing you," he stammered. "It is a liberty, of course, but in the circumstances I am sure Mr. Gay will not mind."

"Mr. Gay is away for the day, and Mr. Herepath has gone with him," Enid said coolly. "Mrs. Gay is shopping in the village. Did you know that Mr. Herepath was here! Are you over for the day, Dr. Gilray? Or are you staying at the hotel?"

Gilray felt just a little easier in his mind. Things were not falling out so badly, after all. At any rate, he would have Enid to himself for a time.

"I am staying the week-end," he said. "I came down at your father's suggestion. He is very distressed that you should have left home. There are many reasons why he wants you to be near him. I do so hope I can persuade you to return to him."

"Will you please stop," Enid said quite coldly. "I quite fail to see, Dr. Gilray, how our family affairs should concern a stranger like yourself. I left home of my own free will, and I am not in the least likely to return. Nobody can know better than yourself how impossible it is for me to do so."

Gilray shuffled uneasily from one foot to the other.

"May I sit down for a few minutes?" he asked.

"There is no reason why you should not do so, if you choose. But really, Dr. Gilray, you are wasting your time here. That is unless—"

The girl hesitated with a wild wave of colour flooding her cheeks. She was looking firmly and squarely into Gilray's eyes, and they dropped and blinked before her gaze.

"I'm all attention," he said "Pray command me in any way you choose."

"Then I will take you at your word," Enid replied in a hard tone. "Dr. Gilray, you are wasting your time here unless you are prepared to give back to Geoffrey Herepath that which you helped to take away from him."

CHAPTER XXXIII

PLAIN WORDS

Gilray's face flushed a dull red. It was no easy task he saw before him and he braced himself for the ordeal in the ordinary way; he would not have cared, but then this slip of a girl knew too much. He had had it from her own lips that she had heard most of the conspiracy whereby Geoffrey Herepath had been deprived of the most precious possession a man can have.

How far was she prepared to go, what sacrifice would she make to save her father. If only Gilray could find this out the path would be easier for him. He had expected tears, and would have known how to deal with them. He had hoped Enid would make an appeal to him, in which case he could have dictated terms. But he saw no suggestion of tears in her eyes, no desire to throw herself on his mercy.

"I am afraid I don't quite understand you," he said.

"Yet I tried to make my meaning plain," Enid replied. "Why did you become a party to this wicked crime?"

"Again I must ask you to be a little more explicit, Miss Harley."

Wild, angry words rose to Enid's lips, but she restrained herself. Not that way would it be possible to get the better of Gilray. He had risen to his feet, and with a gesture of contempt she bade him be seated again.

"I am not sorry you came," she said. "Dr. Gilray, if I told Mr. Herepath all I know, what do you think would happen to you?"

"I have not the remotest idea, Miss Harley. Would you be so good as to explain."

"He would kill you," Enid went on quietly. "And he would be justified in doing so. Let me go back some little way so that I can explain more clearly. Ever since I can remember I have been living in that dreary old house amid the deserted wharves. My mother died when I was quite young, and from the day of her death my father became a changed man. I have always understood that he was passionately attached to my mother, and that she was the only friend he had in the world. She caught scarlet fever from me, and died just as I was getting about again. My father has never blamed me for her death, but I have always felt that in his heart he considers that my life was saved at the expense of hers. I have done my best to be a good and dutiful child to him, but he has always kept me at arm's length. He may be fond of me but assuredly he has never shown it. Any love that was left in him has been lavished only on one object— money. Has he ever told you why he is everlastingly in search of money?"

"I have met your father but a few times, Miss Harley. I should say that he is not the sort of man to confide in anybody."

"That is true. But it occurred to me that you might be somewhat in his confidence. So you cannot tell me what project he has in view: why it is that day and night he thinks of nothing but the getting of money?"

"Honestly I cannot. He struck me as the average type of miser—a man in whom the greed of gold has become an overwhelming passion."

"To a certain extent I agree with you," said Enid thoughtfully. "But I am also sure that his avarice is not due to greed alone, but is dictated by some purpose he has in view, and that every coin he can scrape together goes to the furtherance of that purpose: What it is I do not know, but to aid in its achievement he sticks at nothing short of crime; indeed, I have reason to fear that even that mark has been overstepped, that you, Dr. Gilray, know it has. Oh, I begin to see things all too clearly now! I begin to understand what the coming and going meant of the many strange characters with whom I came in contact in that dreary old house of ours. I am well aware that I have been used as a go-between when money was to be made. But I was told nothing. I was kept in the blackest ignorance, save that I knew that my father had a purpose for which money, much money, was needed. Oh, it was a strange life for an innocent girl to lead."

"That is why I have always felt sorry for you," Gilray murmured.

"Dr. Gilray, I have no need for your sympathy. I am accustomed to loneliness and lack of friends. I never knew what it was to exchange a smile with a single person till I made the acquaintance of Madame Desterre. And about the same time Geoffrey Herepath came. Am I beginning to interest you?"

Gilray muttered something under his breath. He had never admired Enid quite so much as he did at that moment. There was a calm, tranquil strength about her that added to her beauty. A woman had taken the place of the child.

"I repeat that Mr. Herepath came," Enid continued in a level voice. "I need not go into our story, the story that is so old and yet so new. And when I found that he loved me it seemed to me that I could at last see my way to happiness."

Gilray listened moodily. The fires of jealousy were burning hotly in his breast. Herepath's place, he thought in his conceit, might so easily have been taken by himself. A few months earlier, and he might have been saved all this trouble and crime which now involved him. It was gall and wormwood to catch the rapt expression in Enid's voice, when she spoke of Herepath, and to see the love light in her eyes. His heart grew bitter and venomous with hatred of this man she loved so.

"I said nothing to my father," Enid went on, "for it seemed to me that my happiness was entirely my own concern. Had I mentioned the subject I should not have been allowed to see Geoffrey again. We were to wait till he had made his fortune and then we could go our own way. And at that time the fortune did not seem very far off. You understand?"

"I'm afraid I don't," Gilray muttered.

"Dr. Gilray, it will be far better for you to be candid with me. When I think of what has happened, I feel very hard and bitter against you. If it becomes necessary I shall not hesitate to disclose all that I know. So be warned. If you like, we will close this conversation now and I will go back to my book."

Clearly here was no child to deal with, but a determined woman ready to do battle on behalf of the man she loved. Gilray hastily changed his ground.

"I beg your pardon," he said. "I—I was thinking of something else. You were alluding just now, weren't you, to that invention of Mr. Herepath's?"

"You were not thinking of something else, and I was alluding to that invention. Unfortunately, Geoffrey Herepath mentioned the matter to my father as well as to me. It was a mistake on his part, and I dreaded the consequences. Mr. Herepath needed a thousand pounds; he was anxious to find somebody who would advance it. When he told me some little time later that he had been successful in getting the money I had an intuition as to its source, and feared the consequences. When he told me who had advanced the money I knew my fear was justified. The ostensible lender was a man called Brigden, a little shifty rat of a man who has been my father's tool and cover for years. I felt certain then that desperate steps would be taken to deprive Mr. Herepath of the fruits of his work and genius.

"I warned him as fully as I dared. I found that he had been robbed before, and that he had learnt caution from his past experiences. Possibly he might have won through but for the misfortune that happened to his eyes. Here was the golden opportunity for the thieves, and you came on the scene to help them."

"I beg to assure you," Gilray protested, "that I did nothing to injure Mr. Herepath, that I knew nothing of any plot—"

"Don't lie!" Enid cut in with a tone that stung like a lash. "You had better hear me out. You came to our house in the dead of the night to operate on a young man who had met with an accident. I let you in. We had to observe the greatest secrecy, for your patient had done something rash, and a visit from the police was feared. This, however, is conjecture on my part, because I was allowed to know as little as possible. But it struck me as a strange thing that a doctor in your position should consent to come to such a quarter of London at the instigation of Dr. Vorley, and with every chance of compromising your reputation."

"I came because Vorley was an old friend of mine," Gilray said.

"That is another lie, Dr. Gilray. You came because the fee was an enormous one and you were in dire need of money. That much I gathered from what my father said. I was sorry for you at the time but—not afterwards. By the irony of fate, Mr. Herepath came to consult you about his eyes. You had seen my father, and at his bidding practically sentenced your unsuspecting patient to a living death."

"Indeed I didn't," Gilray protested. "I told him to be very careful. I told him—"

"To do nothing for months. It practically came to the same thing. You killed his hopes, and sent him away a beaten and a ruined man. A great deal happened between his first and second visits to you, Dr. Gilray."

"It pleases you to be mysterious," Gilray muttered.

"Not at all—I will speak as plainly as you like. In the interval you established a kind of understanding with me. You discovered me in what you deemed to be a compromising situation at Madame Desterre's house, and on that discovery you traded. I never thought it possible that I could ever hate and despise a man as I have hated and despised you since that night."

The words stung Gilray to madness. The colour flushed his cheeks like flame.

"I did my best to shield you," he almost shouted. "If it had not been for me—"

"If it were not for you I should be a happy girl to-day," Enid cried scornfully. "You wanted money, you thought that a rich wife would rid you of all your troubles. You did me the doubtful honour to fall in love with me, and say that you would marry me without a penny. No, you did not tell me that—you told my father, and he confided so far in me. You were useful to him, and I was to fool you to the top of your bent—he would know how to get rid of you when the time came. Oh, my cheeks tingle with shame when I think of it."

"Then why unnecessarily give yourself pain?" Gilray asked, feeling that he must temporise.

"Because it is my plain duty to do so," Enid cried. "Because I know now in what way you have been useful to my father. Remember, I listened, remember I heard all that passed between you the last time you visited the purlieus of Shadwell. It was a good thing for my father to know that Geoffrey Herepath was out of his way, that he was practically blind, and that he could not go on with his great work. You were the judge, and from your lips came the verdict of the court. But you were a corrupt Judge, Dr. Gilray."

No reply came from Gilray, he was feeling dreadfully helpless before this contemptuous, scornful girl.

"Geoffrey Herepath was too clever for you," Enid went on. "It was very nice for you conspirators to know that he could not use his eyes, but the position totally changed when he destroyed that little disc and with it the whole value of his invention. The situation is equally hopeless for you now, because it is imperative for you, if you would avoid utter ruin, to give back that which you have taken away. In other words, you have been ordered to restore his sight to Mr. Herepath. Can you do it?"

Gilray muttered oaths under his breath. He was aflame with rage and despair, but he knew he was helplessly enmeshed, that, if he would avoid utter ruin and public-degradation, he must obey Harley's behest. No, he was beaten. Enid was hopelessly lost to him, but he must placate her if he could.

"I—I should like to see Mr. Herepath again," he stammered.

"Then you think that perhaps you were mistaken in your view of his case?" Enid asked mockingly. Then she added with threatening sternness: "Dr. Gilray, I would not stand in your place for all the money in the world if Mr. Herepath should prove to be really blind."

CHAPTER XXXIV

THE FIRE

Enid had risen to her feet. She confronted Gilray with flashing eyes.

"Now I can speak plainly," she said. "Dr. Gilray, you are guilty of one or two things—either you are a cheat and a liar, or you have deliberately deprived a fellow-creature of his sight. If your first verdict is true, I accuse you of tampering with Mr. Herepath's eyes so that you could get a rival out of the way. If you have lied to Mr. Herepath, your crime is only a little less repulsive. In any case, you gave judgment against your patient for money, and now to get that money you have to reverse that judgment. What shall you say to Mr. Herepath the next time he comes to see you—if he comes at all?"

"You—you think that he would not be safe in my hands?" stammered Gilray miserably.

"Would anybody be safe in your hands in your present desperate position? I begin to respect that there is nothing very wrong with Mr. Herepath's sight, that you have wilfully deceived him so as to put money in your pocket. Knowing what I know now, I shall advise Geoffrey Herepath to consult another oculist. And if my suspicions are confirmed, you will hear of this again. This wicked conspiracy shall be exposed, even if my father goes down under the ruins. Oh, to think that a man who calls himself a gentleman should stoop so low—should be so base and vile!"

"Now what are you two quarrelling about?" a gay voice floated across the lawn. "Fancy a difference of opinion in this peaceful old spot. Shame upon you both."

Ninon Desterre flitted across the grass, a lovely little butterfly in some foamy, frothy white garment, a black picture hat on her head. She dropped lazily into a chair, and surveyed the other two with charming impertinence from under her nodding plumes. To Enid the intrusion came as a positive relief. She was the first to recover herself.

"We have been having an argument," she said, "on what I call the verdict of the Court. Dr. Gilray represents the judge, and I am counsel appealing against his judgment. I have been trying to convince Dr. Gilray that the sentence will be revoked on appeal."

"Not if it comes before the same judge," Ninon said maliciously.

Gilray made some inconsequent reply, but it sounded false and hollow in his own ears. He could not stay any longer; he had remained too long already. He wanted to be alone with his bitter thoughts. Ninon watched him with twinkling eyes as he walked towards the gate.

"He is very good-looking and successful," she said; "but he does not strike me as being quite on such good terms with himself as usual. To use one of your vigorous metaphors, he has gone off with his tail between his legs."

"I have been speaking pretty plainly to him," Enid said. "No. I am not going to tell you the subject of our conversation."

"No need," Ninon said coolly. "You were discussing Geoffrey Herepath and his eyes. Oh, there is going to be plenty of fun presently. And I shall have a word to say when the time comes. And so you have actually run away from home! Why did you do it?"

"Oh, I can't explain," Enid said uneasily. "There are many reasons why I could not remain there. You know it is the last straw that breaks the camel's back. If you only knew the life I had been leading in that gloomy old house!"

"Well, you will not be worried much longer," Ninon said. "I happen to know that. And your troubles will be over in a few weeks. And you will marry the prince, my dear."

"I don't see any sign of it at present," sighed Enid. "But what are you doing down here? Have you come to see me as a kind of ambassador from my father?"

"Nothing of the kind. I found out what had become of you from that young man of yours, and I decided that a long week-end in the country would be the very thing for my nerves. So I borrowed a cottage in the neighbourhood from a friend, and here I am. And I am quite sure that you are very glad to see me!"

Enid smiled. She was very fond of this kind-hearted, volatile little Frenchwoman, despite the fact that she was a mystery, and that she was in some way connected with the shady dealings of Daniel Harley. But that there was anything really wrong with her Enid did not believe for a moment. Probably she would explain everything when she was ready to do so.

"Now I wonder if the owner of this very charming house would give me some lunch," Ninon went on. "I'm very fond of Blanche Herepath—I mean Mrs. Gay—and it has always been a regret of mine that I have not seen more of her. And the prince is staying here, too, eh? What a delightful family party! And how your father would enjoy being one of us. Does he know you are here, or are you still supposed to be in hiding?"

"My father knows that I am staying near Camford," Enid said demurely. "It is the one place in the world where he dare not come—as yet."

"More mysteries," Ninon laughed gaily. "Am I to be allowed to share the secret?"

"It is not mine to share," Enid said. "But if what you said just now is true, why then all the world will know the story before long."

"Well, it is a good thing that I am not curious," Ninon said. "Perhaps I am the less curious because I have a tolerably shrewd idea of what is at the back of your mind. Now take me inside, and show me something of this charming old house. I have a perfect mania for old houses. When I retire from business and take pity on my faithful Hector Marsail and marry him, this is just the lovely place I should like to live in."

Blanche was pleased enough to see Ninon Desterre, and delighted at the opportunity of playing hostess to her. And Ninon was frankly enraptured with all she saw. She flitted like a bee from flower to flower, she was everywhere at once, her tongue tripped on heedlessly. She seemed to have left every care and trouble behind her.

But her face was grave and her eyes eager when at length she found herself alone in the garden with Herepath. She was the woman of business once more.

"I have come here to-day on purpose for this," she said. "Did you think I had forgotten you?"

"I was beginning to wonder," Herepath replied. "I have some property in my possession that I am anxious to get rid of. It presumably belongs to you?"

"Well, as a matter of fact it belongs to Mr. Harley," Ninon said drily. "I dare say that remark puzzles you, but many things will be made plain before long. I'll take those jewels away with me, if you don't mind."

"I shall be exceedingly glad to get rid of them," Geoffrey replied.

"I thought so. Don't worry any more about them, and don't run away with the impression that you are liable to a long term of imprisonment for receiving stolen goods. But I want to talk to you seriously about yourself. I understand that you owe Daniel Harley a thousand pounds."

"It might be a million for any chance I have of repaying it," Herepath said bitterly.

"Oh, never talk in that despondent fashion," Ninon smiled. "You never can tell where your friends are and when they are coming to your assistance. You went into the city to get that money, and you fell headlong into a trap that Harley had laid for you. Now, why didn't you come to me? If you had told me what you needed, you could have had the money with pleasure. I should have loved to be your partner."

"It's no use crying over spilt milk," Herepath groaned.

"But, my dear man, I don't believe the milk is spilt," Ninon cried. "If I found you the money, could you get rid of Harley by paying him off? Would you let me be your partner—"

"With all the pleasure in life," Herepath exclaimed. "And give you half the proceeds. If I offered the money to Harley he would be bound to take it, especially as he has already threatened me through his solicitor. But you forget the state my eyes are in. In all probability I shall never be in a position to use them again, and in that case your money would be thrown away. My dear lady, why should I rob you?"

"I am going take all that risk," Ninon said gravely. "If you had the use of your eyes again, could you make another disc? You see, I know all about it. There is very little I fail to discover when I set out to find anything. If we could get Dr. Gilray to admit that his diagnosis was wrong, could you make another disc?"

Herepath smiled at the apparent simplicity of the question.

"I could do it in a week," he said. "I am not quite sure that I could not do it without my eyes at all. But what is the use in building on a foundation of sand? Nothing good can come of it, Ninon."

"We shall see," Ninon cried gaily. "Then it is a compact! I find you the money, and you get that elderly cormorant out of the way. Meanwhile, we shall have a word or two with Dr. Gilray, or, perhaps, happy idea! consult another eye specialist. Give me the chance to tell Gilray you are going to do so—what?"

"It is only throwing good money bad, Madame Desterre."

"Oh, but it shall be my money, if necessary. It is all part of the compact. You must run over to Germany, and see the great man on eyes there. If I give you my card he will be only too pleased to work what you call con amore. Now do."

Herepath said he would consider the matter. It sounded very much like a waste of time, but there was something in Ninon's cheeky optimism that gave him hope. Eminent men had made mistakes before, and why not Gilray? All the afternoon Herepath brooded over the point. He had been a coward to give way so easily. At last he went over to Madame Desterre again, and told her that if she would give him the address of the oculist friend she had mentioned he would certainly pay him a visit.

"Now, that is the way I like to hear you talk." said Ninon, as she rose to leave. "My word it is nearly dark, and I have a mile or two to go. Will you send to the village for some conveyance for me? I have never enjoyed a day more, and I am sure, Blanche, that I never sat down to a dinner that was better served than yours. Enid, are you not delighted to hear that this young man of yours is going to another specialist?"

"I am indeed pleased," said Enid quietly. "The idea had occurred to me this afternoon, and I shall be most bitterly disappointed if I do not hear good news from the visit."

For some time after Ninon had gone Herepath remained in the garden, a prey to new hopes and fears. Was it not just possible that the sentence of the court would after all be reversed on an appeal? Was it not strange, too, that it was so light this evening that there was so red a glow in the sky? Down the road a man was galloping as fast as his horse could carry him. He seemed to be shouting something as he dashed along towards the village. The words came clear and low.

"Fire, fire!" he cried. "Up at the Hall—Camford is ablaze."

Herepath turned and ran swiftly towards the house.

CHAPTER XXXV

IN THE GALLERY

Herepath reached towards the house with a strange feeling upon him that he had been through all this before. He wondered why he had half expected it to happen. It was very absurd, of course; but there was no putting the sensation aside.

But there was no time to waste on self-analysis. The old house was on fire, and willing hands were needed to cope with the disaster. At Herepath's call Gay came running into the garden.

"What on earth is wrong?" he demanded.

"Camford is on fire," Herepath explained. "A man on a horse yelled the news as he passed. Probably he is on his way to Castleton for the engines. But hadn't we better run across and see what we can do?"

The suggestion was so obvious that Gay made no reply except to dash across the garden in the direction of the road. The glow in the sky told its own tale; indeed it looked as if Camford was well alight.

"I can't understand it," Gay gasped, as he raced along. "The last tenant was very nervous on the subject of fires, and they spent any amount of money on the very latest appliances for its prevention. All the chimneys and grates were overhauled periodically, and the roof tanks kept supplied with water. Besides, no fires have been lighted there for months."

Herepath made no comment. A theory was shaping itself in his mind. It would have been difficult to have put this theory into words or to give it any practical shape, but all the same Geoffrey could not get rid of it. He would be able, perhaps, to definitely formulate it later on. They were drawing nearer and nearer to the burning house. They could see a score or more of men hurrying to and from the lake with buckets of water, which was all that could be done to check the flames, pending the arrival of the engines.

From one of the windows in the picture gallery there came a dense volume of flame. By the side of the window was a ladder, and from the top of this one man after another dashed his bucket of water, and dropped back hot and exhausted. Gay shook his head as he took all this in. It was very praiseworthy and energetic, but quite useless. If the fire was to be coped with properly it would have to be done from the inside. And how could that fire possibly have broken out in the gallery?

"Here, this won't do," Gay cried. "We shall have to tackle this in another way. Why hasn't old James opened the doors? Where is James?"

A score of voices called for the old caretaker. He had been seen only a few minutes before. Some youth with his eyes sharper than the rest presently found him sitting dejectedly on a heap of curtains dragged down from the gallery window.

The old man seemed to be dazed with fear and fright. He cried aloud as Gay grabbed him by the arm and dragged him forward.

"I didn't do it," he moaned. "It bean't me; I didn't do it, sir."

"Who on earth said you did?" Gay asked impatiently. "What I want to know is, how did it happen? There's nothing to burn in the gallery. Who found it out?"

"'Twas me, sir," James almost blubbered. "I'd just gone to bed—a little late for me 'twas, which 'twere a good thing, sir. An' it seemed to me like as 'ow I could smell burnin'. And my old 'ooman, she snifted the same thing. So I goes as far as the gallery—fust I do—"

"One moment," Herepath asked. "Why did you go to the gallery first?"

The question was a simple one, but it seemed to stagger the old man like a blow. If Herepath had flung at him an accusation of murder he could not have looked more ghastly. Gay shook him by the shoulders none too gently.

"Why the dickens don't you answer?" he asked. "It's a simple question. Oh, what's the use of our wasting time on him, Geoff? The poor old fool is in his dotage. What we've got to do is to open all the doors and work from the hall. There are water tanks on the roof, and a proper system for flooding every room if necessary, but I've never been over the roof, so I don't know anything about it. Here, you fellows—fill your buckets and carry them up the stairs. This way—"

So far, the fire had not done any great damage. It had broken out, apparently, on one side of the gallery, where it had attacked the panelling, which, being hard oak, as firm in grain almost as steel, was resisting bravely. One or two of the pictures were in flames, and Gay gave orders for the others to be removed.

"Not much damage so far," he said.

"That is just where you are mistaken," Herepath said grimly. "It so happens that I know a great deal more about the pictures than you do. On the wall yonder was perhaps the most treasured canvas in the house—I mean Raeburn's Countess Cynthia. At a fair estimate I should say it was worth 10,000 pounds. And apparently it has been destroyed."

"You don't say so," Gay said blankly. "The whole thing is a mystery to me. How the dickens did the fire begin? There is no grate here and no hot water in the heating pipes at this time of year. Why, what are you doing?"

At the risk of burning his hands, Herepath was tearing down all that was left of the famous picture. It was now a tattered mass of charred canvas, with dabs of blistered paint here and there. The action seemed a useless waste of time to Gay, who looked on with something like contempt as Herepath rolled up the painting, or what was left of it, and conveyed it to a place of safety.

"You would be using your time to far better advantage if you came with me and helped to find these tanks," Gay said. "I wonder if old James has sufficiently recovered his wits to be of assistance. You see that trapdoor overhead? Well, beyond that is a tank, and connected with it is a pipe with a canvas hose and a stop-cock. The tank contains some ten thousand gallons of water. If I can only find the way to it we shall have the whole thing settled long before the engines arrive."

But James was far too muddled to give any assistance. He could only cough and gasp in the smoke-laden atmosphere, and gaze with terror on the glowing walls as the fire gradually and surely ate its red way into them. He had heard all about the tanks, of course, a day or two ago, and he could have shown them what to do; but now he could not fix his mind on anything. And every moment the peril of the flames increased.

"Go and get me a ladder," Gay cried. "Two ladders. You see there is another trap at the far end of the gallery, Geoff. You take one tank and I'll take the other. Now, then, you fellows, hurry up with those ladders."

The ladders were brought, and the trapdoors were lifted. Inside was nothing but black darkness, and more precious moments were lost in obtaining candles. So far as Herepath could see, there was a long space where the rafters crossed at intervals, and where he had to walk carefully lest he should put his foot through the plaster that formed the ceiling. He stumbled more than once, and nearly lost his light. As he scrambled to his knees his spectacles slipped from his eyes and disappeared altogether down a crack so deep and black that any hope of recovering the glasses was entirely out of the question.

He cursed himself under his breath. What was he going to do now? How was he going to find his way out of that trap without his eyes? And how utterly helpless he would be until he could go to London and get another pair. And just at the moment, too, that he felt convinced he was on the verge of a great discovery.

He must make the best of it; he would have to use what sight was left to him, despite all Gilray's warnings. He opened his eyes to the widest extent and stared defiantly around him.

Then he started and trembled violently from head to foot. For everything was as clear as crystal before him. He had not been able to see so well for years. He could make out the dust upon the walls; he could see tiny spiders scuttling away fearful of the candlelight. He stared into the flame, which only slightly dazzled him.

What did this mean: what miracle had come to him? Just for the moment he forgot his errand, he forgot the flaming house, and the suspicions which were gradually and surely shaping into certainty. His sight had come back to him, and with it all his ambitions. He would be able to cope with Harley again, he would wrestle with that old rascal and bring him to his knees. He could avail himself of Ninon Desterre's offer now.

He came to himself as he heard shouts from below, and dropped from the clouds to earth again. It was easy to work now that he could see properly. Here was the great tank which he had come to find, a huge iron arrangement with a stop-cock at the base, with a long length of cotton hose-pipe attached. He wrenched the stop-tap over; he saw the hose begin to fill and wriggle like a brown snake.

He dragged the pipe across the rafters with infinite care, and stood presently over the trapdoor at the top of the ladder. He had only to direct the nozzle now in the direction of the blazing panelling and turn the tap.

Gay welcomed his appearance with a cheer. "Good man!" he cried. "You've hit on the right spot. My tank was too far away, and, anyway, I couldn't get the tap to move. Let's have it."

The solid jet of water as thick as a man's arm struck the flames till they fairly hissed again. Long before the tank was empty the panelling that had been burning was reduced to cold, wet charcoal. The smoke began to clear away, and the atmosphere grew cool.

"Now, then!" Gay cried. "All the mops and brooms you can get together, and sweep up the water so that it does not get down below. Not so much damage done, after all. Beyond that one picture nothing much seems to have suffered, Geoff."

"That was pretty bad," Herepath said gravely. "All the same, I daresay it was insured. If so, it makes matters all the worse."

Gay stared at Herepath in frank astonishment.

"All the better, you mean," he said. "What's the matter with you? And how grave you look. Oh, it's the absence of those glasses. What have you done with them?"

"I slipped down, and they fell off my nose," Herepath explained. "You need not worry. I am by no means sure that their loss is not a blessing in disguise. But all that I will discuss with you later on. I think I shall be able to astonish you presently."

But Gay had already turned away to give directions to his army of willing helpers and despatch somebody on horseback to stop the engines. The danger was all over now, the damage done by the water had been minimised as far as possible. Herepath turned in search of something, and at length he found it in old James crouching in one corner with his head in his hands. The guilty, startled look was on his face as Herepath spoke to him.

"Come this way," he said grimly; "I want a word with you."

CHAPTER XXXVI

THE SHAM AND THE REAL

The old man put up his hands as if to ward off a blow. Herepath took him by the arm and led him into the open.

"Now listen to me," he said. "I am not going to injure you, and you are not going to suffer. That is, if you tell the truth. How did the fire break out?"

"Oh, lor', sir, I don't know, sir," the old man stammered. "I just snifted smoke, and my old 'ooman she snifted smoke. And I ups an' get along fust to the gallery—"

"Yes, I know you came first to the gallery. You said that before. But what I want to know, and what you have got to tell me, is why you came first to the gallery. There are no fireplaces there—there is not hot water in the heating apparatus at this time of year. And yet the fire starts in the gallery, and this is the spot you make for at once. Why?"

The old man made no reply. He half raised his hand again with the suggestion of a fear of personal violence. His lips quivered strangely.

"Very well, don't reply if you are afraid to," Herepath said. "I don't want to force you to talk against your will. But don't you think it would be far better to tell me the truth than to have it dragged out of you by the police?"

The old man bent his head and burst into senile tears.

"It bean't no fault o' mine," he blubbered. "I've allus bin taught to do as I be told."

"You mean that you are afraid of Daniel Harley, eh? What did he say to you?"

But apparently Herepath had gone a step too far. The old man suddenly ceased his whimpering, and his face grew resolute again. Evidently the name of Harley was not one to conjure with so far as he was concerned.

"Now you jest take my advice and drop it, mister," he said, quite truculently. "You be young, and no doubt you thinks as 'ow you knows a great deal. Maybe you do. But you don't know Daniel Harley, and what 'tis to get up agen the likes of he. If you've a-got a grudge agen him, you put it a one side. If you're a-trying to get the best of him, you leave the job be. Because you'll be mortal sorry for it if you don't, mortal sorry for it, as long as you lives. If ever there wur a cunnin' old fox 'tis Mester Daniel Harley."

James stopped suddenly, frankly conscious that he was going too far. This rapid change in his manner was puzzling. And it behoved Herepath to be careful.

"Very well," he said. "I'll come and have another chat with you to-morrow. Meanwhile, as all the danger is over, and most of our helpers have cleared out, you had better go to bed and think it over. If you only knew it, I am your friend."

James shuffled away, only too glad of the opportunity to go. The hall was dark and silent now, and the park was deserted. The clock on the village church was striking two as Herepath and Gay turned into their own house.

"I want one whisky and soda before we go to bed," Gay suggested. "I'm as dry as a limekiln, and I am sure we have earned it. What do you make of this job?"

Herepath poured himself out a drink slowly and thoughtfully.

"Are you satisfied with it yourself?" he asked. "Do you call it an accident?"

"Well, to be quite candid, I don't," Gay said. "From a common-sense view such a fire as that is impossible. And yet the impossible happens. If I could see any object in it I should say that the thing had been done deliberately."

"The thing was done deliberately," Herepath exclaimed. "The panelling was sprayed with petrol and a match applied. And old James did it."

Gay jumped excitedly to his feet, and took his whisky and soda at one gulp.

"Here, steady on!" he cried. "Be careful what you are saying, old man. James has been a trusted servant of the family for over fifty years."

"Precisely. And it is because James is a trusted servant of the family that he has behaved in this way. My dear fellow, I have found something out. I have made a discovery so startling that I smile when I think of it. And yet I am absolutely certain that I am correct. Still, I dare not tell you what it is as yet. I've got to see old James again to-morrow first, and when I have done with him I shall get the whole truth. Once that is in my possession I will let you hear all the details. But I can assure you that old James is responsible for the fire."

"But, my dear chap, what could he gain by it? He doesn't want money; he could retire on his savings at any moment. And he's devoted to the family."

"That's just it. He is too devoted to the family."

"Oh, well, if you are going on with these enigmas, I'll be off to bed. Tell me what you like and when you like. There will be plenty of awkward questions asked a little later on, when I come to face the insurance company."

"Yes, if you ever do come to face them, which I very much doubt. I'm open to bet you a level five pounds that the trustees of the estate make no claim. If they don't, of course the insurance company will do nothing. There will be no claim made for the picture—the excuse will be that it is capable of restoration."

"Why, my dear chap, the picture, as you know, is a mass of charred rags!"

"Precisely. A mass of rags that I have taken the liberty of hiding. Oh, there are lively times at hand, I promise you! Only it is not wise at this moment to talk too plainly. Let's go to bed. I have lost my glasses, and I may be further injuring my sight."

But Herepath was conscious of no added defect of vision when he awoke in the morning. On the contrary, he could see better than ever. All those aches and pains had gone, there was no longer any irritation, no spots danced before him. He looked in the glass, and his heart rejoiced to see how clear the pupils were, how transparent the whites. As he dressed he was busy with a new set of thoughts altogether, he had forgotten old James for the moment. He began to suspect a conspiracy of quite another kind.

He finished dressing and strolled out into the garden. Enid was already there getting a basketful of roses for the dining table. A little cry of alarm broke from her as she saw Herepath.

"How imprudent," she said. "Where are your glasses?"

"Lost them," Herepath said, cheerfully. "Dropped them during the fire last night. I'm sure that it was a very happy accident for me, darling. Enid, look at me. Do you see anything wrong? Don't you begin to ask yourself a few questions?"

"You mean that there has been a mistake?" the girl asked.

"Perhaps," Herepath said, drily. "And again, perhaps not. My eyes are better than they have been for years. At the present moment there is nothing whatever the matter with them. And I don't believe there ever has been anything radically wrong. I am prepared to let it go at the fact that Gilray was in error. On the other hand, I may be the victim of a conspiracy. And, if I am, then your father...I hate to say it, Enid."

The tears gathered in Enid's eyes as she laid her hand on Herepath's arm.

"I am afraid so," she said. "Oh, it is a dreadful thing, Geoff. At one time I was almost forced to believe that Dr. Gilray had—had blinded you. I was doing my best to get the matter put right in such a way that you would never know. It is not much that I owe to my father, but I have always tried to remember that he is my father. I hoped and prayed that I should never have to make this confession, Geoff."

"Better tell me, dear," Herepath said gently. "You will be glad of it afterwards."

She told him almost in whispers all that she knew. Once the confession was begun it did not seem so difficult. Herepath's face was stern and hard as she finished, but the arm he had about her waist was tender and loving enough.

"So that was the plot," he said. "I suppose Gilray did not dare to go too far. He contented himself by saying that my eyes were in a perilous state, and gave me those glasses that I could hardly see through. That little operation and rest was all that I needed. Well, I shall know how to deal with Gilray when the time comes."

"There must be no scandal," Enid pleaded. "Once you make the matter public—"

"Oh, I am not going to make the matter public," Herepath assured her. "That would create a scandal reflecting on a noble house. But of all the vile tricks ever played on a man this is the vilest. Still, I am not going to be vindictive. And, after all, those people have placed all the weapons in my hands. I shall make all the money, and I shall compel your father to come to your wedding. But Dr. Gilray is not to practise any more—I shall make that a stipulation. He will have to give up Harley-street and go abroad. But not a word of this to our good friends here for the present. I have certain important things to do to-day, and then I propose to see your father. When I have done with him I have a shrewd idea that our troubles will be over."

For an hour or more after breakfast Herepath busied himself in the village shops buying a few odd things and asking a great many questions. Apparently the answers were quite satisfactory, for just before 12 o'clock he made his way across the path in the direction of Camford, and demanded to see old James.

The latter crept out into the garden rubbing his hands uneasily.

"Good morning to you, sir," he quavered. "Hope as 'ow you're none the wus' for last night? 'Twere a mercy we weren't all burned in our beds."

"You're a sorry old humbug!" Herepath said, half pitifully. "And Daniel Harley was a fool to trust you with so dangerous a job. Now answer me a question. What was the price of petrol yesterday?"

"One and two a gallon," the old man blurted out. "Leastways, so they do tell me. But what do a poor old man like me want wi' petrol? I don't hold wi' they new-fangled things."

"That's the very question they asked me at Tomsett's in the village," Herepath said drily. "What did old James want with a gallon of petrol? You were a fool to get it in the village, James; but then, you've been a fool all through. What did you want it for?"

"Come in handy it do to clean clothes wi', sir," James stammered.

"What, a whole gallon? You could clean all the clothes in the village with that. Still you may be right. If you are, show me your can. I want to see that the can is full or I shall have some very nasty questions to ask you, James. Now trot along and fetch the can, or if you like I will come with you and see it. I want to feel quite sure that your petrol was not used to make that little blaze last night. By which you will perceive that I have a nasty suspicious nature, James."

The old man bent his head lower and lower. Herepath could see that he was trembling from head to foot.

"Perhaps you have had an accident and split the petrol, James."

"That be zackly what it wur, sir, 'twas that zackly," cried the old man, eagerly clutching at the suggestion. "My old 'ooman, she be got turrible clumsy and short-sighted, sir. An' she goes an' hits herself agen the can, she do."

"And knocked the petrol over. Dear me what a sad thing! Now, I thought you might have wanted that petrol to clean a picture with—I mean the picture that was put up in the gallery after the Raeburn was spirited away by Mr. Daniel Harley. Take your time, James, take your time! There is no hurry."

CHAPTER XXXVII

A HALF-CONFESSION

In spite of the sternness of his purpose, Herepath was feeling just a little sorry for the poor old man who was wriggling like a worm on a hook. Here was not the chief conspirator by any means, nor had old James benefited by the plot which Herepath helped to lay bare. But he had gone too far now to draw back, even if he were disposed to do so.

The old man stood there trembling and shaking pitifully. It was useless for him to lie any longer. He glanced at Herepath's stern face as if hoping to find some trace of mercy there. The silence was growing intolerable.

"I am waiting for you to go on, James," Herepath said.

"I know you be, sir," James mumbled. "And turrible hard it be on an old man. 'Taint as if I'd got anythin' to gain, sir."

"There I am absolutely in agreement with you," Herepath said, drily. "I am quite sure that you never expected a penny for that senseless folly. What I want to know is why you set fire to the house."

"Happens as I was druv to it," James said. "Happens as 'ow I was telled as no harm 'ud come to me if so be I did as I was axed to do. When you've lived man and boy for 69 years under one roof you as to do as you're telled, an' there 'tis."

"But, my good fellow, nothing could protect you from such an act as this! If the police knew as much as I do you would be arrested within the hour. No excuse would be listened to, even if Lord Southlands suddenly appeared after all these years and gave evidence that you started the fire by his orders. He would be told that he was not really the owner of the property, but what the law calls a tenant for life. Moreover, that if he was the owner the law did not allow him to commit arson. Certainly, nothing could save you from gaol."

James looked with blank terror at the speaker.

"Do'ee mean to say, sir, as what you're a telling me is true?" he asked fearfully.

"Indeed I do. Houses like Camford belong to the family and not to the individual who is head of the house for the time being. Besides, no man is allowed to set fire to a house, even if he owns it. Now if I were to go to the police with Mr. Gay and lay information against you—"

"But you wouldn't do it, sir? You wouldn't have the heart. Me an old man as I be with one foot in the grave, so to speak, and gettin' nothin' for the job neither. He comes to me an' he says—"

James broke off again. He appeared to be struggling between justice to himself and loyalty to some person whose name he was fearful of uttering.

"You are speaking of Mr. Daniel Harley," Herepath said. "Go on."

"An' sposin' I do go on, sir, will'ee promise to see that 'tis all right."

"I will do my best for you, certainly. I dare say Mr. Gay and myself can manage it between us. After all, there is very little damage done, and the trustees may be disposed to make the best of it. Mind you, I am only assuming that. I want to know how the mischief was done. Also what Mr. Daniel Harley expected to gain by burning the Raeburn portrait."

The old man looked quite cunning for a moment. Herepath read exactly what was going on in his confused mind. He was wondering just how much Herepath really knew, and if it was possible to fool him.

"I bean't up in these 'ere things, sir," James went on. "I'd never be one to make a fuss over a lot of painted calico, I wouldn't. How folks can give thousands of pounds for them 'ere picters fairly 'mazes me. Ay, and sometimes they gets what's called forgeries. There do be tricks in every trade 'sides horse-copin', it seems, sir."

"I dare say, James. So the Raeburn was a forgery?"

"I be thinkin' as 'ow it might a been summat o' the sort. But Mr. Daniel Harley could tell'ee for sure. He does a deal of work among picters for Lord Southlands."

"You mean that he acts as a kind of agent for his eccentric lordship? In that case he comes here pretty often, I suppose?"

"Lor' bless 'ee, yes, sir. Once a month, he do surely. Comes very quiet-like, he do. And allus allowed to do as he likes. 'Twere a matter of a few weeks ago as he comes an' says to me as that there Raeburn was a forgery, and that 'twere time the real picter was put back in its place. Lord Southlands he took and pawned the proper portrait, he did, just afore he cut off out o' the way hisself. And now he's made a bit of money, and the picter's 'out' again. I be a-telling you zackly what was telled me, sir. We're a-gettin' at it a bit now."

"Very pleased to hear it, I'm sure," Herepath said drily. "So that was the ingenious way in which the picture was to be got rid of. Most complicated. You are a silly, foolish old man, James, and I'm very sorry for you. What you are telling me now makes it easier for me to keep you out of trouble. Now tell me everything."

"Well, sir, Mr. Harley he gev me all them facks. He wanted that there forgery destroyed, and the real picter to turn up again like as if it had been in some other part of the house all the time. Very nice and affable about it he were, too—for him."

"Um! Then Harley is not particularly genial and good-tempered as a rule?"

"That he bean't, to be sure, sir. He was all right then, though. And he told me just zackly what I were to do. I was to buy a gallon o' petrol in the village—"

"You are sure that he said you were to get it in the village, James?"

"Lor', sir, but you do seem to know everythin'," James said admiringly. "To tell'ee the truth, sir, 'twant in the village as I wur to get it; I wur to go over to the town for it. But I bean't so young as I were, and jogging along in that there market cart do stir up my rheumatism summat chronic. So I took the liberty I did of gettin' the stuff in the village at Tomsett's."

"Now we really are getting on," Herepath smiled. "I thought we should come to something of this kind presently. Mr. Daniel Harley is far too sharp to suggest getting petrol in the village. Never you tell him you got it in the village, James. The fact might get you into serious trouble. But the secret is safe with me. Go on."

"Well sir, as I was a-saying, I was to get this 'ere petrol and fling some over that there forgery. 'Twas to be done just afore me and the old 'ooman went to bed. And I done it, I did, done it most alarmin' well as it 'ave turned out. I was to let the stuff dry afore I touched a match agen the picter, but I didn't get neer a chance, I didn't. Directly I get's that there candle within a yard of it, blest if the thing didn't fizz up like a firework, an' all the mischief was done. You should have seen that there blaze for the first 'arf minute. If that old oak warn't as hard 'as iron itself the house would have gone surely. Then I s'pose I got addled an' lost my head; for I rushed round to the stables just as I was an' 'ammered to wake John up."

"Oh, yes, I know all the rest. And where was Mr. Harley all the time?"

"He warn't down here, sir; leastways, not as I knows of. I understood as 'ow he was a-going back to Lunnon."

"Just so. The night before the fire. Did he take anything with him, James?"

"No, sir. Went as he came, he did. When he has a night down here, as he sometimes do, he never brings nothin' but a brush and comb and a toothbrush in a paper parcel. I be certain he had nothin' with him when he left for Lunnon, for I druv' him to the station in the market cart, I did, and cruel hard work it were."

Herepath asked no further questions. He was perfectly satisfied James had told him a great deal more than that rustic person imagined he had.

"I'll not keep you any longer now, James," he said. "I believe you have told me the truth, and it's a very good thing for you. And you need not worry. James, no harm is going to come to you. Oh, by the way, when do you expect to see Mr. Harley again?"

"I understand as 'ow he's coming down this very evening, sir," James said innocently. "Only for an hour or two it'll be, and then he's off back to Lunnon by the midnight train from the junction. I dare say he'll pop down in that there little car of his."

Herepath smiled as he turned away. This was exactly what he had hoped for. He began to see his way very clear now, everything was straightening out before him. He had his battery all ready and he would know how to use it at the right time. It seemed to him that he had never enjoyed a cigarette more than the one he smoked on the way back to Gay's house. He wanted to be alone for an hour or so now to think matters out and get everything in trim for the evening.

Therefore he was not altogether pleased to meet by the lodge gates Madame Desterre, accompanied by no less a personage than Princess Helena of Pau. Ninon made a dart at him in her own characteristic fashion.

"We have been looking for you everywhere," she cried. "Positively we began to fear that you had run away. That would have been a terrible business. Had you departed with the jewels of the Princess I should have been disturbed."

Herepath smiled helplessly. What did this inconsequent woman mean? It seemed incredible that she should speak thus before the unfortunate lady who had been robbed of all those precious stones. And here was Ninon actually confessing that she had been a party to the robbery. Herepath flushed uncomfortably.

"You have been making a confession to the Princess?" he asked.

"I have told her that you are in possession of the 'swag,' yes," Ninon said coolly. "Her Highness knows all about the little escapade at the restaurant, when our good Count Player came so near to serious trouble. The Princess also knows how the stones came to you. And now, will you be so good as to restore them—"

"To you?" Herepath asked. "I have them close at hand. I shall be delighted to hand them over to their proper owner at once."

"Ah, well, you can't do it, Mr. Herepath," the Princess laughed "Unhappily the proper owner is a long way off. If I could get the stones back I would do so, but so long as I remain in England so long my elderly husband is obdurate. It return home he gives me all I need—if I stay here I go my own way, and live more or less on what you call my wits. And I am getting terribly hard up. Positively before long I must go back to the land of my fathers if only to replenish my purse. Unhappily I have no more diamonds to dispose of."

"Do I understand that you have disposed of these, Princess?" Herepath asked.

"Alas, alas! I am desolated to make the confession. It would not do to say that I had sold my gems; that would have produced a too wonderful sensation. So my brilliant friend, Ninon, arranged the whole scenario, and—my stones were stolen."

"You mean that the public have been deceived, that the story of the robbery was made up to disguise the real facts."

"Precisely," Ninon laughed aloud. "Poor dear public! A cruel deception, mon enfant. The diamonds were sold for twenty thousand pounds to our charming old friend, Daniel Harley!"

CHAPTER XXXVIII

THE REAL MAN

Herepath was seeing daylight now with a vengeance. In the next minute or two a hundred things grew plain before him. All this had been in the light of a revelation, and on his side also he would have a revelation or two to make before many hours had elapsed.

"Won't you enlighten me a little further?" he asked.

"Not for the present," Ninon said. "You would not have learnt this much had not I wanted to make you feel quite easy in your mind as to these jewels. I invented the whole pretty little play of the robbery, and it went from first to last without a hitch. The way we got hold of Zana and kidnapped him was a stroke of genius. And Victor Player took his place. Oh, I dare say I should be ashamed of myself; perhaps I am, a little. But I like adventure and excitement. I cannot get on without them. It was I who brought the Princess in contact with Daniel Harley, and arranged for the sale of the stones. They had to change hands without anybody knowing that they had been sold, and I am rather proud of the way in which I managed it, hey, what think you?"

"I congratulate you," Herepath said gravely. "It was indeed a brilliant performance. And I presume that Harley made a very good thing of it. But that night in the restaurant we came very near to exposure and scandal."

"Rather!" Ninon exclaimed, her eyes sparkling at the recollection. "Count Player had just come back from Amsterdam, where he had been trying to sell the gems. We have a customer for them now in America, so there is no longer any occasion to try elsewhere."

"I am beginning to understand," Herepath said smiling. "The case of those Cosway miniatures, for instance. And other problems that have baffled the police. I begin to see quite plainly."

"Which reminds me," Ninon said with a sudden gravity of manner. "I hope you can see in every sense of the word, Mr. Herepath."

"I am becoming positively sure of it, Madame Desterre," Herepath said as gravely. "Has Enid been saying anything to you about it?"

"She has told me practically everything. A dear, sweet, transparent child, is Enid. Well, it is not for me to judge other people. Still, what I have done has harmed nobody, and ladies of fashion must have money, pardieu. But that Gilray is a cold-blooded scoundrel. We have him tightly now, and if you take my advice he will not escape. He has asked the Princess and myself to take tea with him this afternoon. The Princess does not propose to go—she prefers a walk with Enid. But I am going to this tea, Mr. Herepath, and I suggest that you come with me. For I know, and you know, that we will bring that scoundrel to his knees between us. What do you say?"

Herepath hesitated for a moment. He was anxious to have the matter out with Gilray, but he had other important things to occupy his attention. Still, he might spare an hour or two for Gilray's discomfiture. He must be made to understand once and for all that he must put Enid out of his thoughts. He must be made to comprehend that he was powerless for further mischief.

"Very well," he said. "It shall be as you suggest, and many thanks for the opportunity. I will call for you at your cottage at 4 o'clock if that will suit."

Gilray was sitting on the balcony of his pleasant sitting-room overlooking the garden. He rose as he heard his visitors coming, but his face fell when he saw that the princess was not one of the party, and that apparently Herepath had taken her place.

"It is very good of you to come, Madame Desterre," he said. "The Princess has another engagement? I am sorry. Won't you sit down, Herepath?"

"I prefer to stand," Herepath said grimly. "I shall not detain you long."

"Order in the tea," Ninon suggested. "Without my afternoon tea I am useless...Ah, that is delicious; I could not refuse tea even when offered by my bitterest foe. Mr. Herepath tells me he never touches it."

"I should not touch it here in any case," Herepath said pointedly.

Ninon lay back in her chair with the cup in her hand. She smiled with the pleased air of one who is going to be much amused.

Gilray flushed angrily.

"If that is intended for a joke," he said, "it is not in very good taste. If you have anything to say, Herepath, please say it. This is more or less private. But remember that a lady is present."

"Oh, please don't mind me!" Ninon cried. "Besides I am partly responsible for things. Mr. Herepath, I think the stage is yours."

Herepath crossed over to where Gilray was sitting, and dragged him to his feet. There was bitter contempt on his face as he spoke.

"Now regard me fairly and squarely," he commanded. "Look into my eyes. You are a judge of such matters and speak with authority. What is the matter with my sight?"

"Really, this is most extraordinary," Gilray blustered. "You came to me professionally, and I gave you advice. Surely you have not forgotten what passed when you called on me."

"I am not likely to forget it, nor will you by the time I have finished. I came to you when my eyes were really queer and you advised me, pending a more careful examination, to do no work. At that time you spoke the truth. I came to you again, and you gave me what was practically to me a sentence of death. It was the second occasion that you acted like the despicable scoundrel that you are."

Gilray advanced as if to strike Herepath. Then he changed his mind and sat down.

"It is very unfortunate for you," he hissed, "that there is a lady present."

"Oh, please don't mind me," Ninon said coolly. "I should probably enjoy it. And I am afraid that I agree with everything that Mr. Herepath says."

"I am fortunate in my audience," Gilray said bitterly.

"You are indeed," Herepath retorted. "We might so easily be the police. Now, what I accuse you of is this. When I came to see you my eyes were very queer. I had forgotten till a day or two ago that I had been experimenting weeks back with some iron filings, which probably was the cause of all the mischief. You operated on my eyes on the second visit and removed the source of the trouble. But you did not tell me so—you gave me some glasses that made me practically blind, and told me never to be without them. And all the time my eyes were as good as yours, you cold-blooded scoundrel."

"But what object could I have?" Gilray stammered. "What could I possibly gain by such an action?"

"Oh, don't patter with me!" Herepath cried. "You thought to get rid of a rival. You thought to grind me down in the dust and ruin me. You tricked me into believing that I should never be able to do any work again. I was even to lose the fortune my invention promised me. And you deemed your path to be clear.

"But you reckoned without me and Daniel Harley. I beat him all right. I convinced him that without my eyes the invention was useless. He paid you to give me what was my death sentence, or he promised to pay you. And when I destroyed the little glass disc, it became necessary for you to eat your words. If you did not do so, you got no money, and that meant ruin and disgrace.

"You were held fast in the cleft stick, Dr. Gilray. Either you were ruined, or you had to put the broken man on his feet again. You and Harley were both too clever, a little bit too quick. So you came down here to see me—to make a show of bringing about a wonderful recovery of my sight. The recovery is made already."

"If you go on this assumption," Gilray said sulkily, "you will find that—"

"I shall find nothing. I lost your precious glasses, an accident deprived me of them. And I can see as well as you can. There never was anything the matter with my sight. You can spare your diplomacy, and go back to London. The next time this matter is discussed, it will be in a court of law."

The dull, sullen red on Gilray's face gave way to a ghastly pallor.

"No—we all make mistakes," he said. "And as to Harley and myself you are wrong."

"I am not going to listen to any attempted excuses," Herepath went on. "I have evidence of the vile conspiracy you entered into from the lips of two people. It can be proved up to the hilt. As Daniel Harley had no mercy on me, so I shall have no mercy on him. I could force a confession from you—I could have you on your knees crying for mercy if I pleased. But that would not save you—nothing can save you from disgrace and exposure. Did I say nothing? Well, there is one saving course you can take, and that is to give up your practice and go abroad. If you do this, I shall not follow you; but if you defy me and remain in London, then you must take the consequences. For my own part, I do not care a jot which course you pursue."

"You—you will give me a day or two to decide?" Gilray asked.

"I don't want to be too hard on you," Herepath said. "You can have your day or two, all the more willingly, because I desire to have you and Harley together before me. That meeting may take place here this very night, but as regards that I cannot speak definitely. Madame Desterre, are you ready? Dr. Gilray, would like to be alone."

Gilray sat there dejectedly. He forgot to rise as his guests departed. His head was bent forward, his moody glare was fixed on the ground. He did not hear Ninon Desterre's light laugh as she passed into the road.

"So far so good," she said. "You did that well, my friend. But I should like to be present when Mr. Harley is there. It would be splendid."

"You shall be," Herepath said grimly. "And it may be sooner than you expect. The drama may be played out at any moment at Gay's house. If so, I will send to your cottage for you. Really, I look upon you as quite one of the necessary characters."

"That is very flattering," said Ninon archly. "Won't you tell me a little more?"

But Herepath refused to go further. He was silent and thoughtful during dinner, and it was still light when he made an excuse to get away from the house. For some time he lingered in the park, where he could obtain a view of the house. The light was fading fast as he rose at length from the grass and made his way across to the spot where a man was shuffling along with a parcel under his arm.

"Good evening, Mr. Harley," he said. "Good evening. It will interest you very much to hear that my sight has been entirely restored. It will also interest you to know that I have heard the story of the conspiracy between yourself and your fellow-scoundrel, Gilray. And, further, it will interest you to know that I am aware of the fact that you have under your arm a Raeburn stolen from Camford."

Harley started and smiled. He looked like a bulldog driven into a corner.

"What do you think you are going to do about it?" he sneered.

"Take the picture from you, by force, if necessary. Write to Lord Southlands and—"

Harley showed his teeth in a bitter snarl. He fairly quivered with passion.

"Out of my way, you fool!" he yelled. "What mischief can you do? Dolt and idiot, step on one side! Curse you, I am Lord Southlands!"

CHAPTER XXXIX

LORD SHYLOCK

Herepath expressed no astonishment at Harley's amazing statement. He merely stood in the other's way grimly blocking his path. He knew that he had all the cards in his hands now, and he was in no hurry to play them. As Harley tried to pass along he gripped him firmly by the arm.

"What are you up to?" the latter asked angrily. "What are you doing here? Don't you know that this is private property? I tell you I'm the owner. I tell you that I am Lord Southlands. Get out of my way."

"Won't do," Herepath said crisply. "Won't do at all. Surely you're not going to pretend that you are not Daniel Harley, of the riverside slum in Shadwell?"

"Call me that if you like, Mr. Herepath. If I like to disappear and have a fancy for using another name, is that any business of yours or of anybody but myself? I've got to catch a train."

"You'll catch no train to-night," Herepath said grimly. "You are coming with me, my dear sir. It's my turn now. Now I am quite strong and able enough to compel you to what I want by force. We are all alone here, and any resistance on your part would be futile. Do you suppose that I would lose a chance like this? If you like it better, we can go to the village police station, where I can charge you with stealing a picture, the property of the Earl of Southlands. Now you can make your own choice. Which is it to be, my lord?"

Harley was rapidly losing his truculent manner. He began to realise that Herepath had him at a disadvantage. And there was that picture under his arm. He was wondering precisely what Herepath knew. This meeting had been a staggering surprise for Harley, and the cool confidence of Herepath's manner shook him sorely. If he only knew what was at the back of the other's mind.

A day or two ago he had dismissed Herepath from his mind as a ruined man, whose invention with its millions of profit was as good as his. Herepath had rather turned the tables on him over the matter of the glass disc, and it had become necessary to reverse the policy so far as Gilray was concerned.

Still, the patents were practically at his command.

And here was Herepath springing out of nowhere and acting as if he were entirely master of the situation. Harley crushed down the anger that shook him. He would have liked to have flown at Herepath like a cat. But not just yet, wait till he was a little more sure of his ground, and then—

"You are taking a good deal for granted," he said. "Does a man with your deficient eyesight generally wander alone in the dark like this?"

Herepath smiled at the diplomatic suggestion underlying the question.

"That was very clever of you," he said. "You are very wily and very cunning, Mr. Harley; but I assure you that cunning will not help you now. The lure was spread too broadly before me to give you any hope of scoring by its means. You want to know if I have had an interview with Dr. Gilray on the subject of my eyes. I have."

"Hope they are better—then," Harley said, more or less ungraciously.

"Thank you for your good wishes. Very awkward breaking of that glass disc, wasn't it? Upset your little scheme altogether what? Quite a fortunate thing for you afterwards if Gilray could be proved to be wrong in his diagnosis. In that case I could use my eyes again and proceed with my invention. And you could rob me of it afterwards. Well, I have seen Dr. Gilray, and I have given him a piece of my mind. He did not examine my eyes again, for the simple reason that there was no necessity to do so. That little fire you arranged with poor old James was a perfect godsend to me, Mr. Harley."

"Don't know what you are talking about," Harley muttered wildly.

"Oh, yes you do. And you are going to admit it, or, by Heavens, I'll have the whole thing out in court, with you standing in the dock. Now, none of your nonsense. I know everything, or next door to it. You bullied old James into setting fire to the gallery so that you could steal the Raeburn, having previously put a forgery in its place as a substitute. With the forgery destroyed you would be all safe. As a matter of fact, the forgery was not quite destroyed, and I have the remains of it in my possession at this moment. The whole story would make pretty reading for a newspaper. And what a witness I should be, especially as I intend to take the real picture from under your arm, and hand it over to the police."

Harley was growing more quiet and watchful. This was no moment for passion. He was realising the danger in which he stood.

"You were talking about your eyes," he suggested tentatively.

"Oh, yes, I was going back to that. It was a cunning scheme of your miserable tool and accomplice to induce me to wear glasses utterly unsuitable to my sight, and thus confirm me in the belief that something was very wrong with my vision. But, you see, I lost those glasses when I was helping to put out the fire in the gallery. I am staying here with my brother-in-law, Mr. Harold Gay, who is steward of the estate. I merely mention this incidentally. Anyway, I lost those glasses, and I found that I could see as well as ever. And, by the way, that is another charge that will be made against you when you are in the dock."

"You're mad," Harley cried hoarsely. "What have I to do with Gilray?"

"Everything. You paid him a large sum to give his verdict that my eyes would be useless to me for months to come. At least, you promised to pay him 5000 pounds to do so. Then, when I checkmated you by destroying the glass disc, you had to alter your plans altogether. I was to be made whole again, and it was left to Gilray to bring this apparent miracle about. But he was too late. The conspiracy was overheard by your daughter and reported to me. I have only to raise my hand and you get a long term of penal servitude, Mr. Harley."

The hard old man was beaten at last. The vindictive gleam was still in his eyes, but he shook and trembled, and his lips quivered. Herepath could hear how fast he was breathing.

"So far so good," Herepath went on. "You see that the man you despised and looked down upon is now your master. I am not going to tell you how I found out all about the picture and your visits here at night. But the old man, James, has made a confession to me, and I shall use it if there is occasion to do so. It is very lucky for you that you have a daughter."

Harley broke out in a torrent of impotent rage.

"Confound her," he cried. "I wish she had never been born. A pretty daughter. A nice loyal child to her father. A white-faced sneak."

"Stop," Herepath commanded. "Stop, or old man as you are, I'll close your mouth for you. How you came to be the father of such a girl passes my understanding. Pah, you never have been a father to her in the proper sense of the word. You have never shown her one sign of affection since she was born. You have used her as a go-between, you cared nothing whether you got her into serious trouble or not. And I am not going to stand quietly by and hear my future wife abused like that."

Harley rubbed his hands slowly one over the other.

"Oh, so you are going to marry her, eh?" he croaked.

"Yes, I am. She will be part of the price of my silence. It is for me now to dictate terms, and for you to listen to them in humble gratitude. I shall marry your daughter, and you will give us your blessing. I might stipulate for half your money into the bargain, and you would not dare refuse. But it is tainted gold, and I do not need it. Still, you will give me a receipt for the 1000 pounds I owe you, and with that I shall be content. I shall have my invention; I shall be able to restore that broken part, and in time I shall be rich."

"And this is the programme that I am to give my consent to?"

"My dear sir, I don't care two straws whether you give your consent or not," Herepath went on coolly, "in any case it is a mere matter of form. You will quite see why I shall not be particularly proud of my father-in-law. A man who is at home with conspiracy and arson and robbery is not exactly the relative that one produces before one's friends, even if he is Lord Southlands."

The old man twisted and wriggled, consumed by impotent fury. With all his agility and cleverness he could see no way out of the trap that he had laid for Herepath, and in which he himself had been caught.

"You rogues are all alike," Herepath continued. "You never give honest men credit for any brains. You regard us all as fools. Then you go on and on, thinking that nobody can see your juggling till you find yourselves in trouble. Why do you do these things Lord Southlands?"

"Oh!" the other sneered. "Then you do believe that statement of mine. You are prepared to credit the fact that all this property belongs to me."

"Quite," Herepath replied. "It came to me more or less as an inspiration. You see, I have spent a good deal of time in Camford Hall lately, for I am fond of pictures. And I made a discovery. I found that certain pictures had been removed quite lately and rubbish substituted in their stead. I was lucky enough to find those pictures in an old public-house called 'The Green Man.' They were in the custody of one Count Victor Player. What is the matter? Have I said anything to disturb you?"

"Go on," Southlands said harshly. "Put all your cards on the table."

"I am doing so, my lord. I had certain suspicions from one or two innocent remarks dropped by your daughter. They came back to me when I found she knew Camford well, to say nothing of the old house where my sister lives. A half-uttered sentence came back to my mind. Was Enid born in that old house?"

"Yes, she was. Has that anything to do with our discussion?"

"No, except that it confirms my theory. The theory seemed sufficiently shadowy at that time, but it grew more substantial when I was hidden in the gallery the night you were there with old James—persuading him to set the house on fire. I knew by his manner to you, and your manner to him, that you were the eccentric Lord Southlands who had so dramatically disappeared. I began to understand your point of view. I suppose these eccentricities grew upon you till they became a habit. Your idea was to free the estate from debt; it was a mania with you. And you stooped to crime."

"No," Southlands said swiftly. "Not till I came in contact with you. And this picture under my arm is my own, after all."

CHAPTER XL

THE REASON WHY

"But surely all the pictures are heirlooms?" Herepath suggested.

"Not this one. Nor were the others that Player had to sell for me. They belonged to my mother, and came to me in her will. My mother was my father's cousin, and she originally brought the Raeburn from her side of the house. But I see there are certain things that require an explanation. Where can we go to discuss them?"

"What better place can you have than my brother-in-law's house?" Herepath suggested. "It is close by, and Enid is there. Madame Desterre is not a mile away, and the same remark applies to Gilray. It should be quite a pleasant party."

Southlands curtly indicated his approval. They walked on side by side in silence till the old house was reached. Out on the balcony in the warm and peaceful night were seated Gay and his wife with Enid. The girl rose with a little cry, and her face grew pale as she saw who Herepath's companion was.

"Don't be afraid, darling," he whispered. "Everything is coming right. Our troubles are all over. Within an hour they will be things of the past. Blanche, Harold, let me introduce you to Lord Southlands. All this is very irregular, perhaps, but his lordship is not wedded to conventional ideas. And, Harold, would you mind going as far as the hotel and asking Gilray to come along at once? Also, perhaps, you will act as escort to Madame Desterre. Lord Southlands wants to catch the midnight train at the junction."

Gay asked no questions. He seemed to have an intelligent grasp of what was happening. It was some half-hour before he returned, accompanied by Madame Desterre and Gilray. The latter looked white and anxious, while Ninon Desterre was smiling and debonnaire as usual.

"Sit down," Southlands said sharply. "My time is limited, and I have a lot to say. Mr. Herepath has found me out. He has caught me stealing my own pictures. He talks about imprisonment for arson and many other unpleasant things. Still, we have come to an understanding. He says nothing, and he takes my daughter as the price of his silence. And I make no claim on the insurance people. I daresay everybody is wondering why I am reduced to stealing my own pictures. Well, I don't want the world to know it, but I have sold them. And they represent the last 20,000 pounds or so of mortgages on the estate. Once they are disposed of the estate is free. I had intended about a month hence to return home and open Camford in state again."

"On the proceeds of stolen property," Herepath said coldly.

Southlands made no reply. He turned to Ninon Desterre with a gesture, intimating that she should take up the story where he had dropped it.

"That is not quite correct," she said. "So far as I know, Lord Southlands has never had any traffic in stolen property, Geoffrey Herepath is thinking of the Princess's jewels and the Cosway miniatures. They were not stolen."

"I beg your pardon," Herepath said politely. "Then what was it that happened to them? In both cases the matter was handed over to the police."

"And yet they were not stolen," Ninon responded, laughing merrily. "My dear Geoffrey, you have a good proverb in this country to the effect that one half the world does not know how the other half lives. That proverb was at the bottom of Lord Southlands' policy. He was anxious to clear his estate, so he disappeared and went into business to do so. Gradually he became a sort of pawnbroker to the aristocracy, and a lender of money. I had little or nothing of my own, and I became a kind of commercial agent. I made a lot that way, and Lord Southlands enabled me to live in the style I do. You see, I am popular—I know so many people. I can introduce clients of stability and worth.

"Now it happened sometimes that my friends went too far. Then came the moment when they could not redeem their valuables, and they had to sell outright. Nobody must know this, not even their husbands. It was I who hit upon the idea of those, what you call bogus, robberies. They were not robberies at all—merely little comedies to save the faces of the ladies who were compelled to part with their valuables. When the police were looking vaguely for the thief the gems were in the strong-room of the old house at Shadwell. The victims had everybody's sympathy, and nobody was any the wiser. Witness the affairs of the Princess's diamonds and Mrs. Van der Knoot's miniatures. Oh, I am not defending the business, I am no champion of the morality of it. I only say that it was very good fun. Nobody was robbed and our profits were good."

"Were there only two of you?" Herepath asked.

"Four," Ninon went on. "Lord Southlands and myself, together with Mr. Vorley and Count Victor Player; ah, yes, my dear old Hector Marsail. Sometimes we worked in disguise, so that we did not know one another; but there was a green and orange scarf or sash or tie we wore on these occasions. It was the green and orange tie that puzzled Dr. Gilray."

"It was," Gilray muttered. "I am obliged by the explanation."

"We took Victor Player in a year or two ago," Ninon resumed. "To begin with he was a victim of one of the robberies. We found him very useful afterwards. But he has come into money now, and has become entirely respectable. He is turning that lovely old inn into a private house, and is about to be married. Dr. Gilray will remember the inn. We led him a fine dance there the night the Princess lost her diamonds."

Again Gilray muttered his thanks for the information.

"Oh, well, there is little more to tell," Ninon said with a sigh. "Now that Camford is cleared there will be no more of these delightful adventures. Besides, I have promised my dear Hector Marsail that I will go out to Brazil with him in the autumn. I am going to marry the dear boy. And now that I have sown my wild oats, I shall settle down as an exemplary character. Am I forgiven, Enid?"

"As if anybody could be angry with you for long," Enid said between smiles and tears. "It is all very shocking, but some people seemed to be permitted to do anything. Father, are you really going back to Camford?"

Southlands smiled sardonically at the question.

"With Mr. Herepath's permission," he said. "Provided, of course, that he has not set his heart on seeing Gilray and myself in gaol."

"I give you my word of honour," Gilray said unsteadily, "that I never intended to harm Herepath's eyes."

Herepath turned upon him with a sudden spurt of anger and contempt.

"You will be well advised not to say a word," he exclaimed. "A viler plot than that devised by you and Lord Southlands, to rob a man of his sight and property was never conceived. I can hardly control myself when I think of it. But the scheme failed, and in time, I daresay I shall not feel so hard about it. As for you, Dr. Gilray, you may go. My idea was to drive you out of an honourable profession, but I have changed my mind. You will have trouble and difficulty enough before you as it is. If I am any judge of Lord Southlands, and his methods, you can expect nothing from him. Go."

Without another word Gilray rose and departed. An awkward silence followed, until at length his footsteps died away in the distance. It was Southlands who spoke first.

"You are mistaken, Herepath," he said. "I shall have to help that fellow. He did a good deal of dirty work for me, and it was no fault of his that he failed. No, I am not going to express any regret for my past doings, for I should do the same things again to-morrow. There is only one thing in the world worth living for and that is money. I have known what it is to be without it. And I have got all this back by my own exertions. Herepath, will you walk with me as far as the spot where my little car is hidden? I have a few words say to you. Good-night, Enid; good-night, Mr. and Mrs. Gay. We shall see a good deal of one another in the future, no doubt."

The cold, hard old man moved away with his hands behind him till he and Herepath were out of earshot of the others. He was quite at his ease now.

"You have a great deal more brain than I gave you credit for," he said. "As you have the whip hand of me I cannot prevent you marrying my daughter. It would never do for me to come back here feeling that people about me knew the story of the last twenty years. But, mind, you will get no money from me. I have cleared the estate, and for a few years perhaps I shall enjoy my good fortune. After I am gone everything passes to my cousin's boy, Albert Barrington."

"I would much rather not have your money, my lord," Herepath said coldly. "I have my invention, and I shall hold your receipt for 1000 pounds before long. Within a week everything will be exactly as I dropped it a short time ago. Within a month I shall have people eager and willing to find me capital. I prefer to make my own fortune."

"Yes; and you will," Southlands said quite pleasantly. "You are born to get on. Some men are that kind, and I am a good judge of the genius. Oh, yes, I'll post you the receipt to-morrow. And you won't make any scandal, will you? I mean you'll wait a reasonable time for Enid, and marry her from Camford as soon as I can get settled. We can appear to be friends, at any rate."

"I should like nothing better," Herepath said. "Everything must be made as smooth as possible for Enid's sake. Is this your car? Let me light the lamps for you. Goodnight, my lord. No, there is no necessity to shake hands."

Enid was quite alone on the balcony when Geoffrey returned. Gay had gone off to see Ninon Desterre to her cottage, and Blanche had found something inside the house that called for her pressing attention. The girl rose as Geoffrey came forward. There were tears in her eyes, her face was pale; but there was a suggestion of happiness there.

"What a wonderful evening it has been, Geoff," she whispered. "And how happy I could be if I could only forgot one or two things."

Geoffrey took her in his arms and kissed her tenderly.

"Ah, but there are so many lovely things to remember, sweetheart," he said. "Besides, we are not responsible for the acts of other people. And whatever happens, you are always my sweet and innocent and lovely Enid to me. We have won, too, we have won all along the line. Your father's only suggestion was that I should wait a reasonable time for you, and that we should be married from Camford. I was glad to hear him say that, as there is no necessity to set idle-tongues wagging. And I daresay we shall be able to forgive him everything in time."

Enid lay back in her lover's arms smiling gloriously. She pressed her lips to his, and he gave a little sigh of infinite content.

"I am too happy to bear malice against anybody," she whispered. "And only a day or two ago the world looked so dark and dreary for me. Shall I wake up presently and find it is no more than a pleasant dream?"

"No dream," Herepath said as he kissed her again. "Thank heaven, it's no dream."

FRED M WHITE – A CONCISE BIBLIOGRAPHY

NOVELS (A-Z)

Ambition's Slave (1916)
The Argus Eye (1919)
Blackmail (1902)
The Blue Daffodil (1934)
The Brand Of Silence (1911)
A Broken Memory (1929)
The Bubble Reputation (1908)
By Order Of The League (1886)
The Cardinal Moth aka The Accused Orchid (1903)
The Case For the Crown (1918)
Claxton's Mill (1912)
A Clue In Wax (1930)
The Corner House (1905)
The Councillors of Falconhoe (1922)
Craven Fortune (1904)
A Crime On Canvas (1909)
The Crimson Blind (US title: The Mystery Of The Crimson Blind) (1905)
A Daughter Of Israel (1892)
The Day: Or The Passing Of A Throne (1914)
A Deal In Letters (1923)
The Devil's Advocate (1924)
Dropped From The Fast Express, or A Daughter's Sacrifice (1911)

The Edge Of The Sword (1907)
The Ends Of Justice (1906)
A Fatal Dose (aka Behind the Mask) (1907)
The Fight For The Child (1925)
The Five Knots (1907)
"Found Dead" (1930)
The Four Fingers (US title: The Mystery Of The Four Fingers) (1907)
A Front Of Brass (1910)
The Garden O' Dreams (1909)
A Golden Argosy (1886)
The Golden Bat (1924)
The Golden Rose (1909)
The Green Bungalow (1923)
The Grey Woman (aka Sinister House) (1928)
The Happy Exile (1920)
A Harbour Of Refuge (1918)
Hard Pressed (1910)
The Honour Of His House (1920)
The House Of Mammon (1913)
A House Of Sorrows (1911)
The House Of The Schemers (1906)
The House On The River (1925)
In Trust (1892)
Jim Crowshaw's Mary (1911)
The King Diamond (1927)
Lady Clara (1913)
Lady Edna's Awakening (1920)
The Lady In Blue (1915)
The Law Of The Land (1906)
The Leopard's Spots (1920)
The Lonely Bride (aka The White Bride) (1907)
The Lord Of The Manor (1907)
Love, The Foe (1910)
A Maker of Millions (1909)
The Man Called Gilray (1911)
The Man Who Found Christmas (a novelette) (1915)
The Man Who Knew (1932)
The Man Who Was Two (1921)
The Man With The Vandyk Beard (1925)
The Midnight Guest: A Detective Story (1907)
A Mummer's Throne (1910)
My Lady Bountiful (1905)
The Mystery Of Crocksands (1923)
The Mystery Of The Ravenspurs (aka The Black Valley) (1911)
The Mystery Of Room 75 (1922)
Naboth's Vineyard (1889)
The Nether Millstone (1906)
Netta, The Story Of Sin (1909)

New Century Calendar Clue (1948)
Number Thirteen (1914)
The Old Secretaire: A Christmas Story (novelette) (1887)
On The Night Express (1930)
The Open Door (1907)
Paul Quentin (1908)
Paul, The Sage (1910)
The Phantom Car (1929)
Powers Of Darkness (1912)
The Price Of Silence (1925)
The Psalm Stone (1905)
Queen Of Hearts (1930)
A Queen Of The Stage (1908)
The Riddle Of The Rail (1926)
The Robe Of Lucifer (1896)
A Royal Wrong (1913)
The Salt Of The Earth (1918)
The Scales Of Justice (1908)
Secret Of The River (1934)
The Secret Of The Sands (1911)
A Secret Service (1913)
The Seed Of Empire (1916)
The Sentence Of The Court (1913)
A Shadowed Love (1905)
The Shadow Of The Dead Hand (1926)
The Silver Stream (novelette)
The Slave Of Silence (1906)
A Society Jezebel (1917)
The Sundial (1908)
Tregarthen's Wife: A Cornish Story (1901)
The Turn Of The Tide (1923)
The Weight Of The Crown (1904)
The White Battalions (1900)
The White Bride (aka The Lonely Bride) (1910)
The White Glove (1910)
The Wings Of Victory (1919)
The Yellow Face (1906)

SHORT FICTION SERIES

THE MASTER CRIMINAL (1897-1898)

A series of 12 short stories featuring Felix Gryde, who describes himself as "a really clever soldier of fortune."

The Head Of The Caesars
At Windsor

The Silverpool Cup
The "Morrison Raid" Indemnity
Cleopatra's Robe
The Rosy Cross
The Death Of The President
The Cradlestone Oil Mills
Redburn Castle
"Crysoline Limited"
The Loss Of The "Eastern Empress"
General Marcos

THE LAST OF THE BORGIAS (1898)

A series of stories featuring Professor Victor Colonna, a vigilante physician who murders undesirable people with undetectable poisons.

The Scrip of Death
The Crimson Streak
The Holy Rose
The Saving Of Serena
The Varteg Necklace
The Three Carnations

DRENTON DENN - SPECIAL COMMISSIONER

Drenton Denn is a tough newspaper reporter on the payroll of The New York Post. His hallmarks are a straw hat, a Norfolk jacket, a perennial cigar, and a terrier by the name of "Prince."

The Yellow Moth
The Red Speck
Dust
The Fire Bugs
The Great White Moth

THE ROMANCE OF THE SECRET SERVICE FUND (1900)

This series features Newton Moore, the top agent at The Secret Service Fund.

By Woman's Wit
The Mazaroff Rifle
In The Express
The Almedi Concession
The Other Side Of The Chess Board
Three Of Them

THE DOOM OF LONDON

This sci-fi series of six stories describes a variety of catastrophes which ravage London.

The Four White Days
The Four Days' Night
The Dust Of Death
A Bubble Burst
The Invisible Force
The River Of Death

THE SAGE OF TYBURN (1905-1906)

Each of these stories was preceded by the header The Sage Of Tyburn.

No. 1 - The Chronicle Of The Yellow Girl
No. 2 - The Chronicle Of The Blue-Eyed Syndicate
No. 3 - The Chronicle Of The Inconsequent Princess
No. 4 - The Chronicle Of The Elderly Adonis
No. 5 - The Chronicle Of The Libelled Velasquez

THE DRAGON-FLY (1909)

Six stories about an impecunious but brilliant amateur criminologist, entomologist and ornithologist by the name of Horace Daimler. Each of the stories was preceded by the header The Dragon-Fly.

No. 1 - How Horace Daimler Got His Name
No. 2 - The Three Red Rats
No. 3 - [title unknown]
No. 4 - [title unknown]
No. 5 - A [illegible] Crime
No. 6 - The Mirror Over The Fireplace

REAL DRAMA (1909)

A series of stories published under the subtitle "Being Some Leaves From The Notebook Of A Late Theatrical Agent."

His Second Self
An Extra Turn
"Not In The Bill"
The Plagiarist
The Man In Possession
A Pair Of Handcuffs

THE TELEPHONE STAR (1912)

A series of stories about Keith Marrit, a star journalist working for a fictitious newspaper called The Telephone.

No. 1 - The Case Of El Hamid, The Seer
No. 2 - The Case Of The Genuine Counterfeit
No. 3 - The Case Of The Yellow Car
No. 4 - The Case Of Lord Wintercotte
No. 5 - The Case Of The Rusty Nail
No. 6 - The Case Of The One-Eyed Chauffeur

GIPSY TALES (1903-1916)

A series of stories describing the adventures of a wily British navvy with Romany roots, who is known only as "Gipsy." In his fantasies Gipsy portrays himself as a playwright, and tries to stage-manage the dramatis personae and the situations that feature in the stories.

A Matter Of Kindness
A Liberal Education
A Stranger In Bohemia
Drops Of Water
The Unpremeditated Curtain
Mere Details
Out Of Season

THE DIARY OF A LONELY SOUL (1915)

The Diary Of A Lonely Soul - Story 1 [title unknown]
The Diary Of A Lonely Soul - Story 2 [title unknown]
The Diary Of A Lonely Soul - Story 3 [title unknown]
The Diary Of A Lonely Soul - Story 4 [title unknown]
The Diary Of A Lonely Soul - Story 5 [title unknown]

AN A-Z OF OTHER SHORT FICTION

According To The Statute
The Ace Of Hearts
Adventure (aka A Trick of Fate)
After Reynolds

Alias "James Jones"
An Ally
And This Is Fame
Anonymous
The Apple-Green Plate
Applied Mechanics
The Arms Of Chance
Art Critics
At Short Notice
Aunt Mary
Autumn Manoeuvres
The Azoff Diamonds
A Bad Cold
The Balance Of Nature
The Barrister At Bay
Below Zero
The Better Way
Big Fish
The Big Thing
Billy's Xmas
A Bit Of Egypt
The Black Admiral
The Black Cat
The Black Narcissus
The Black Prince
Blind
Blind Chance
The Blindworm
A Block Of Marble
A Bootless Errand
Brayton's Secret
The Broken Lute
A Broken Sceptre
The Broken Trail
The Buff Gauntlet
Burglar Bill's Pupil
By Grace Of His Majesty
By Wireless
A Call On The Phone
A Captious Critic
The Case For The Prisoner
The Charlatan
A Christmas Bride
A Christmas Deputy
Christmas Cards
The Christmas Carol
A Christmas in Peril
A Christmas Star

A Gamble In Love
A Game Of Draughts
A Garden Of Pearls
Gentlemen Of The Jury
The Gates Of Ramshi
The Grey Bat
The Grey Raider
The Guiding Star
The Half-Crown Princess
The Hand Invisible
Hardy's Big Coup
The Heart Of The Anarchist
Heavy Metal
The Heels Of The Dawn
Her Christmas Dawn
His Christmas Gift
His Majesty's Mails
A Hole In The Net
The Hospitallers
Ice In June: A Playwright's Story
Icky Of Oluk Lake
Imperial Preference
In Black And White
In Rosemary Lane
In The Dark
In The Fog
In The Pit
Introducing Mr. Pentsymon
The Joinville Tunnel
Judgment Reserved
Karma
Kindergarten
The Kingmaker's Token
Lady Mary's Bulldog
The Language Of Flowers
The Last Drive
The Law Of The Jungle: A Tale Of Mean Streets
The Leather-Pushin' Private
The Left Hand
The Lesson The Ants Taught
The Livery Of Death
The Lonely Furrow
The Long Arm Of Bronze
Love In Aether
The Luck Of The Game
Made In England
The Man Himself
The Man Who Got Through

The Man Who Rang The Bell
The Man With The Eyeglass
A Masked Battery
The Master's Voice
A Matter Of Habit
'Merica
A Message from the Flood
The Midnight Call
The Missing Blade
The Missing Note
The Mistletoe Bough
Moray The Traitor
More Than Coronets
The Morning Glory
Music Hath Charms
A Musical Treat
The Mystery Of Room Five
Natural Selection
Nerves
The Night Express: The Story Of A Bank Robbery
The Northern Light
Not On The Records
An Object Lesson
The Odds On Zero
One Day With A Working Ant
One Foggy Night
One Of The Old Guard
On Peace Night
The Onus Of The Charge
The Orpheusia
Ostentation
The Other Man's Story
The Pardon
A Parrot Cry
The Path Of Progress
The Pawn And The Rook
Pearls Of Price
Photo By Lesterre
Pictures In The Snow (a Christmas story)
A Place In The Sun
The Platinum Chain
A Popular Novelist
Poste Restante
A Prize Crop
Proof Positive
The Purple Terror
A Queen In Hiding
A Question Of Money